WIT
FOR

GU00890228

A
WILD
JUSTICE

Also by Kenneth Royce

The XYY Man
The Concrete Boot
The Miniature Frame
Spider Underground
Trap Spider
The Woodcutter Operation
Bustillo
The Satan Touch
The Third Arm
10,000 Days
Channel Assault
The Stalin Account
The Crypto Man
The Mosley Receipt
No Way Back
The President is Dead
Fall-Out
Exchange of Doves
The Proving Ground

KENNETH ROYCE

A WILD JUSTICE

Hodder & Stoughton

LONDON SYDNEY AUCKLAND TORONTO

LINCOLNSHIRE
COUNTY COUNCIL

British Library Cataloguing in Publication Data

Royce, Kenneth
 A wild justice.
 I. Title
 823[F]

 ISBN 0-340-55973 X

Copyright © Kenneth Royce 1992

First published in Great Britain 1992

All rights reserved. No part of this publication may be reproduced or transmitted in any form or by any means, electronic or mechanical, including photocopying, recording, or any information storage and retrieval system, without either prior permission in writing from the publisher or a licence permitting restricted copying. In the United Kingdom such licences are issued by the Copyright Licensing Agency, 90 Tottenham Court Road, London W1P 9HE.

The right of Kenneth Royce to be identified as the author of this work has been asserted by him in accordance with the Copyright, Designs and Patents Act 1988.

Published by Hodder and Stoughton,
a division of Hodder and Stoughton Ltd,
Mill Road, Dunton Green, Sevenoaks, Kent TN13 2YA
Editorial Office: 47 Bedford Square, London WC1B 3DP

Typeset by Hewer Text Composition Services, Edinburgh
Printed in Great Britain by Biddles Ltd, Guildford and Kings Lynn

FOR STELLA

1

The beams reared like a huge V, the square-shaped bridge squatting low behind them. Visibility was good, the sea calm. The only turbulence was created by the trawler itself, widening layers of froth bubbling back from the rounded bows leaving a foaming white carpet astern. Conditions were ideal and Ryan contentedly sucked his empty pipe as he controlled the wheel. The observation windows facing him were free of spray and his vision was only partially obscured by the huge beams themselves, soaring above the bridge and hanging over the sides as if the ship needed a balance like a trapeze artist's pole.

Declan O'Dwyer joined his skipper on the bridge, noticed the unlit pipe, and said, "Can you breathe through that thing? Or are there still fumes enough in it to satisfy you?"

Ryan grinned; the leg-pulling about him giving up smoking was wearing thin, but he was good-natured and tolerant. Both men were on the short side, but were stocky and tough like the trawler.

As they gazed ahead they could feel the drag of the nets. And then they felt something else. The trawler yawed and inexplicably gathered speed. There was a terrifying sound of grating beneath them as though the keel was being ripped out. The two men stared at each other and Ryan's hand shot out for the throttle in an instinctive act of desperation. In the split second left, O'Dwyer could have raced for the door but chose to stay with his old friend and skipper. Perhaps it was already too late.

The trawler rolled over and was gone in seconds. The small crew below stood no chance. Ryan and O'Dwyer died on the bridge with the hull above them, and in the time it took them to die both knew why. Mercifully, it had all happened so quickly. The sea was calm again and below its surface the fouled nets slowly coiled themselves round the trawler, as it slowly sank to the bottom, like a shroud.

There was a good view of the sea from the Marine Office windows. The outside door opened and a man stepped in, closing the door quietly behind him. Shaw looked up, his features drawn; he had been up most of the night after the news of the disappearance of the *Mary R* had reached him. A search had quickly been organised and the RAF in Britain had responded to conduct a search off the coast of County Cork over Irish territorial waters. The Irish Naval vessel *L E Ciara* was also searching with other vessels. Nothing had been found; not a trace.

Shaw did not like the look of the man who entered and yet there was something vaguely familiar about him; something disturbing, too. He gazed into the bleak eyes and said, "Is it important? I'm up to my eyeballs. We have a ship missing and right now I'm on my own."

"Sure you are. Didn't I make sure you were?"

Shaw reached for the telephone. "Whatever it is, can you wait until the others are back?"

The man gazed round the walls, at the pinned-up notices, nautical charts, press clippings, the three desks covered in papers as if everyone had left in a hurry. There was the tang of the sea in the room and it was clear that Shaw himself had served some time afloat, his features crusted from the effect of wind and spray.

"It's about the *Mary R* that I called." The stranger smiled at Shaw's reaction. "The brother of one of the crew is a mate of mine." He pulled out a piece of paper from his worn seaman's jacket. "That's the name. Did you know that the brother was on board as well?"

Shaw did not like what he was hearing. He took the roughly torn piece of paper and glanced at the crudely printed name on it: Con Daley. It was to his credit that his fingers remained steady and that he did not flinch. But his mind was racing and he was confused and anxious. Daley had escaped from Maghabery Prison in Northern Ireland two days ago, with four other terrorists, two of them Ulster Loyalists.

Shaw searched for something to say. There were thousands of Daleys, perhaps, even, Con Daleys; but only one who had a brother in the crew of the *Mary R*. The two brothers were notorious political enemies, one profound PIRA, the Provos, the other, Mike, hated everything Con was doing. Both had the same aims but their methods were totally polarised. The two brothers had not met in years and now they never would again.

"Well?" demanded the hard-eyed stranger.

"It's impossible. They hated each other's guts. And, anyway, Sam Ryan would never have allowed Con on board."

"The brothers were trying a reconciliation. Have you not heard of that before?"

"Con has just broken out of prison, for God's sake. He was in for murder. There's no way they would have got together. Anyway, what's your interest?"

"Killing Brits in the six counties is war not murder. My interest is to put the record straight; Con was on that ship. Issue his name with the rest."

Shaw felt a strong thread of fear. He should call the Garda but knew that he would not. Many Irishmen disliked officialdom. But there was another good reason why he should not go to the police and it stood in front of him with dark, empty eyes. "I can't do it," he said flatly.

"Just start a rumour and let it develop from there."

"You start it. You know more about it than me."

The stranger hooked a chair towards him and placed his foot on the wooden seat. He leaned forward, elbow on knee. "So you're not willing to take my word?"

This was dangerous ground. Shaw said again, "Sam Ryan, the skipper, wouldn't have let Con Daley come within spitting distance of the *Mary R*. I have no notice of him being aboard. That's all I can tell you."

"Ryan did it as a favour to Mike who was going to persuade Con to give himself up. It wouldn't have worked but

9

that was the idea. Look now, it was hardly a thing to advertise. Believe me, Con was on board. We just want the record put straight to take the pressure off his relatives and girlfriend. They don't deserve to be left in suspense. How would your family feel if someone kept your whereabouts a mystery after you were dead?"

Shaw accepted the remark as intimidation. "What's your name?" he asked.

"Now don't spoil things. And what does it matter? They're all dead, aren't they? Who can prove anything? All you've got to do is to say Con was on board."

"We're not yet sure that they're dead. Strange things happen at sea."

"Of course they're bloody well dead. A Brit submarine tore the guts out of them in our territorial waters like they've done before. Those 'beamers' roll over in a flash in the right circumstances. We all know it and Sam Ryan knew it."

It was true that there was a history of submarine collision with trawlers in and around the Irish Sea. Not only British but American submarines had been involved; not only Irish but continental trawlers had suffered. At best costly nets had been fouled, and at worst lives and ships had been lost.

Shaw sat back. Was it worth resisting? Did it matter anyway? He could see that it did, particularly to Con Daley who would then have the heat of a nationwide search for him removed. As he gazed up he noticed the stranger was smiling slightly, as if to say, we could have avoided all this palaver, what choice have you if you don't want trouble?

The FBI referred to the IRA as street hoods. And Shaw recognised that he could not cope with them. Going to the police could make things worse, and he would not know from day to day when retribution would take place. Fear was an effective weapon. He struggled with his conscience and thought of his wife and four children. "I'll see what I can do," he said.

The stranger grinned. "You'll do better than that. Let it slip out reluctantly that it was the memory of Mike you were trying to protect, not Con. What better meeting place could they have had than at sea? You know how to do it. I'll expect to see something in the evening papers and hear it on radio and television. If I don't I'll be back."

Shaw felt a rising anger and frustration. He sat there glaring back and wanting to strangle the man in front of him.

The stranger straightened and pushed the chair back. "- Good of you to set the record straight. The family will appreciate it."

2

Jamie Patterson lay crouched against the wall, the rain pouring down on him, trickling inside his clothes. He was close to another huddled figure and tried to turn his back. The low farm wall was no protection but the bad weather was a blanket cover against almost everything except dogs. It kept the choppers at bay and made searching troops noisier as they squelched over rough ground and intermittently complained. They had been lucky to get clear quickly and, with more luck, the car they had stolen might not be missed until morning. The original six escapees had split up as soon as they were clear of the prison and Patterson and Daley had been united by circumstances.

The heavy rain had helped them from the start. When the home-made bomb went off in the prison all attention was attracted to it and the damage it did. The six men were the other end of the yard and, although startled, reacted instinctively. While mass attention was concentrated on the destruction caused by the bomb, they had found themselves in an isolated group. The sudden downpour gave good cover and, as the fire spread, increased the smoke pall. Fire-engines clanged in to create more confusion. It was a wonder there had not been a far bigger breakout. None of them knew who had made the bomb.

Patterson and Daley had made for the same car and the situation was far too critical for argument. Their combined force helped. Both knew how to open and start a car without keys and they had worked silently and well. Shortly after crossing the border by one of the many tracks so difficult to police, they ditched the car, hiding it in some woods, and had then gone across country by foot, and it had rained all the way.

"Are you sure we're over the border?" Patterson asked.

"I know this very farm. I've used it many times."

"So you used to sneak over the border, shoot some poor sod dead in front of his wife and kids and then sneak back."

"Jesus, I thought you were a black-hearted Prot. So who did you kill?"

"You, when I get a chance." Patterson's voice was full of hatred.

Daley was equally seething and, had he had a weapon, would probably have tried to kill Patterson there and then. Of all people, he had landed one of the enemy as a companion. Their common predicament, for the moment, bound them.

Daley believed he was in a stronger position than Patterson. He was on more familiar soil for a start and knew many of the boltholes on the Republic side of the border. But he was not sure he wanted to use them. The Garda might know some of them and wait for him but his reluctance was founded on a stronger feeling than that. He had been in prison only a short time, yet had already received a death threat which he knew to be from his own kind. And he knew why. There was a peculiar kind of comfort in being with Patterson right now.

"Hadn't we better get moving?" asked Patterson irritably.

Daley did not reply immediately. After a while he said, "Come on," and disappeared into the downpour with Patterson following.

Both men spoke with the harsh, difficult-to-understand accent of the Northern Irish which would be a give-away the further south they went. But that was a future problem. Patterson followed Daley's direction because there was no option except to return over the border to almost certain capture.

The rain stopped just before dawn and they hid themselves deep in some woods, covering themselves with bracken, and slept the sleep of the exhausted, wet through though they were. Occasionally, the sound of helicopters penetrated their sleep but they knew they were safe from all but ground discovery. When, about mid-morning, they did finally wake they did so in uncanny unision as if each was prepared against the other.

13

They were chilled through and wet. But they were hungry and thirsty now. Movement would be a problem in daylight. They were reluctant to leave the woods which would become a logical place for the police to search. They started to walk again, silently, hatred suspended by a common peril.

"Have you any idea where we are going?" Patterson asked again.

"As far from the bloody border as we can. We could do with some wheels."

The only way they could get transport was to steal it and that would create new problems. Once the car they had ditched was found, the police would know they had crossed the border and the usual pleas for co-operation from the Garda would start. That was how Patterson saw it but Daley destroyed the impression.

"Don't kid yourself that the Garda won't be searching. "They'll be out there. It's just that they've more ground to cover. Crossing the border doesn't solve the problem, it just gives us a little more space." The distant sound of a helicopter seemed to bear out Daley's judgement.

They stopped to hide under a tree but the trees would soon peter out and they would have to cross open country and there was a lot of it. Patterson wondered why Daley was not using one of the boltholes near the border. The farm had been one.

Once the helicopter had gone they trudged on, heading south towards the east coast. They were south of Dundalk, a near border town, but could not be sure how far they had travelled. As the crow flew it was about fifty miles from the border to Dublin but they could not afford to risk so direct a route.

They approached another farm and kept beside a hedgerow along a narrow tractor lane. The drone of tractors reached them from across the fields. They located the farmhouse and then dived through a gap as a car came slowly down the lane. A battered Morris 1000 passed them with a middle-aged woman at the wheel.

Daley nudged Patterson. "The farmer's wife. Off shopping, I bet. The men are in the fields; we'll have to take a chance."

14

They approached the farmhouse cautiously but the last stage had to be tackled as if they were openly visiting. They were met by two barking mongrel dogs but quickly made friends with the animals. Their luck was holding. The door was wide open and the house seemed to be empty.

They worked fast, putting a loaf and a packet of farm butter in an old carrier bag. They found some home-cured ham in the huge kitchen-pantry and took enough to arouse curiosity but not enough for suspicion. They drank from the tap, tasting the freshness of well-water. There was a portable transistor radio on the wide window ledge and they found another, a pocket version, on one of the kitchen-dresser shelves. Daley reached up and took it, then by unspoken consent the two men left, breaking into a run once they found the cover of the hedges.

By mid-afternoon the sun was shining and they had dried off and decided to find somewhere safe to eat. They found a stream but once they had slaked their considerable thirsts they moved away from it; streams attract people and they were still in their prison garb.

The bread, butter and ham were deliciously fresh and they fell upon them, sharing a solitary knife Patterson had stolen. When they had finished eating they felt like sleeping again but were far too vulnerable. To get rid of their prison clothes was the next priority. There was an aimlessness about Daley that increasingly worried Patterson. The PIRA man seemed to have no direction except to hope for the best. They needed clothes and transport. These two facts had become increasingly important.

They sat against the bole of a tree and Daley produced the radio which he switched on low volume. He played around searching for a news report but it was another half-hour before one materialised. The two men hunched over the tiny set to listen to the distorted sound.

Three of the men had been recaptured, three were still loose although it was believed that one of them had died. Daley learned that he had been drowned late the previous day off the Cork coast, south of Ballycotton. He had apparently gone to see his brother, a crew member of the *Mary R*, although no

15

details were known as the brothers were sworn enemies. There was some garble about a reconciliation and the fisherman brother's desire to persuade Daley to give himself up, a statement apparently made by Mike Daley before setting out to sea. Nobody knew to whom this statement had been made, but it had come from a reliable source.

The fugitives looked at one another in surprise as they continued to listen. The question of how Daley had got from Belfast to Cork the same day was a mystery, but it was thought that he had been provided with a fast car, or even a light aircraft or helicopter. Patterson was named, as was the other man still on the run. Patterson had known Daley's identity before the escape and it was possible that Daley had known his, though neither had given an indication.

"My God, you're in the clear. You're dead." Patterson eased his body away from the rough bole of the tree. But when he gazed at Daley he saw raw fear, not relief.

Daley stared into space, stunned and clearly uneasy. They had been so busy escaping that Patterson had not really taken a good look at him until now. Instead of a hardened killer he saw a scared man no longer sure of himself. Daley was slight of build, medium height, but there was a tough wiriness about him. In his late twenties, Patterson supposed, Daley had been grabbed and indoctrinated early, as so many of them were. Daley was quite good-looking in a hungry sort of way, his pale blue eyes at the moment reflective. He had probably known no other life than belonging to the IRA since leaving school, or even before.

Patterson, slightly older at thirty, was a schoolteacher who did a little journalism on the side. Prison had not changed his views on what he had done but it had given him much more time to think, and observation of those in prison had merely hardened his views. He was a thinking man but along the line his thinking had taken a wrong turning and was far from finding the right road again. It did not help that his sister had been murdered by the IRA, and that he had seen what had been left of his mother, after the same IRA bomb, die slowly and in agony. His bitterness went deep and he felt it rising now as he gazed at Daley.

16

"We've got to cross the water," Daley said lifelessly.

Patterson pulled himself round. He pushed his still-wet dark hair away from his face. He was taller than Daley, bigger in every way but still on the lean side. There was nothing superfluous on either man. "To the UK? I'm not against that but we can't go like this and it's too soon. We'll be picked up. What's gone wrong? Someone's fixed your death nice and thoughtfully and you've lost your bottle. Where's all your bullshit bravado now, boyo? You should be over the moon."

"It's a long story. But nobody has done me a favour. It wasn't done for my sake."

It was obvious that Daley was rattled by the announcement of his death and Patterson did not like the way things had suddenly turned. A new element had emerged and he wondered whether it was such a good idea to stick with Daley who suddenly seemed to be bad news. "Have you had your hands in the till? Kept some of the extortion money? Creamed some off the top? Are your friends after you?"

"If you don't like my company, piss off." Daley spoke quietly when he might have raged. He did not want Patterson to go yet; the Prot might shop him.

Patterson was suffering a dilemma of his own. He did not know his way around down here. At least Daley had avoided towns and villages. They simply had not been prepared for the escape; none of them had, which was why half had already been caught. He probed just the same. "If that's what you want. It doesn't matter any more. We'll be picked up for sure." Patterson climbed to his feet and brushed off some of the bracken.

Daley sat with his knees up and his head held between them. He suddenly looked up at Patterson, realising something of his recklessness; there was almost an air of defeat about him as he replied. "I can't stop you. That radio announcement means I can't use the usual places. They've arranged my death to make it easy for themselves; I can't die twice. They think I did something I did not do. I'm not in a good position to explain."

"Nice bunch."

"Your lot do the same. There has to be rigid discipline."

17

"Sure, but we get a trial. A chance to explain."

Daley offered a sickly grin. "That makes a difference?"

"So what do you want to do?"

"There's one place I helped set up myself. That's where we were heading. There will be clothes and food. I arranged it with another guy."

"And he'll keep quiet? He won't go along with the rest who want to put a bullet in the back of your head?"

"He's in Albany. We have a little time."

Albany top security prison was on the Isle of Wight, regarded as part of mainland Britain. It could take just a little time for communication to be effective. "Then we'd better get cracking. How far?"

"Another five miles, I reckon. It's difficult to judge distance under these conditions. We fixed it further back from the border because the border spots are being picked off or under observation by the SAS."

Patterson did not reply. He believed in shoot to kill. The IRA had declared war on Britain and he saw no reason why Britain should not declare war back and shoot the bastards as they showed themselves, armed or not. It would be no more than what the IRA had been doing for years. Certainly innocent people might get killed, but fewer than were already being killed; that was war. People who did not deserve it got hurt. But as Patterson saw it, it was the only way to stop the ultimate carnage. They trudged on, following the lines of the narrower lanes and burying themselves in the hedges whenever they heard anything approach.

The coming of dusk was a blessing. The sky clouded up but the threatened rain held off. It was easier now; until they saw the dark shape of a road block. Again their luck held. A policeman was smoking and the glow of a match showed up like a forest fire between cupped hands.

Daley swore vehemently under his breath. For once he was absolutely sure of where he was and reckoned they were no more than a quarter of a mile from his hideout. The two men drew back. There were two cars drawn across the narrow road, lights out. It was impossible to say just how many Garda there were and it did not matter.

"Now what?" whispered Patterson. They were both tired, their feet sore and they were hungry and thirsty again. Weariness had probably been responsible for them losing concentration at a critical time.

There was silence then the muffled tones of whispered conversation further down the lane. And then, just when they thought they had reacted in time, a voice by the cars said, "There's someone up there. Let's see."

The running footsteps drew closer all too fast as Patterson and Daley gazed at each other in the gloom. Suddenly, legs that had been moving all day would not move at all and they were rooted.

3

Hans Steinbach drove into a side street and stopped the rusting Opel. He had been on the run since the Berlin Wall came down. When that happened East German protection went out of the window. Many of his colleagues, and his girlfriend Ingrid, had been picked up quickly as the speed of the co-operation between both Germanys took everyone by surprise.

As each Eastern Bloc country threw out its Communist government, security services had disintegrated as everyone looked after themselves, in much the same way the Nazis had scuttled after the war. Everything changed overnight: Presidents were ousted, imprisoned, killed.

Schools for terrorism hastily closed down. Terrorists who had kept the West busy with their acts of violence and had been harboured in Eastern Europe, where most of them had been trained anyway, were now on the run.

Steinbach had been trained at Dolni Brezany, ten miles from Prague and at the famous East German camp at Finsterwalde, near Dresden, which had been called the 'Stasilager', after the state security police. Over a period of twenty years thousands of terrorists had trained in these camps including Italy's Red Brigade, Germany's Red Army Faction, African liberation groups and the armed wing of the ANC. Carlos and Abu Nidal were frequent visitors. And the doors had always been open for men on the run from the West. Where terrorists had trained with guns at Finsterwalde, children now laughed and played; already it had been turned into a school. It was another kind of war.

Now, apart from the Middle East, there was suddenly nowhere to run and safe houses had become an open invitation to imprisonment. There was little that was safe to go to in Europe, but even the few exceptions were now treated with massive suspicion. Suddenly nobody wanted their violent services any more and few were keen to go to Libya or Syria. They had been thrown back on their own resources which were suddenly revealed as being painfully thin. The terrorist groups had grown used to being nurtured by the Eastern Bloc camps, which at times had been almost like holiday centres.

Steinbach had refrained from going with the original exodus. For one thing it was all too soon and he needed time to work out a strategy. For another, once over the border most had been herded into schools and camps, until it was decided how to deal with them. Steinbach preferred not to take such a risk.

By the speed of the round-up of some of his friends he knew that border police would be on the look-out for such as him. He had to get to the West, though. Far too much recrimination was happening all around him in East Germany and his face had appeared too often in the Western press. The police had seized an opportunity they could not have expected to come their way so swiftly.

Steinbach had always worn a beard but that had come off and he looked quite different clean-shaven. He also wore brown contact lenses over his blue eyes, and an unruly dark wig over his naturally fair hair. Whether or not he cared for it, his undisguised appearance was Aryan. Hitler would have been proud of him except that Steinbach was some way left of communism.

He had extra passports, one readily to hand fitted his present appearance. The passport supply had dried up when Nicolae Ceausescu's Rumania had collapsed. The Securitate had supplied hundreds of forged passports as well as bugging equipment to Arafat and the PLO. All these people were going to miss the excellent service which so unbelievably quickly had been taken away from them. And Steinbach was one of them. It had taken him some weeks to get himself organised and not to panic as friends were picked up all around him. There were weeks when he dare not stay more than one night at a time in any one place. But he had kept his head while others lost theirs.

21

He would miss Ingrid. They had been together for years. Her political passion was a reflection of her sexual intensity and he would be lucky ever to find someone as satisfying. He thought about her often, but now the only certainty was that he would never see her again. Once he had discovered at which prison she was being held he had smuggled in some poisoned confectionery to her through a friend. It had taken a little organising but in the past both of them had managed to smuggle in arms to friends.

Ingrid knew too much about him and might predict what he would do. He had trusted her but did not know her breaking point and how far her captors would go. He had been trained in a certain way and expected all police forces to act as he had been taught to do. He survived by not taking chances; now it was even more important not to lose concentration.

Steinbach's concern was the possibility of failing to travel freely with his forged passport, and that arms around the car might be discovered. Should he ditch them and try to start again elsewhere?

As he sat in the old car he finally plumped for safety. He would have to start again, build up his contacts. Perhaps a few of the old ones had made it to the West and could be located.

There was a small canal on the outskirts of the city and he thought it best to dump his arms there. It was a noticeably poorer area even for East Berlin. He backed into a cobbled alley, made sure he was unseen, pulled out the car seats and the floor covering and produced parts of a sub-machine gun, two 9mm semi-automatic pistols, three grenades and a small quantity of Semtex, fuses and detonators, and rammed them all in two shopping bags.

He worked with thin gloves on, wiping the parts as they appeared. There was little refinement in what he did, but all he needed to do was to lose the weapons until he was safely in West Berlin. Even if the police were not at the old crossing points, even if they were totally lax, State Security would have plain-clothes men there looking for men like him.

Which was why he was concerned when, as he reached the

low bridge in the unimaginatively named Wasserstrasse, and was about to drop the two bags over, an old lady appeared. He had not seen nor heard her approach, which angered him for it showed his nerviness.

"Don't litter the canal," she yelled at him, approaching quite fast now. She was poorly dressed and grey-faced but clearly had her standards. "Just what do you think you are doing?"

The small canal was already filthy with litter. Facing him across the bridge was the blank wall of an old factory which almost certainly discharged its own waste into the narrow canal. The central base of the building was arched so that the canal could flow through; litter had fouled the passage creating a mild turbulence. The water stank. On the opposite side of the bridge was a row of boarded up shops and the whole area was one of decay. As Steinbach turned to face the woman it was difficult to understand her complaint when so much had been tipped over the bridge before.

"I shouldn't think it will make the slightest difference," he said, "but, OK, I'll find a bin." Anything to avoid trouble.

"No you won't. As soon as I'm gone you'll come back and tip your rubbish in the water. It used to be so nice here; so pretty. Until it was spoiled by people like you."

She lashed out at him with an ancient umbrella and caught him across the side of the neck, making him reel. As he fell back against the bridge he realised that she was slightly crazy. She came at him again, striking wildly. He had not really been hurt by the first blow but she now caught him across the knuckles and he dropped one of the bags. A grenade rolled across the cobbles.

She did not notice at first but it was still rolling and her weary eyes suddenly filled with fear as she realised what it was. She backed away, chin sagging. It was too late. Steinbach took a quick look round, reached out and killed her with one sharp pressure on the throat. Almost in the same movement he tipped her over the bridge and threw the bags after her, followed by the loose grenade. He went straight to the Opel and drove off. He did not think he had been seen.

As he motored towards the West he had no feelings about

the old woman. He had been quick and he could not leave her alive to provide a description; he needed his disguise for a while yet. But it was a nuisance and a timely reminder of the unexpected.

Detective Superintendent John O'Neil gazed at Shaw across the desk. Nothing had changed much since the stranger had issued his veiled instructions to Shaw about the disappearance of Con Daley. Now, a day later, he was being interviewed by a top copper from Dublin, of all places. What was wrong with the Cork coppers? What the hell did Dublin know about the Cork people?

Shaw had taken O'Neil into a box of an office off the main one with the three desks, for a little privacy. It was his own office but was so small he preferred to work with his colleagues with more space.

O'Neil felt sorry for Shaw. Intimidation was an old problem and family men were most vulnerable. He doubted that the tiny office offered the kind of privacy Shaw would have liked; those in the other office had only to stand close to the door to hear what was going on. So the big, burly, but usually amiable O'Neil tried to keep his voice down. But he was from Dublin and he could not disguise that from the moment he opened his mouth. It was a disadvantage down here, but it was a Special Branch matter rather than criminal.

"I know you're straight," said O'Neil, glancing towards the door. "The local boys tell me you're as honest as they come and I can see that for myself. But you're holding out on me, you see. Someone has put the frighteners on you. I ask you, that little shit Con Daley on the *Mary R* with his brother. I know about Mike Daley; it was thrown up when we did our first check on our darling Con. Con would be sea-sick standing on the edge of a quay. The two brothers could not be more different and Con was in for murder. There can be no attempted reconciliation with that. So who called on you and put on the pressure?"

Shaw was out of his depth. He was so basically honest that he had no idea how to lie convincingly. But he was still worried about his family. "No one called."

24

"Look," said O'Neil, searching for a pipe in his many pockets, "they won't hurt you or yours. We are not going to contradict the story. On the contrary, we shall help it along a bit. We would like it to be true; people like Con Daley need a few permanent fathoms above their heads. But we don't believe we're that lucky." He finally found his pipe and started to foul up the small room. He smiled across the minuscule desk. "It might help us if they believe we believe. But, you know, they haven't done it for us. They wanted the news to reach Con. They want him to sweat. And then they want to get their hands on him before we do. That's why they did it. You've done your bit; you're in no danger."

O'Neil searched for something to put his smoking match in. He had the feeling that a little carelessness on his part could send the whole building up in smoke.

Shaw pushed a coffee lid across for O'Neil to drop the match into. He felt easy with this man, although still puzzled why a local affair had attracted Dublin. Everyone felt easy with O'Neil, even those who swore, cursed and threatened him as he helped them on their way to jail.

"Now tell me exactly what happened," said O'Neil comfortably. "Take your time and then I'll get out of your hair and your staff can get on with their jobs."

4

Patterson and Daley broke the spell and turned to run back up the lane. Desperation was on their side. Neither man spoke or called out, their voices would be an immediate giveaway. As matters stood, they could be poachers, thieves, anyone. They knew where there were gaps in the hedge, it was instinctive to record them, but running destroyed the pattern. They ran faster than the police who could not know whether or not they were armed.

Daley, who was slightly in front, dived head first to his left and Patterson had just enough time to check and to follow. The animal instinct in Daley surfaced as he immediately headed back towards the police cars which were now the other side of the thick hedge.

This meant slowing right down or be heard. It also meant heading out into the open field away from the lane to cut sound right down. They were more exposed but further away from the cars and the police weren't sure which way they had gone.

Flashlights came on but the beams followed a crazy pattern as the police were still running. Cars started up and headlights flashed on. Patterson and Daley threw themselves flat in the stubble of a harvested field. One set of headlights broke through the hedge to send broken shafts of brilliant light and strange, confusing shadows, across the field.

Both cars shifted position. One sped off to follow the running policemen who switched off their flashlights as the car's beams approached to cast their elongated shadows up the lane, until it seemed that the two men were actually following their own shadows. If it created extra light it also caused a confusion which helped Patterson and Daley.

The second car remained stationary after repositioning to keep its lights trained in the direction of the others. Under cover of the noise of the moving car, Patterson and Daley raced across the field into the comforting darkness. By the time the police decided to split up and diversify the search the two men were well to the south and still running.

When shortage of breath forced them to stop, they bent over, hands on knees trying to recover. The car lights were well behind them and facing the wrong way.

Daley gasped, "We'll have to take a chance on the bolthole."

Patterson nodded in the dark. They could not stay in open country. If the police could not find them now they would start again at first light and would bring reinforcements and dogs. They continued south as the least likely direction the police would expect them to take.

Daley found the bolthole. It was inside a small copse. In the dark it seemed to Patterson to be no more than a series of spaced-out sheds and as far as he could see most of them were falling down. Daley guided him around, feeling his way, for there was no light and if there had been they dare not use it.

Then they tumbled across the old still, drums and bottles and pipes and a copper cylinder. Patterson did not like the idea. "An illegal still? This will be the first place they'll search come daybreak."

"They'll have done that already. Many times. The still is all broken up, in a state of complete disuse. In its present state nobody could make poteen here." A touch of pride came through as Daley added, "We deliberately made it like this. Run-down, disused, derelict. Ideal."

"Clever bugger. Or was it the other bloke's idea?"

"He helped me assemble it. Cost a song; half the timbers are rotten, the still has bloody great holes, and the pipes are broken. It was designed for the Garda to find and then leave alone. All the local coppers will know about it. But they won't expect us to."

"Is there food and water here?"

"Not on show. That would be stupid."

Daley led the way into a long hut which had a table with a

broken leg and a couple of rickety chairs. The floorboards were rotten in places and he walked carefully. "It might be better to stay outside. One of us must keep awake. There's not much we can do until daybreak. Then I'll show you where there's food and water."

Patterson was suddenly suspicious; it was as if they were starting out all over again. "We'll both stay awake."

"That means we'll both nod off. We're tired out. Do you think I'd top you while you're asleep? If they find you dead or alive they'll find me too. Nothing's changed."

"Okay, I'll stay awake and will call you when I can't do it any more."

But Daley was right. The two men were so exhausted that soon after Daley fell asleep, so, too, did Patterson. He struggled to keep awake but it was made more impossible by not being able to move about. It was too precarious to walk with so much lying around to trip over. Exhaustion took over and he dozed off, back against one of the buildings, and then he fell sideways in a deep sleep.

Even the October chill did not rouse Patterson who knew nothing more until he felt an excruciating pain in his thigh, and then another. He struggled to a sitting position to find it was broad daylight and Daley was standing over him, about to kick him again.

"You useless bugger," said Daley. "We could have gone down the tube."

Patterson felt terrible, as if he had been drinking all night. He struggled up, unable to speak, rubbing his thigh where Daley had kicked it. Eventually, he said, "You do that again and I'll throttle you."

"You sure you've got the strength? Come on, I'll show you the set-up."

Patterson limped after him and Daley led the way to where the still was kept. It was even untidier in daylight: there were jars and tin cans strewn all over the place, and the amount of twisted copper piping made it look like a derelict plumber's yard. Daley picked his way through to a covered area beyond the hut which might have been a bicycle shed. To add to this illusion were a couple of buckled wheels and an old rusted frame.

28

Sheets of corrugated iron lay in a shallow pile, with a few scattered randomly. The only reason they had not been stolen was that most of them were broken or holed.

"Help me with this one." Daley pointed to one of the separated sheets. They moved it aside to find a mass of slugs. Daley used one of the broken pieces as a shovel and scraped away the earth. There was about three inches of soil on top of a few planks of wood which Patterson helped him lift. Underneath was a hole resembling a small slit trench. At its bottom, about three feet down, were grimed tins of food, and bottles of water. There were also some big black plastic bags which looked like bin-bags, filled and sealed.

Daley lowered himself down and passed up some cans and water to Patterson. An opener was taped to one of the cans and he handed up an unopened box of paper cups and plastic utensils. He heaved two of the heavy plastic bags out.

"Basic rations," said Daley, as he climbed out of the pit. "Let's see if the clothes fit first and then we'll put everything back as it was."

They stripped naked where they stood. Daley broke open a bag and tossed one to Patterson. "I know these will fit me because I chose them and put them there. Those are for a bigger man but I don't guarantee they'll fit you."

They were silent all the time they dressed. Daley was ready quickly, having donned clean underwear, a white short-sleeved shirt, light-blue jeans and jacket, and a raincoat. He had included a pair of his own shoes. Patterson was faced with a bigger problem because of his extra height and Daley made him jump into the pit himself to bring up two more bags. When he had finished he looked much the same as Daley except that he wore canvas shoes because the more conventional style would not fit him.

They tidied up, sealed and returned what they did not want, put back the sheet of corrugated iron, and everything looked much the same as before. As they carried the cans into the main building, half its roof hanging down and a big, jagged hole in the other half, Patterson was thinking that if there was a hole to keep foods, where was the one to keep arms.

They sat against the soundest part of the wall and Daley opened some cans. There were no plates and nothing with which to heat the food; a primus might be a giveaway, whether for heat or light. The place was nothing more than a survival transit camp. Patterson did not mind eating cold stew and meats direct from the can with a plastic spoon, and the tinned fruit was an added luxury. Daley must have thought it out very carefully. It showed another side to the man and Patterson wondered what else Daley had prepared for. His early uneasiness returned.

The pattern Daley had set in his bolthole was a harsh one. There was no spade or shovel which would have made clearing the earth and burying the tins much easier. He had thought every detail through. If it was to appear derelict then that was what it would be so the Garda would find nothing suspicious. If they found the holes then that was too bad, but Daley had provided no reason for them to think that they might be there.

When they had buried the rubbish, including their prison clothes, in a pit Daley had prepared a little distance from the bolthole, Patterson said reluctantly, "You've done a good job here."

"I had a lot of time to plan it."

"So apart from your friend in Albany, nobody else knows about this place?"

Daley wiped his lips: "Only you."

They entered the main building again, feeling quite different now that they were dressed normally. Yet Patterson was disturbed; he had his own reasons for staying with Daley but their liaison was unnatural, even though forced together by circumstance. Yet Daley had supplied food and clothes and it had not been for love – which suggested Daley had something in mind and that would not be to Patterson's advantage. There was also the inevitable religious difference, but each was capable of slipping in and out of religion as it suited them. Both were practised in calling on the support of those institutions, religious or political, when convenient and true allegiance was obscured.

"I can't understand why the police haven't come back."

Patterson squatted with his back to the wall wondering what happened next, for he was now very much in Daley's hands.

"I reckon they had already done this area. They were working their way up. Anyway, so far as they are concerned we could have been any villains. The road block might not have been for us at all."

"Put the radio on low and see if we can pick anything up."

"I dropped it crossing the fields."

Patterson slowly digested the implications of that news. "So if they find it they will know which way we came. And if the farmer reports its loss we'll have shown up our trail. Great. What next?"

"The farmer won't report it. It was stuck up high on the dresser; it wasn't being used. If the Garda find it we could have been going either way. I think it best to wait until later in the day before we move; unless we're forced out. It will give time for things to settle. Then we head south again."

Patterson gazed across the dilapidated room to the man sitting against the opposite wall, as if they needed the distance between them. Now they had got rid of their uniforms, natural positions were already being adopted.

"We need some money," said Patterson bluntly.

"I have some. Enough for the present." Daley smiled knowingly. "It was buried with my clothes."

"What about lending me some?"

"No. I'll use it for both of us, mind."

"Why? Why should you give a damn about me?"

"I thought we'd already decided why. Until we're really clear we need each other. If one gets caught the other will soon be picked up. We stand a better chance together. For the moment."

"Did you bury some arms, too?"

"We don't want to be caught with arms. We might get searched crossing the water."

"So why have you got an automatic stuffed in the back of your waistband?" There was an underlying steeliness in the question.

"You're sharp. Or I've been careless. Didn't think you'd notice. It's to blow your bloody head off if you try any funny business, like chickening out to the police." Daley smiled. "Self-defence. You're a big boy and you're black-hearted, so you are."

"Now we know where we stand. If we can't trust each other to escape together we'd better split up."

"We've always known where we stand. But we still need each other. I can get you arms, but at the right time. I don't want an execution on my hands right now. Think about it."

Patterson did. He felt naked against an armed Daley. He tried to keep it light. "I suppose you could have put a slug in the back of my head had you wanted to. You must have been tempted against one more soft target."

"Don't push your luck, Patterson. There's the enemy and there's us. And you're one of the enemy. You bastards killed my wife and injured her friend."

"And you bastards killed my mother and sister. Perhaps it's as well you have the gun. You need it."

The venom from Daley could be felt across the room but he made no move and the two men simply stared at each other, hatred flowing out.

After a while, Patterson stood up. "This won't get us anywhere, will it? You have the gun, there's not much I can do. I shouldn't have fallen asleep last night; I suppose that was when you got it."

Patterson gazed down at Daley whose vehemence was still simmering. "You'll have to shoot me in the back because I'm off. I don't know where, and it doesn't really matter." He gazed round the wreck of a room. "You can't use this again anyway. It's blown and I think you are giving too much time to your mate in Albany. The UK police will have contacted him by now, if only because you two were old buddies. You haven't the time you think you have." Patterson nodded in farewell. "Send me a postcard."

Daley scrambled to his feet. "You're probably right. Let's get moving."

Patterson was puzzled. Every time he tried to break away, Daley blocked it one way or the other.

"Look," Daley said. "I've got to get rid of the gun before

32

we leave Ireland; it's too risky to take. I can get you arms the other side. As many as you want."

Daley was on the verge of pleading but all that did was to make Patterson more uncomfortable. Patterson needed to find a telephone but with an armed Daley hanging on like a leech it was going to be a big risk. Yet somehow he had to try.

5

'Pongo' Waring rose from his desk, looked down into the street and decided that nobody worked any more. It was barely four o'clock and already people were scurrying home. They could hardly blame the weather, for it was a pleasant October afternoon, the sort of day he enjoyed.

He was a big man, once a great sportsman, and had obtained his nickname from being a life-long supporter of Aston Villa Football Club, and was called after the great soccer centre forward of long, long ago, although the unkindly suggested he was a contemporary. But never to his face.

A Police Commander at New Scotland Yard, Pongo Waring did not suffer fools gladly and had a low flashpoint with idiots, not that there were now many around him. He drove his staff hard but most worshipped him and his results were plain to see. Which was why he had been assigned to C13, the Anti-Terrorist Squad.

He had been in constant touch with the RUC about the breakout from the Maghabery prison because four of the escapees were terrorists. The home-made bomb had resulted in the death of the man who had made it, and the rest were minor injuries. But it had thrown security out of the window for a brief period and six sharp-witted prisoners had made their escape. They could hardly have expected the opportunity.

The news media had been quick to report that three men had been recaptured, a fourth was reportedly holed up somewhere in Armagh surrounded by police, and Daley had been drowned at sea. That left Patterson on the loose. As both the RUC and the Irish Special Branch in Dublin had expressed disbelief about the drowning, that still left Daley, and if he was with Patterson that concerned Waring very much indeed.

He crossed to his desk and pressed the buzzer. A fair-haired man in his late thirties entered and crossed the room, slowed down by a slight limp; he had been shot in the thigh close to an artery nine months previously. Detective Inspector Peter Gaunt bore a resemblance to his name, but he had not always been thin in the face, which his height exaggerated. Gaunt had suffered and was lucky to be alive. His wounding had not been reported, and for once, reporters, with good reason, having sniffed out a story, left it alone.

"That's the report on Patterson," said Gaunt.

Waring sat at his desk and looked up giving a nod to Gaunt to indicate a chair; he knew what it cost his subordinate to stand too long. He studied the report and said, "I thought this fellow was in Hull."

Gaunt sat down. "Then it's a different Patterson."

Waring picked up the print-out. "Where did you get this?"

Gaunt stared in surprise. "From central records. What's the problem?"

"Who did you see at records?"

"Young. He was transferred from SB some few months ago."

"And who did he take over from?"

"Kenny Graham. He's now retired. Vetting Status lifted some four months ago."

"The stupid dozy bugger. Is he responsible for this?"

Gaunt leaned over the desk to read the print-out heading upside down and backwards. "Yes. That's his reference." He could see that Waring was quietly fuming. "What's wrong?"

"How can a man be in two prisons at once? It's bloody impossible"

"He's *that* Patterson? The name is not uncommon. I did not make the connection."

Waring was pensive for some time, fingers across lips. "I want this straightened out with records at once. *At once*, Peter. And check with the RUC. I hope they're not playing silly buggers. The last thing we want is another enquiry. Now where's the Daley file?"

35

Gaunt looked embarrassed. "It was borrowed by Bradbear of Five. I think he's still using it."

Gaunt thought Waring was going to explode. The commander half rose from his chair, then subsided slowly. "Just what the hell is going on? Two consecutive cock-ups: first Patterson, now Daley. Are you telling me the file has been released to him?"

Gaunt was quick to pacify. "He has the clearance; he's got it in the reading room. It's all under control."

Waring tried to reduce his steam. "What's wrong with their own files? Do Five think they can play me for a fool because I've only been with C13 for a few weeks. They had better not forget how long I've been a copper. Get Daley's file at once and tell Bradbear to clear it with me first the next time he wants to see something of ours. Anyway, I want to see him before he leaves the building."

Waring stared at the door after Gaunt had left. He was used to interdepartmental rivalry but the higher up the tree the sneakier it became. Once the Security Service came into it they seemed to think they could override everyone about everything. There had been too many slip-ups between the services and too often at crucial times. Terrorists had got away because of lack of liaison between the Security Service, Special Branch, and the Anti-Terrorist Squad. Waring could see most problems as sporting analogies, and, too often, individual departments wanted to hold the ball too long when others were better positioned to use it.

Waring was a copper through and through, a fine detective, or he would not be where he now was. To him terrorism was a straight issue of getting the bombers. Dealing with the political side was not his job, nor did he entertain it. Politicians came and went and the problem remained the same and people got killed, all too often in horrendous circumstances. Detection was the major part of his job and ordinary villains could often be just as elusive as terrorists. The difference was that all terrorists were willing to kill; if they made a mistake and got the wrong person it was too bad and they expressed the view that they should not have been driven to it.

Waring hated violent killing but most of all he hated indiscriminate violent killing. Nobody would believe that he became emotionally involved when he visited a scene where someone had been blown to bits by a car bomb. He was supposed to be a hardened copper and personal feelings should play no part. One could never become completely hardened against that sort of thing and contact made it worse. Only the killers got satisfaction but they seldom saw the final result.

In the few weeks since Waring had taken over C13, he had been to the site of four bomb outrages, three of the victims had been blown to bits, the fourth had lost his legs and was in a critical condition, and was the wrong target anyway. It was Waring's ambition to bring as many bombers to justice as he could. And for that he needed the help of the general public. And no party games from MI5 and the Special Branch. The first evidence of either of these organisations going their own way on the terrorist patch, or of interference into his own enquiries, then he would take steps even if it meant committing suicide by going public.

Waring accepted the obvious, that there was a vast amount of good liaison between the departments almost all the time, in fact. But self-interest was always a factor, and he was too experienced not to know that he was sometimes impeded by accident or design. He kept his eyes open.

Carmel Daley was taken in for questioning by the RUC in Belfast. She had been expecting it but had done nothing to avoid it. She was a pretty girl in a hard sort of way and, at the moment, wore no make-up. Dressed in tight jeans and jacket she was bundled into the car as a small crowd shouted insults at the police, while an army patrol stood by as back-up. Her departure was watched by many people, some with a direct interest in the outcome of her police visit.

Carmel was Daley's common-law wife. She had changed her name to stop people talking about her living with Con Daley. It only made matters worse but it made her feel better in herself and gave her a false sense of respectability.

What the police wanted to know she could not tell them.

She had absolutely no idea where Daley had gone. He had not contacted her, which upset her, and she knew of no hideouts where he might be. She did not know if he was north or south of the border. She knew nothing. But it took five hours of questioning for the police to arrive at this, and still they were not completely satisfied; not even when she eventually broke down in tears. That was a first, but it tugged at no hearts amongst a constabulary which had seen its numbers murderously eroded over twenty years and more.

Carmel refused the police car offered to take her home and took a bus, walking the last half-mile. She was no sooner inside her small terraced house than the bell rang and two men were leaning against opposite walls when she opened the door. She would have slammed the door in their faces but knew they would finally break the door down if she did not let them in. She stood aside wearily.

"Nice to see you, Carmel. You're looking great."

"Sure. I always look my best when I've seen the police."

"It's a habit, is it? We thought it was the first time, so we did."

She led the way into the kitchen, refusing to give them the satisfaction of the front room. She knew both of them well. They were known as the 'terrible twins' although they were not related. Flynn and Mooney. But there was a similarity between them. Both were short and stocky and both wore untidy beards. They appeared to be, and were, tough, with the hard eyes of their calling and an evident lack of feeling for the nicer side of life. She knew why they were there but it did not help her come to terms with them.

When they were all sitting round the kitchen table, she made no offer to make tea, she said, "I can tell you no more than I told the police."

Mooney grinned, arms folded across his thick-set chest. "That's what interests us, Carmel. Just what did you tell them? They came to hostile territory to collect you. They must have thought you had something for them. Tell us what you told them."

Carmel felt she had had enough. "I told them that they had made a mistake picking me up for as soon as I got back

38

Mooney and Flynn would call on me to check out what I said."

Mooney leaned across the table but it was Flynn who delivered the backhander to send Carmel crashing to the floor taking the chair with her.

Carmel cracked her head on the old quarry tiles and passed out. The two men leaned forward to see where she finished up and waited patiently until she came to. They made no effort to help her up. She clung to the edge of the table and gradually pulled herself upright, and then she bent down to scoop up the chair. Her mind was reeling as she said, "You pigs. It must make you feel good to hit a woman." She was beyond caring whether or not they hit her again.

As if nothing had happened, Mooney said, "Come on, Carmel, don't mess about. Just tell us what happened and we can be on our way."

She sank slowly on to the chair. The two men were indistinct across the table to which she clung for support. In a quivering voice she answered, "I had nothing to tell them. I don't know where Con has gone. He hasn't contacted me and I don't suppose he will."

"Where would he be likely to go?"

"How would I know? And if you're his friends, as you always claim, why don't you know?"

"We'll put your teeth through your lip next time, Carmel. Don't play around with us. You must have talked about it some time."

"How could we? He didn't know he was going to be picked up. And as sure as hell he didn't know he was about to escape either. All the papers and TV say it was a freak thing to happen. There were five others, for God's sake. Unless he gets in touch there's no way I'll know." She gazed from one to the other and added, "You know damn well that if he had somewhere in mind he wouldn't have told anyone, especially me."

It was something they could believe. They pushed their chairs back and rose. "We'll take your word for now. But God help you if you hear from him and don't tell us. You understand?"

Carmel nodded and wiped blood from her mouth. "Why do you need to find him?"

The two men exchanged glances and grinned. "That's obvious," replied Mooney. "We want to help him. He'll never make it on his own." He paused, gazing down without compassion. "If you need money let us know. We always look after our own."

Before she could stop herself Carmel said, "And we all know how." As Flynn stepped towards her she added hastily, "Anyway, how do you know he's on his own? What about Patterson?"

It was as if an ice age had entered the room.

Ingrid Lotz was ushered into an interrogation room and struggled all the way. She had made life so difficult during the short time she had been in prison that she had been put in an isolation cell. There she had curled up and shouted insults at the door until exhausted.

She should have saved her energy, for while she lay alone and empty she could think only of Hans Steinbach. She needed him badly and felt his loss. At that stage she was helpless and on the verge of weeping, but still had sufficient spirit and fanaticism not to show her feelings to her captors.

It took three wardresses to get her into the room and make her sit down at a bare table, wrists handcuffed behind her. She had no intention of making it easy for them and she was up in a flash and running round the room kicking over her chair and another the other side of the table. She was trying to heave the table over when they grabbed her and held her down. Someone called for a restraining harness and it was only then that Ingrid began to calm down; she hated being in a strait-jacket, it was the one piece of apparatus which could deter her. To be harnessed was like being imprisoned inside herself; she felt she could explode like a bomb.

They got her back on the chair but by then the harness was on view and they made sure it stayed in her sight. By this time she was breathing heavily from the strain of resisting and sagged on the chair.

She was slight of build, a slim, attractive figure, and her

features were pleasant in repose, which usually meant when asleep. Her bone structure was good and, had she looked after herself, she could so easily have made a living from modelling. But she did not want or need money; her middle-class family had plenty of money and it was against them and their smug kind that she had rebelled. Like many converts to a cause or religion, she had gone madly over the top, helped by the company she picked up along the way. It was too late for Ingrid to turn back, nor did she want to. She had got used to killing. Like so many terrorists she saw herself as a saviour, the rest of the world was rotten, but she could not see beyond the destruction. Perhaps she did not want to.

When she yearned for the comfort of Hans she baulked at accepting it was the only comfort she had in life. There was nothing else left for her to turn to. The euphoria arising from the success of a bloody mission, the destruction of someone she hated because of the way they lived, was short-lived. It provided the same effect as drugs would have done and lasted only so long before the pangs for another injection of violence became crucial to living.

She sat on the hard wood, arms behind her, and watched a wardress pick up the chair the other side of the table. The wardress avoided the baleful stare from Ingrid and joined the other two women near the door.

As Ingrid sat there facing across the table she could feel the presence of the women behind her. She was calming down rapidly now. Tantrums, all part of her eternal protest, took up energy and she felt drained yet still full of hatred. There was a knock on the door and she heard a man's voice and felt the faint draught of the door opening and closing.

Two men appeared in front of her. They wore plain-clothes, and had police written all over them. One, the taller, dark haired, took up a standing position in a corner. The other, work-weary eyes concentrating on a parcel he placed on the table, sat opposite her. He was in his early fifties, balding, and was clearly the senior.

The Stasi, she thought. And then she reflected that the East

41

German Security Police were already on the run and was puzzled as to who these two experienced men might be. Surely not from the West. But did it matter?

The seated man glanced over her shoulder and said, "Undo her cuffs and then leave us alone."

"She's violent. I think we should stay?"

"Just do as I say. Please." His smile was not unpleasant and his weary eyes almost came to life.

When the cuffs were off and the door was closed Ingrid sat rubbing her wrists. Scathingly she said, "Aren't you afraid I'll claw your eyes out?"

"No. Try anything and I'll break your jaw and an arm, and if you get too rough, Geyer there will put a slug or two into you to stop you breeding other little shits like yourself." He smiled quite warmly. "To be honest, we're hoping you try something. Your mob killed a good friend of ours. My name is Krempel, so let's get on with it."

So they were from the West. Everything had moved so quickly. But they must surely have been invited here, or had made a request to visit. She was suddenly uneasy, thinking it might somehow involve Hans.

Krempel placed his hands either side of the paper-covered parcel. "Could be a bomb, couldn't it?" He carefully took away the covering to fold it neatly and put it on one side. A box of chocolates lay between them. The outer cellophane had already been stripped off but that would be done with anything suspicious, and with someone like Ingrid whatever was sent to her would be examined.

Krempel eased off the lid. "These are Belgian. Not easy to find this side of the wall. Must have cost a bomb."

In the corner Geyer smiled at his chief's weak joke. He noticed that Ingrid had stiffened up, gaze on the note just inside the lid.

"The note came separately," Krempel explained. "We put it in the box as it was easier to carry. Here, it's for you. You had better read it."

Ingrid snatched it from him. She held it up as if trying to keep its contents from the others who must already have read it. Her heart thumped but she managed to keep her expression blank. Only her quivering hands gave her away. It was from Hans, of course, although there was nothing to indicate that in the note. It was not even signed, it did not need to be, but it did offer all the love of the sender and that was enough for her. She had known he would be in touch. "How long have you had this?" she demanded.

The two men exchanged casual glances and Krempel said, "A day or two. You were in isolation and therefore denied all privileges. It's from Hans Steinbach."

She clutched the note to her breast. "You don't know who it's from so don't fly a kite, copper."

"We have a sample of his handwriting. From way back. It's from him." He pushed the box of chocolates across the table towards her. "And so are these."

Krempel had spoken in a way that made her doubtful. She said, as if expecting to be contradicted, "The note makes it obvious that the chocolates are from the same person."

"Ah! I am glad you accept that. Aren't you going to have one?" Again Krempel spoke in a way that made Ingrid nervous.

"I'll eat them when I feel like it. Certainly not in front of you."

Krempel again glanced at Geyer. They seemed to have a private joke going between them. He turned back to Ingrid: "We were rather hoping you would have one now. Just one. You wouldn't want another."

Ingrid felt cold. They were playing with her. She examined the chocolates; they appeared fresh enough. "What have you done with them?"

"Nothing, but open the box." Krempel chuckled. "I have to tell you that the cellophane was already off when they arrived. Hans knew that, as a matter of course, it would be removed before the box reached you. And you would expect it to have been removed, so nobody would be disappointed. Go on, have one."

Ingrid tried to control her hands and put them below table level. What were these two playing at? What were they suggesting? "Why don't you come to the point, you stupid bastard?"

"The point is that if you take one you would not be alive to take another."

Ingrid, already pale, lost all colour. Her normal reaction would be to dive at them, and she noticed that Geyer had slipped his hand inside his jacket where the gun would be. But instead of fury she felt fear; a cold hard fear of a kind she had never experienced. And she felt sick. Barely able to speak, she said, "You've poisoned them, you shits."

"You're not thinking, Ingrid. Whatever you might think we can get away with, poisoning a prisoner in an interview room is not one of them. Whatever our temptation we'd never get away with it. Give us credit for a little common sense."

"Then what are you saying?"

"You know damn well what we are saying. The reason delivery to you was held up was because the chocolates had to be examined. You people get up to all sorts of smart dodges. Half of them might have been Semtex and the other half mini-detonators. They were sent to forensic. More than half of them contain cyanide. Perhaps he knows your favourites; point them out to us and we'll show you if they are marked as poisoned."

But Ingrid could not move. She was now shivering as if she had malaria. Neither man moved; Ingrid was so unpredictable that it would be folly to go near her in her present unbalanced state. And it could be all part of an act.

"He would never do that to me. Never." Her voice had suddenly become small, like a young girl over her first real disappointment.

"He obviously reasoned that you know where he might be going and was taking no chances. Hans is free, at the moment, Ingrid, he wants to stay that way if he can. If he wants to kill you then there has to be a damned good reason. Where would he go? Where is it that he knows you know?"

Ingrid had her arms clasped across her chest in an effort to stop shivering. Then she suddenly looked across the table at Krempel and spat at him. "You bastard. That's what you want, isn't it? You want me to betray him, so you spin this crap about poisoned chocolates. Let's stuff your lie down your stinking throats." She suddenly grabbed the box

44

in front of her and started to cram the chocolates into her mouth.

Krempel dived across the table and Geyer rushed round the side. They yelled for help as they grabbed her, Krempel from behind gripping her round the stomach and jerking hard to make her retch. He succeeded in large measure, for Ingrid had crammed in so many chocolates that she could not chew or swallow any of them. She choked on them as Krempel kept up the pressure, and they began to eject. Meanwhile the door flew open, and the wardresses ran in to help the men and Geyer called out for a doctor.

"We must clear her mouth. Stop her swallowing or biting." But by now Ingrid was being violently sick and they made sure she kept at it. She was lying face down on the floor, writhing and retching by the time the medicos arrived to stretcher her off. The women began to clear up the mess and the two policemen collapsed on to the chairs.

Krempel looked pale. "Let's hope she pulls through."

"What chance has she got?" asked a breathless Geyer as he pulled his legs aside to allow the mop through.

"God knows. She's still alive. She would have to bite deep into the chocolates to get at the cyanide. Steinbach injected it as far as he could; he did not want easy discovery. We'll just have to hope." He rubbed his face wearily. "We need her. If she pulls through this it might convince her we told her the truth. Hopefully she'll want revenge. If you believe in prayer, Willy, now is the time."

6

Their accents were too distinguishable to disguise. The Republican Irish were tolerant of strangers taking them off but a 'stage' Irish accent would deceive no-one down here. They were from the north and it would be evident every time they spoke. Which precluded possibilities like hitching a lift, or hiring a car. Prisoners on the run from up north would be remembered.

They would have to walk unless they could somehow find transport, and short of stealing it there was nothing they could do. The dryer weather was holding and they now carried canned food in two worn canvas grips with some other items Daley had produced from the broken-down still, and which he was secretive about.

They reckoned they were doing about twenty miles a day. They were young and reasonably fit and could have done more but most of the terrain was rough if they were to stay mainly clear of the roads, and there were times when they had to take cover.

When they reached the outskirts of Drogheda they realised they had not made as much ground as they had believed. They skirted the small town and found a car abandoned about four miles south of it. It was a red Ford Fiesta, covered in dust, locked and empty.

The car was on a country road and there was nobody in sight. It was almost too good to be true. As they worked to open the doors there was a strong smell of petrol as if there was a leak or the carburettor had been flooded. Once the wires were crossed the engine started straightaway.

They looked across at each other and burst into laughter. It had been so easy they were suspicious, but nobody could have known they would go that way. Daley drove because he knew the territory better and how to keep to the country roads where traffic was sparse.

"She must have flooded it and panicked. It couldn't have happened too long before we pitched up," Patterson observed.

"She?"

"There are tissues on the shelf and a woman's magazine in the pocket. She must have legged it to the main road and hitched a lift. How long dare we use it? I don't fancy going to Dublin in it."

Daley kept his eye on the road. "We're not going to Dublin. We'll head for Rosslare."

Patterson did not like the way Daley controlled things so easily. There had been no discussion.

Daley took a tight bend and then added, "Look, I've had more time to think. If they reckon we're south of the border they'll keep an extra eye on Dublin and the sea services from Dun Laoghaire. Rosslare is about a hundred and fifty miles from the border; they won't expect us to go so far. It might even be better to go on to Cork. I don't know how much juice these things hold. Even at a self-service station we'll be expected to pass the time of day."

"I'm not keen on spending too long in a stolen car in daylight."

"So who is? Just what can we do about it?" Daley snapped. "We're on the run; sure it was never going to be easy."

That was part of the problem. So far it had been so easy that it almost seemed that they were being allowed to get away. Luck had kept them company all along the route.

They now accepted that they needed each other, for the time being at least. They had entered another kind of prison, barred themselves in. They could not even enter a café for a cup of tea or a pub for a drink. Prison had at least supplied variable company. Now they had only each other and an engine that became more monotonous with each mile. And it would be far from easy to reach England with all the ports on the look-out for them.

"Why don't you lose yourself with the Dublin crowd?"

asked Patterson cagily. "They'll take care of you, pug you up for as long as you want."

"They wouldn't take you. You'd disappear six feet under."

Patterson turned to look at Daley without learning anything. "I didn't realise you were doing this all for me. God bless you, Con. Is it that you dare not turn to them? Or you'll be six feet under yourself?"

"Don't push your luck, Jamie. I haven't noticed you wanting to go back north to the protection of your crowd."

"It's more difficult up there and you know it. Even if we're caught down here extradition is a strong and emotional thing. We might be on opposite sides but we carry the same political argument. But you're right; I'll drop it. Bickering won't help either of us."

Daley glanced across. A contrite Patterson somehow did not fit, which made him uneasier than before. He knew the truth was that they could never trust each other. It was not possible. They were on opposite sides of a highly charged war of fanatical belief. When he thought about it, it was a miracle that they had remained so long together. And yet he knew something bound them other than escape.

After a while Patterson drove under Daley's direction to give the IRA man a break. They had been concentrating so much on getting clear of Drogheda that it was some time before they woke up to the fact that the car had a radio. They tuned in to wait for the news. They rated only a tail-end snippet but discovered that all the other escapees were now back under lock and key. They had all been caught in Ulster.

They did a huge loop around Dublin, not even touching the back streets, and continued south to be held up by a tractor on a very narrow country road. By this time Daley was driving again and he pulled up and waited for the tractor to move; there was no room to pass.

The tractor driver climbed down and walked back towards them. His lean, hardened body was all sinew and muscle. His creased face showed the struggle of years. "She's broken down. Paddy's gone off to get a tow."

"How long will he be?" asked Daley.

48

"It's just four miles up the lane. He's been gone ten minutes."

"Can't you move her just enough for us to squeeze past?"

"You can help me push her."

Patterson and Daley weighed it up. It was difficult to see where the tractor could be pushed to with the high hedges either side. Somewhere there would be farm tracks leading off and passing points at intervals, but so far as they could see, the tractor had broken down in a most awkward position.

"What do you think?" asked Patterson.

"It's a bloody big tractor. I can't see it moving. And the four miles will be Kerry miles. We'd better take a look, though. I don't like the idea of turning back."

They climbed out and followed the farmer to the tractor. The nearer they got the more impossible it seemed. The wheels were huge below the cab. They were well aware that the farmer was watching them curiously, but he climbed into the cab with the agility of someone half his age and called out, "I'll take the brake off and you take a wheel each and push with everything you've got."

They took up positions knowing they were wasting their time but not wanting to show undue hurry. They tried to move the tractor until they could try no more. When they stood back the farmer was standing behind them with a lethal-looking crowbar. They had neither seen nor heard him climb from the cab, but then they had been straining against the wheels.

"You two are from the north," he said, holding the bar across his body.

"You don't get any prizes for that," Patterson replied. "Of course we're from the north. Donegal. In the Republic, man. Why are you threatening us with that thing? We've been trying to help you."

The farmer kept his distance. "You've been trying to help yourselves. You just stay there until Paddy comes. You might be those two who escaped from Belfast."

Patterson was about to reason again when he saw Daley draw his pistol. He seemed to see it in slow motion, his mind trying to reject what he saw.

49

The farmer was rooted, his jaw sagging as he realised he was right about them. As he saw the gun come up to aim at him he dropped the crowbar and put his hands in the air. He was too scared to shout and it would have made no difference anyway.

But Patterson shouted. He shouted as loud as he could and lunged at Daley's gun hand. "No. NO!" It had no effect and Daley did not change position as he fired. The farmer collapsed across his crowbar and Daley stepped forward to put two more shots in him to make sure he was dead.

"You crazy bastard. What did you do that for? Now we've got murder on our hands."

"So what's new? Did you expect us to hang around chatting until his mate turned up? He might be on the radio band. Let's get him in the boot quick." Daley, cold-eyed and controlled, faced Patterson across the body and added, "If you call me a bastard once more you'll join him."

They managed to force open the boot of the car with the farmer's own crowbar. They heaved the body in, it was quite light, and rammed down the lid, having difficulty in making it stay down now they had ruined the lock. They tried to straighten the bent lock using tools from the kit in the boot. But the arrangement was very tenuous and the lid was not completely closed. It was the best they could do.

Daley took the wheel again and reversed back until he could find a spot wide enough to turn. He then drove as fast as the road would allow.

At this stage neither man was talking; they had been too intent on getting the job done knowing their lives depended on it. It was only when they had covered several miles that Daley said, "It's no use you being uptight. We couldn't wait for the other bloke to pitch up; the odds would have been shortened too much. And the more you gassed with him the likelier it was to happen. All I've done is to create a mystery. If we can really lose the car it will never be solved."

Patterson still felt sick at the cold-blooded killing. It had taken him so much by surprise that he had been far too late trying to stop Daley. Yet, reluctantly, from an escape point of view, he knew Daley was right. The farmer's friend would arrive to find the tractor abandoned. Unless they found the body nobody would ever know what had happened to him.

Ever since Daley had produced the gun at the hideout, Patterson had been nervous of him. Now, having seen him use it, he was acutely wary. What had happened to those little uncertainties he had seen in Daley soon after the jailbreak? Had it needed a gun to make the difference? Patterson had not considered himself to be in real danger from Daley before; now he did.

The silence between them became painful as the miles slipped by and sometimes Patterson hoped they would be caught. His depression deepened each time he heard the boot lid creaking at the back. Once the lid did spring up and they had to stop and do a running repair on the lock. But when they moved off again the lid continued to creak.

Supposing the farmer fell out? When Patterson glanced at Daley he seemed to be totally unconcerned. For the first time in months Patterson yearned for Smithy; Donna Smith. He believed he had exorcised her from his system, but for a few seconds she was back and he needed her. He shook her image from his mind and went back to brooding.

The needle on the fuel gauge was creeping towards the empty mark and it would be fatal to suddenly run out of fuel. They pulled on to a side track and went up it until they were out of sight of any passing traffic on the busier road. They examined everything that was in the car. There was no map.

Patterson got out and walked up the track. They were safe for the moment so he took his time and the ground was steep, foothills to the larger range inland. To his left was the sound of running water and he veered towards it. He came across a shallow, narrow stream, pure and sparkling as most Irish streams remain.

He knelt down and cupped his hands to drink the cold refreshing water. Across the stream the ground dipped sharply and he looked for a point to cross without getting his feet wet. In the end he took off his shoes and socks and pulled up his jeans to wade across in the ice-cold water.

Not far from the other side was a gulley that fell steeply to a dense wooded area. To get to the bottom he would have to climb down and getting back would be quite difficult. It seemed ideal.

Behind him, Daley said, "What do you think?"

Patterson controlled his surprise and irritation. "What's the matter, did you think I'd run off?"

"You might have tried."

"Out here? In the bloody wilderness?" Patterson lost his patience. "You stupid bastard, just where do you think I would go?" He deliberately used the insult knowing Daley had shown himself to be touchy about that particular word; it was risky, though.

For a moment Patterson thought he was going for the gun. Then Daley waved a hand in dismissal and said in a shaky voice, "You did that deliberately. You wanted to see how far I would go. You're playing a dangerous game, Jamie."

"Aren't we all! Let's get on with it. If we heave the body down there it might not be found for weeks, months, ever. The stream is too shallow for fish so there should be no fishermen, but even if there were they would be unlikely to go down in that gulley."

Daley nodded. He too had taken off shoes and socks. "I agree. The only ones likely to find the body are dogs or foxes. And maybe kids, but I think it's too far from habitation for kids. Let's do it."

They went back to get the corpse and struggled up the steep slope. Finally they swung the body like a hammock and then let go. It sailed out and disappeared out of sight as it crashed into the trees and shrubs below. When they gazed down there was no sign to show what they had done. Daley crossed himself and they went back to the car.

They agreed to stay the night where they were. There was fresh water and it was incredibly secluded, although they decided against lighting a fire. It was dusk when they opened cans of food and ate hungrily. They had been travelling all day and since finding the car had covered a good many miles. The one thing about most Irish roads was that there was plenty of space. They were sure they were in Wexford and could not be too far from Rosslare Harbour.

When they had finished eating and buried the cans Daley

52

said, "The stream will be an ideal place to dye my hair. My girlfriend, Carmel, calls it a colour wash. I've got all I need in that grip: a bottle of dye, rubber gloves, and some wash-off muck. All you have to do is pour the dye evenly over my hair and rub it in with your fingertips, using the gloves to avoid staining your fingers. Then we wait about half an hour and rinse it out. Bingo, different man."

Patterson was leaning on an elbow at the base of a tree. "And you want me to do it?"

"I could do it myself, there's a vanity mirror with the kit, but it would be easier and better if you did. This is the first real chance we've had."

"And I suppose a forged passport goes along with the package?"

"A driving licence. We don't need passports for the UK and the less we carry the better."

"And what about me?"

"We can't use the same dye. I can lend you a driving licence, though." Seeing Patterson's look of disgust he added, "You've no complaint. I supplied your clothes."

"That won't help my face when we get on the ferry. I don't like it. Neither of us have shaved. What is it supposed to be? Designer stubble?"

Daley smiled. "Didn't I tell you? I have a shaving kit in the bag. We can both use it. A cold water shave won't kill us. Ah, what would you do without me, Jamie?"

Patterson did not answer. Increasingly he wondered why Daley needed him at all unless he was simply afraid to be on his own, like some people are afraid of the dark. But he had no real intention of leaving Daley; his threats to do so were merely to sound out Daley's own feelings. Even so, he was increasingly uneasy about Daley's motives.

They set out early next morning. There was a good deal of mist around and they took it slowly. Patterson had done a good job with the dye and Daley now had dark brown hair and brows and, with his hair combed straight back, looked a different person. And they had both shaven.

Patterson had tried to change his parting but, unlike

Daley's, it always fell back to its customary position. He gave up. The mist was still cloying as they passed a couple of ghostly tractors. He said, "I've got to get to a phone."

"You're mad. Who do you want to ring?"

"That's none of your business. I have to let someone know I'm safe."

"A woman? Oh, no you bloody don't. I've held out on Carmel and you can do the same. Jesus, any friends we have will have their phones tapped. Be your age."

"I must still make a call. This phone won't be tapped."

"Oh?" Daley lifted his gaze from the road, ground mist still swirling. "How can you be so bloody sure?"

"Because I want to call the RUC in Belfast to let them know where we are, you berk." Patterson spoke scathingly.

Daley laughed loudly. "She must be someone special. She's sure got you hooked. Where is she?"

Patterson hesitated. He was looking straight ahead as he said, "She's in the UK. High Wycombe. Buckinghamshire. There's no way she will contact the police. She's my mother, staying with her sister. And she's ill. This uncertainty won't have done her any good at all. All I need is a callbox."

"And some money," said Daley pointedly.

"You can spare me that much."

"I don't like it."

"Okay. I'll go my own way. Drop me off outside Rosslare. I'll do a quick blag to raise enough money for the moment." Again he was pushing Daley to separate in order to see whether the new-found confidence the gun had produced still held. So far Daley had backed down from each threat of splitting up.

"Can't it wait until we get to the other side of the water?"

Daley was already compromising. Patterson could see no sense in it. Daley had a disguise, money, clothes, food and a gun. He was self-contained. Yet he still clung to a companion who was his political enemy.

"It doesn't make sense," said Patterson.

"What doesn't?"

"You wanting me around."

Daley spotted the misty tail lights of a truck in front, but the mist was slowly rising. "I'm superstitious," he explained. "You may be a black-hearted Prot, but we've been lucky together. We're the only two of the six still free. It works."

Patterson took a chance. "It works because you had prepared for the day. It has nothing to do with me."

Daley kept looking ahead. "Sure it does. Like a mascot at a casino. Just being there seems to do the trick. I'm Irish, for God's sake."

"So am I."

"No you're not. You're a Brit. A Scot."

"My family go back three hundred and fifty years in Ireland. How far does yours go? Don't give me all this crap, Con. You're expecting trouble and I might be handy to have around. Isn't that it?"

Daley's grip tightened on the steering wheel and the car veered. "There could be trouble, sure enough. If we're recognised or cornered."

"It's not just the law who's after you. Stop at the next callbox and give me some money to make the call. We've got to ditch this car soon. The mist is lifting and we're pushing our luck." But Patterson was glad they had got rid of the body.

They motored on and approached the outskirts of Rosslare. It would be far too risky to take the car to the docks. They would have to find an out-of-town place to hide it and then walk a few miles back. They needed to check on the boat services.

A telephone kiosk reared in the weak light of early morning, the mist still reluctant to clear completely, and Patterson said, "Pull in and hand me some cash."

Daley hesitated, and Patterson shouted at him. "If it was anything dodgy I'd try to do it behind your back. We're both in it, for God's sake, so give me some cash. It won't take long."

"I'll come in with you."

"Will you hell. Give me the cash."

Patterson walked the few feet to the box and pulled open the heavy door. He could not see the car once he was in the box. Whether Daley had turned off the lights or not was difficult to decide. The dull light in the box formed a vision barrier and he could not clearly see what was happening outside. It worried him, for he knew Daley was suspicious. He opened the door a little and wedged his foot in. He could just see the car through the wisps of mist but no sign of Daley at the wheel.

Patterson let the door close and fumbled with the money. He had to read the instructions about the cost of calls before he could get going at all and began to get nervous. As he dialled, he was surprised to see his fingers shaking.

Being in the box was like being in a coffin with a murderer outside waiting to provide the dead body. He could not be sure that Daley was not outside straining to listen. Suddenly he was very nervous and Daley's gun became a real threat. He pressed the earpiece tightly to his ear as if the waiting Daley might hear.

A woman's voice said, "Royal Ulster Constabulary."

Patterson kept his voice right down, "Detective Chief Superintendent Monroe, please." He was almost whispering.

"I can't hear you. Will you please speak up."

"Detective Chief Superintendent Monroe." Patterson gazed about, trying to pick up Daley's shape outside the box. He felt as if he had just shouted.

He waited, and could feel the sweat begin to trickle. It seemed hours before the operator came back and when she did she said, "He won't be in for another two hours. Can I take a message?"

Oh, Christ. "Can you put me through to his home?"

"I don't think that's possible, but who's calling?"

Jamie Patterson. I broke out of jail a couple of nights ago and am on the run. He was so pent up he almost said it. This was all going wrong. He was a fool to expect Monroe to be in this early. "It doesn't matter." He slammed down the phone to see Daley outside the door.

Patterson backed out of the door to give himself time to recover. Before he turned round, Daley said, "What the hell have you been up to? You've been hours."

So Daley could not have heard him; Patterson began to calm down. "I didn't know the codes from here. I had to look them up."

"Well, did you get her?"

"No. She's not up yet and my aunt didn't want to disturb her. I'll try later."

Daley was angry. "You didn't leave a message?"

"With my aunt? Tell her I'm okay but still on the run? Come on. It's time we ditched the car."

They stopped arguing as the encroaching daylight added to their problems. The car must have been reported stolen long since; Daley eased it into open country. They could not take the risk of leaving the car too close so by the time they found a country spot to abandon it they were some distance from the harbour. They tucked it behind a clump of trees and then started to walk back, first over rough ground for some distance and then along tracks and finally on to country roads. Not long after leaving the car Daley wiped his gun clean and threw it into some bushes. For a while after that he was morose, aware of his loss of advantage. And confidence.

They did not reach the outskirts of Rosslare until late afternoon and they had barely rested on the way. It had become a very warm day, heralded by the early mist which should have warned them, and they were hot, tired, hungry and thirsty. It was almost as if they had been impelled on to their own execution and could do nothing to stop themselves.

In a way, their weariness helped. Caution, relaxed because of fatigue, eased tension and there was little to draw attention to them. They followed the signs to the docks and found they were early. When they enquired, the daily boat did not leave for Pembroke in Wales until eight-thirty that evening.

Daley bought two tickets, gave one to Patterson, and decided it would be safer if they boarded separately. With the fresh clothes, clean shaven, driving licences, and Daley's dyed hair, the odds had been reduced now that the car had been ditched.

But it did not feel like that when they sought out a café and had a meal amongst other people, whom so far they had been avoiding. It was mix-with-the-rest time and a strange, disconcerting feeling. Their main difficulty was in trying to avoid catching each other's glances – hard when seated only two tables away from each other. They took their time over the meal but still had plenty in hand when they went down to the docks.

Cars were already beginning to queue but foot passengers were allowed to board the big ferry. The whole place was now alive, cars and people everywhere. Police were evident as soon as they made for the boat.

It was impossible for the two escapees not to feel nervous, particularly Patterson who had little in the way of disguise. Their nerve ends were drumming and the impulse to run was almost overwhelming. The two men kept well apart. People could move freely between the Republic of Ireland and Britain. But most people carried some form of identity to avoid problems at control points.

Daley insisted that Patterson go first. Patterson believed the IRA man wanted to make sure he boarded the boat, but it also gave him time to get away if Patterson was caught.

When Patterson passed through controls he was certain he was recognised by every official, and by those who were standing back so casually in support. He was surprised when he had no difficulty and was passed through. He carried one of the grips half filled with food and Daley carried the other.

Expecting to be shouted after and almost painfully relieved when he was not, Patterson went shakily to one of the passenger lounges and found himself a seat among some bawling children. The food and drinks bar was just behind him and passengers were already crowding round it.

Daley boarded ten minutes later. He went into a different lounge from Patterson's and fell asleep almost as soon as he was seated.

Patterson was equally tired but was kept awake by the noise and movement of the children who were already bored. The lounge was fairly full. After a while he went to the bar and queued to get a beer. Daley had given him a little money for the journey but no more than that. He was still tied to Daley, but it was the first time he had been separated from him and it gave him time to reflect.

He looked around for a quieter seat but it was too late and he strode out into the alleyway, beer in hand. Even here there were pockets of people, talking, reading notices on the information board, just generally hanging around and trying to escape the noisy hum of voices in the lounge.

He went along to the other lounge and tried to locate Daley. He found him close to the doors, curled up on a seat, fast asleep. He returned to the other lounge and sat where he could, trying to keep awake and sipping his beer. He placed his empty glass on the floor and virtually passed out. The boat had yet to leave harbour.

By the time they reached the open sea a heavy swell was up but even the pitching and tossing and yawing failed to wake him, succeeding only in reducing the noise level. Gradually the passengers quietened down and the boat began to make its own noises, creaking and groaning as it ploughed through the troughs of the Irish Sea.

Patterson drifted, the sickening motion not reaching him. But out of the depths of a deep sleep arose the day when some of his family had been wiped out in a sectarian killing. A whole bus had been blown up, women and children who had been on a Mother's Day outing. The trip had been arranged and paid for by the children, and the local vicar had seen them off.

Twelve had been killed, and as many injured, some badly enough never to walk again and one never to see. Patterson lost a sister and his mother. His sister had finished up in bits, being directly over the blast as the coach passed over a culvert, but his mother had taken an agonising time to die.

He visited her daily, and it had needed all his courage to face what was left of her. Hospital dressings covered the worst, but there were parts missing where no dressing could be applied, like her feet. This was what the media never exposed; the number of dead was always recorded but the injured remained anonymous cases in hospital beds or wheelchairs or parts of people on life-support machines. The cameras never showed the horrifying truth.

Patterson would never forget those last days of suffering his mother had endured. He summoned every bit of nerve just to go to see her. And the tragedy was that she could not see him, nor did he believe she ever knew he was there. His remaining sister had once gone with him and was still under sedation from the shock. It was an horrific side of the business of terror that outsiders never really got to know or understand. The family had been close; now it was shattered. Nothing could be the same again. Ever.

And not long after that Smithy had been forced to leave him as her own life came under threat, and this loss compounded the others. Most of those he loved deeply had been ripped from his life.

The vividness of his dream became a nightmare and he began to jerk in his sleep until someone shook him. As he struggled to wake, someone was saying with good humour, "I had to wake you. You're kicking the living daylights out of me."

Patterson struggled up, sweat pouring off him, and he was shaking. "I'm sorry, I must have been dreaming."

The big man next to him laughed. "A dream, was it? I thought you were taking on the devil himself. I'm going to the bar, would you like a coffee?" The Dublin accent was pronounced, the voice friendly. "Thanks," said Patterson. "That's kind of you."

The big man rose. "You're from the north?" It was said in a friendly way, not prying.

"Donegal."

"Sure, it's beautiful up there." And then, as Patterson offered money for the coffee, "Be my guest. I'll be back in a minute."

And that, thought Patterson, was the other side of the coin. But he was shaken by the realism of the dream. He had suffered the reality of escape but it had taken a dream to shatter him. He wiped his face with a handkerchief supplied by Daley. But at that moment his hatred of Daley and all he stood for was intense.

It was one-fifteen when they docked at Pembroke and most passengers were tired and irritable. Worsening weather had added half an hour to the crossing and it was a difficult time to get anything done.

Patterson and Daley dared not make contact until they were through immigration and customs. When they did link up in the no-man's-land beyond the dock gates, Patterson said quickly, "I've got myself a lift to Cardiff. I'll meet you at the Posthouse Hotel just outside the city. I'll be near reception."

There was nothing that Daley could do about it. He realised he had lost his power over Patterson now they were in mainland Britain. But he still had the money and reminded Patterson that he would need some. Somehow the threat seemed weak now, although Patterson could not get far without it.

They broke up quickly and Daley walked back to where the cars were still off-loading. He felt more in danger here than in his native Ireland and that made no sense. But he did not like being alone, especially now. Everyone he passed seemed to take an unusual interest in him. He knew it was all in his mind but it did not help. He should have thought of getting a lift as Patterson had done.

As he drifted back towards the boat Daley believed he had seen the last of Patterson and suffered a strange emptiness and felt very exposed. He reluctantly conceded that the Prot had guts; even when confronted with the gun, Patterson had shown no fear. He would miss his companionship and the strange sort of security he emanated. Patterson seemed to be a man who was sure of himself even when everything was against him, and he didn't give a toss for anyone, gun or no gun. But that impression could come from his own uncertainties, so Daley finished confused.

On the dock road, Patterson waited with his grip between his feet as the car drifted in beside him. The big man who had bought him a coffee put his head through the open window and called out, "Jump in beside me. My wife prefers to sit in the back."

The lights of the Posthouse hung back from the road but could not be missed, the illuminated antelope of the Trusthouse Forte group, unmistakable. There was a friendly air about the place, the first Patterson had felt since escaping. He now had open opportunity to ring Belfast again, but if Monroe was not available at seven-thirty in the morning, there was no way he would be available at 3.45 in the middle of the night.

61

It was chilly waiting outside the hotel but Patterson did not want to go inside in case he missed Daley, and although he might book a room he had no way of settling the account. So he waited, walking up and down, and sheltering under the hotel canopy during the odd rain shower.

Patterson began to think as Daley had done; that he would not see him again. In a way he hoped that he did not, for he could only see trouble and danger ahead. He had already witnessed cold-blooded murder, and the vision of the poor bloody farmer would not go away. Daley was vicious and deadly and unstable. Give up; call it a day. It was a strong, almost irresistible pull. When he felt like that he had only to think of his mother.

It was almost an hour later before Daley arrived and when he did it was in the cab of a massive trruck that continued straight on once Daley had jumped down.

Patterson had sidled into the shadows when the truck pulled up and for a moment or two he watched Daley look around and then heard him swear profusely before heading for the entrance. As he passed Patterson without seeing him his gaze was on the ground and it was clear that he was no longer looking for him; he was obviously going to book a room for what was left of the night.

"Oh, ye of little faith," Patterson called out behind him.

Daley stopped in his tracks, then turned. "Jamie? *Jamie!*" There was almost pleasure in his voice, and certainly relief.

Patterson stepped out of the shadows. "You took your time."

Daley sauntered back towards Patterson. "I had trouble getting a lift. Then I had to pay through the nose for one; those truckers aren't allowed to give lifts."

Patterson said easily, "Surprised to see me?"

"Not at all." He chuckled. "I've got money and you haven't. We'd better book a twin-bedded room. We need some sleep."

"Tell the receptionist we're on our way to Pembroke and missed the ferry to Ireland. Tell her our car broke down in Bristol and we had to hire one and we'll catch the afternoon boat. She won't be interested but it's something she might remember if questioned. Just slip it in."

For the moment the relationship had changed; Daley felt his original initiative slipping away.

Seeing this, and knowing how touchy Daley could be, Patterson added, "I've had a bloody lot of time to think about it waiting for you. You play it as you see it, but there are still two guys on the run and we are two guys pitching up at a very strange hour. Okay?"

They woke early, had their first baths since escaping, shared the razor, and felt different men when they were dressed. They had breakfast in their room and ordered more coffee. They felt human again and switched on the television for the morning news. They no longer rated a mention. But that did not mean they were safe. Morning news broadcasts were notoriously short.

"What happens now?" asked Patterson, handing the leadership back to Daley.

Daley was sitting on the edge of his bed draining the last of the coffee. "We go to London. There's a place there where we should be safe."

"And then what? What do we do for money?"

"I've still got plenty. But we've got to start earning our way."

"Like robbing banks? What about your friends? Aren't they supposed to help you?"

Daley was pushing things around on the tray. "Robbing banks is not a bad idea. We can pick up arms and explosive. There'll be more than enough."

Jamie looked across the beds; he had been joking but he could see that Daley was not. He noted that the second part of his question had been ignored so he repeated it, wanting to know where they stood. "What about your friends? Aren't they supposed to see you through?"

Daley stood up and preened himself in front of the dressing table mirror. "I don't want to go back to PIRA."

Patterson took interest. "Why not? It's a one-way ticket with those guys. You can't just resign. Can you?"

Daley shrugged and wandered over to the window. "I've had enough of the killing."

That could not be true; Patterson recalled the total lack of concern when Daley had shot the farmer just two days ago. "I need to know if they are after you. My own life is on the line. And they have plenty of men in the UK."

"I worked here myself for a couple of years." Daley spoke as if Patterson was one of his own. "You're right, of course. Over a million Irish live here."

"The vast majority of them happily. So why are you so anti-Brit?"

Daley turned. "Don't get the six counties confused with mainland Britain."

"When are you going to answer me, Con?"

"It's none of your business."

"It is if I stop a slug in the back of my head because I wasn't prepared."

"That won't happen." Daley shrugged his narrow shoulders. "They know I want to leave and are not happy about it. It'll all blow away in a couple of days. As sure as hell they're not going to make big strides to find me. Let's see about hiring a car."

7

Flynn and Mooney returned to Carmel Daley's terraced house to find she had fled. There was all the evidence of a hasty departure, and one or two items of clothing had been left behind in the rush. Otherwise all drawers and cupboards were empty.

"How come we missed her?" said Mooney angrily. "I thought the boys were supposed to keep an eye on her?"

"She probably did a moonlight. Slipped out the back way." Flynn was more philosophical. "They can't watch her day and night, front and back. But where has she gone?"

"The Republic or the UK. She wouldn't hang around up here; we've too many men on the streets."

"We'd better pass the word to London and Dublin. If they can pick up her trail it might lead us to Con." Mooney grinned almost evilly. "And we need him to help us with our enquiries. Let's get the word out."

Pongo Waring read the fax and gazed up at Detective Inspector Gaunt. "What do you think?" he asked. "Hans Steinbach. He's strong stuff. Why would he want to come here?"

"Maybe too many people are looking for him over there. Maybe he has somewhere to go here."

Waring waved the sheet. "That's more like it, Peter; the tourist season is over. And the sort of sights he would want to see are in dark alleys and basements. But there are plenty of those. Ever had the feeling that some of these people know our patch better than we do? And I see it's gone very quiet on the Patterson–Daley front. Why do you think that is?"

Gaunt had his injured leg stretched out, the wound near the

femoral artery particularly painful in the damper weather; a piece of lead was still lodged too close to the artery to operate safely. "The RUC have recaptured four of them, after all. And quickly. That's not bad, sir. They have no leads on Patterson and Daley. They're probably in the Republic."

Waring was not satisfied. Retaking convicted terrorists was not his specific job but he was bound to have more than a passing interest in them, particularly as Daley had successfully operated in the UK some time ago. "And perhaps they are here. Don't you think it a strange combination? Two enemies together like that?"

Gaunt was startled. "How do you know they are together? They might be miles apart."

"I'm clairvoyant," Waring said with a smile. "Ask the RUC what they think of the possibility of them being together."

"You know what the answer will be."

Waring grinned widely. "We might get a surprise." He hesitated. "Ever since the Stalker enquiry into the shoot-to-kill business, I've had the impression that they are reluctant to confide in the mainland police. In the short time I've had this job, I am even more convinced. I can't really blame them. I'd lose my job for saying it publicly but I have a lot of sympathy for their point of view. We are either at war with the IRA or not. Certainly shoot the buggers; there would be fewer innocent people killed." He placed his big hands on his desk and gazed at his younger subordinate. "You never heard that, Peter. Your leg is playing up and is causing you to have hallucinations.

"Send a fax in the usual way. But I'll make a separate phone call to Alec Monroe to see if he gives a different opinion. They are being unusually quiet about this. Almost uncannily quiet."

Hans Steinbach crossed from the Hook of Holland to Harwich. He travelled without a berth and slept on deck, using his baggage as a pillow. He was now carrying a Dutch passport in the name of Joseph van Schutter. He spoke fluent Dutch as he did English and, to a lesser degree, French and a little Arabic.

His background was not dissimilar to that of Ingrid Lotz. He had finished his education at Leipzig University where his father had once held a chair and had been a rabid Nazi supporter who had somehow evaded the net after World War Two. His father had been forty when Hans had been born in 1955.

Eventual discovery of his father's background had a profound and permanent effect on Steinbach who was already inclined towards the extreme left. What he finally found out about his father drove him into having an enormous row which came to blows and near murder. Steinbach left his father, bleeding from the head and face, in a heap on the living-room floor, and they had not met or spoken to each other since. So far as Steinbach knew his father was still alive but they never attempted to make contact. His mother had died when he was seven.

Steinbach did not think of these things now. The trauma had passed and he had shut out his old life as if it had never existed, so he had no emotional hang-ups. And yet, almost in contradiction, he used his own name in all normal circumstances as if to embarrass his father whenever he could. And the few times he had considered it he had thought it strange that, from the beginning, he had found no problem in killing.

After his first two killings he had faced himself and had been surprised to find that the difficulty was easily overcome, if there had ever been a difficulty at all, by thinking he had killed the sort of things his father stood for. So hatred was always at root and that made life and death very much easier to deal with. He had always regretted not finishing the job by killing his father instead of beating him up. He had not given a thought to the fact that his father had not reported him to the police when he was rushed off to intensive care.

After his father recovered and the police demanded some information the episode had all been put down to some psychopathic intruder, and the culprit was never found. It would seem that even a Nazi father was willing to protect a murderous son who had given no further thought to it except one of regret in not finishing the job.

And it became easy, when mixing with people of the same

ilk, to justify what he did, and to discard compassion, the great weakness in the scheme of things. They sought each other out with the ease a masochist finds a sadist, and the world beyond the following pain and ecstasy is forgotten in their closed confines of sick relief. So far as Steinbach was concerned his father and his kind did not suffer enough. It never occurred to him at any stage that he should suffer too; he was one of the great saviours. What did a few lives matter compared to the real issues?

Steinbach took the boat train to London and mixed with passengers as if they were not there at all. He spoke when he felt his safety might benefit from it but otherwise he had difficulty in tolerating the fools around him. What useless lives they led.

In London his instincts for self-preservation took over and he trod carefully. Times had changed and he was not sure how many safe houses were now known to the police. Because of the casual, almost untidy way he was dressed there was a limit to the type of place he could approach. He finally settled on a small hotel in Earl's Court and mixed with the Australians.

Steinbach was not short of money. There were funds in various English banks that were open to him provided he could produce the right passport to satisfy identity. And, of course, the right signature. There had always been available funds, essential when on the run after a job.

After he had locked the small room behind him he dumped his kit without opening it, and lay on the bed to rest. He was tired now and the nearest he had ever been to being upset as he found he missed Ingrid. That had been a waste. They were supposed to help each other, kidnap someone and hold them to ransom and demand the release of colleagues from whichever jail in whichever country. But times had changed and they had done so overnight.

He gazed at the grimy ceiling and for once felt alone. But tomorrow he would get himself organised and do a careful check on an address he had.

The present Chief Constable of the Royal Ulster Constabulary was Sir Charles McRae. He was annoyed about the escaped prisoners. It was difficult enough to get convictions when juries could be intimidated and witnesses threatened, but when a conviction was finally achieved only for the men to escape, then he wondered whether it was worth the terrible uphill struggle. It should be infinitely easier for the Prison Service to keep prisoners in jail than it was for the RUC to get them there in the first place. Police hearts were always heavy after a jailbreak.

And, of course, it was the police who had to round them up again. It was like doing the same job twice; worse, because they were open to press abuse if they failed. Well, they had pulled in two-thirds of the escapees and that was good, so soon, but he was far from happy about the remaining two. The more so when he felt that one of his own officers was showing signs of not being too forthcoming.

When Detective Chief Superintendent Alec Monroe called on him the third morning after the escape he expected some sort of news but Monroe did not raise the issue at all, which irritated McRae.

Following Monroe's usual reports he was about to leave the Chief Constable's office when McRae said, "Are you sure that's all, Alec?"

"Sir?" What was left of Monroe's hair was sandy coloured, and it straggled across a freckled scalp. Monroe was tall and thin with sunken cheeks and a tired expression as if he was half-starved. His eyes were sharp, though, and challenging.

"Are you trying to protect me from something I should know, Alec?"

Monroe stepped back from the door and sat again as McRae indicated the seat he had just left. "To protect you, sir, it would have to be from something you shouldn't know."

"You mean if ever there is another enquiry, praise God there won't be, I cannot give evidence about something of which I have no knowledge?"

"Wouldn't that make sense, sir?"

McRae chuckled, his florid cheeks shaking. Dark, thick brows arched over deep-brown eyes. His nose was slightly out of joint where someone had broken it in his early twenties. "It would make sense if I could judge the importance of what was being withheld from me. And to do that I would have to know, don't you think? Which would mean it was no longer being withheld. How's that for an Irishman?"

Monroe smiled. He liked his Chief Constable even if not always agreeing with him. "What are you particularly referring to, sir?"

"How can I know that if I'm not being informed?" McRae clasped his hands on the desk. "It's a dangerous thing to do, Alec. It would mean that I must have unquestioned trust in my officers in all things they do. Which means their judgement must be infallible and that is not possible. It would also encourage them to hold too much back, and, subsequently, to start acting on their own behalf. It would be human nature for that to happen if the control becomes no more than a figurehead. I hope I am something more than that."

Monroe inclined his head thoughtfully. "Nevertheless, I would ask you to trust me on this particular issue, sir. This is a pretty small matter."

"I do trust you, Alec. And most of the time I trust your judgement. But there are times when a consultation benefits us both. Don't keep me in the dark about something you know and which could rebound on us. If it goes wrong it's the Force that gets the flak, and as I'm head of it, me in particular. So what are you hiding from me?"

Monroe rubbed a finger along his nose. "Not much. The break-out was an opportunist affair. There's no cover-up there. It was a combination of a sudden cloudburst at a time the prisoners were about to leave the yard, and a home-made bomb going off causing a fire and confusion."

Monroe eyed his chief, still not wanting to tell him anything. "The six men happened to be fairly isolated when the rain came and the bomb went off. They took the opportunity to hide behind . . ."

"Cut it out, Alec," McRae interceded. "I know all this and you know I know. The bulk of the prisoners were herded back to their cells. Visibility was suddenly extremely poor. There was one man dying and others injured. The Fire Brigade was called and there was a short lapse when security broke down.

70

It probably wouldn't have happened if it was known at the time that the six men were missing. The six virtually escaped through the gate as the fire engines came in; they effectively used them as cover, in the rain and during the shouting, and at a time of crisis when the damage was thought to be far worse than it was and attention was substantially on the bomb damage. Isn't that what you were going to say?"

"Something like that. It was an amazing set of circumstances all happening at once. In all normal conditions the men could not have escaped that way in a million years. The prison staff were temporarily hypnotised by the shock of the bomb and what followed. They thought the bomb was an escape device and it was on the other side. It did blow a hole in the wall but by that time all but the six prisoners were inside. It was remarkable that more people weren't killed or injured."

"And that's it? What have you told me that I haven't heard before? It's in writing, in triplicate, and it is recorded on computer. If you don't come up with something better I'll suspend you, Alec. I can't have a force within a force. We've been down that road before. And it was a disaster. Haven't you learned anything from it?"

"With respect, sir, I wasn't here then." Monroe knew he had to give something and had been waiting for this moment. "The six were not prepared for escape, which is why we picked up four of them so quickly. Nor could Daley and Patterson have been prepared but they might have been better equipped to take advantage of it." Monroe hesitated for a long time before adding, "It was no coincidence that those two men were together."

McRae impatiently tapped the desk. "Do you intend to leave me hanging there?"

"This is where it is best that you don't know, sir. And if it goes wrong you won't take the can, I will."

"You're telling me that they were thrown together for a purpose?"

"Daley has already been useful to us and then he clammed up quickly. He, like the rest of them, is a mine of information. He could put a lot of people away."

71

McRae sat back and his chair creaked under his weight. "Are you saying Patterson was put on to him deliberately? What information did you expect a Loyalist man to get from the IRA? It's a non-starter."

"Not if the man is wavering. And over a course of time."

"But you said he had already clammed up."

"He mistimed his move. He was already convicted and should have acted at the time of his arrest. Once he was in prison he received a couple of death threats. Whispers, a note. He was scared and had nobody to turn to. There was no way he was going to trust any approach from one of his own. And any ploy from us to get him alone would have been seen a million miles away. PIRA know them all. We moved him from the Maze to Maghabery, away from the hardened terrorists. But not all terrorists in Maghabery have renounced terrorism. Some just prefer it there to work their ticket. The risk to Daley, while not as acute, was still there."

"Is Patterson a plant?"

"He's been useful to police intelligence. He has a case against him but it's been suspended. His name is Patterson, not uncommon, but the man he represents has a nasty record and is dead. It is this I've been trying to guard you against."

McRae looked uneasy. "Then you'd better tell me no more. I hope you know what you're doing, Alec." About to dismiss Monroe he said, "Have you heard from him?"

"No. It will be difficult for him."

"Then why don't you call the whole thing off? It's over now Daley has escaped. Concentrate on getting him back."

"No, sir. It could now be bigger than ever. Patterson can opt out when he likes. Let him have his head."

"If Daley lets him. From his record he seems to be a vicious devil. I say it again; I hope you know what you are doing."

Ulla Geiger stripped down the Erma-Kniegelenk Pistol and checked it once more. She did so with some disgust. A 1964 EP.22 was far from being her choice of weapon and again she wondered who the armourer had been to select such a gun. True, it suited her for weight and balance, but the magazine only held eight rounds. It was not her choice of Parabellums, and she had tried many. But at least it was German.

She sat on the floor, her back against the wall, and, once the pistol was assembled, gazed round the well-furnished room. She had cleaned the windows because dirty windows could draw attention, and the apartment had not been used for some time. She had made one of the several beds, and had checked the amount of supplies.

Food was mainly in tins or in long-term packets full of preservative. There was a microwave, and a built-in electric fan oven. The kitchen was highly modern, lime wood units, end shelves galleried. Electric and telephone bills were regularly paid by a proxy arrangement. To give an impression that the apartment was in reasonable use, someone came in twice a month to turn on the heat in winter, and in summer, casement windows would be opened, and often left open, each one wired. As far as was possible an impression of normality was given.

It was not so difficult to do. An apartment in an expensive block enjoyed privacy. Neighbours often saw little of each other. Wealthy Arabs lived upstairs, but nobody saw them. An old lady lived next door, but she had not been seen either, and next door was round the corner of the corridor. Above all it was bad manners to be inquisitive.

To have a terrorist safe house in the heart of the wealthy élite gave people like Ulla Geiger a sense of satisfaction. The neighbours would be impressed by the furnishings and décor, and by the sophisticated TV and high-fidelity sound equipment in one corner of the drawing-room, the cost of which would keep whole families alive in the Third World whom the users often claimed to represent.

An agency kept it clean but they in turn had to go through another agent who had overall control of the welfare of the apartment. The carpets and scatter rugs were of the highest quality, and the furniture throughout was superior. The best of preserved foods were available and drink was plentiful, though carefully rationed. Drunken parties were out.

Ulla Geiger was dark, with wild hair and clothes that seemed to have come from street barrows after several rounds of selling. Her Greek blouse was faded and her dark, heavy skirt almost reached the ground. A big buckled belt encased a slim waist. She justified her odd dress sense by arguing that girls did their own thing these days and that her voice, in English or German, was 'highly cultivated' and always satisfied the hall porters who seemed to think that only the very wealthy could dress so outrageously.

In fact Ulla was one of the odd ones out. She had clawed her way up the educational ladder, mainly teaching herself. Her parents were, and always had been, poor, and her accent was affected, though well entrenched by now. She could be charming and witty and marvellous company and could kill someone in the middle of a laugh; she did not even have to dislike them. Ulla was part of terrorism because she felt she belonged and her friends cared about her, and, more importantly, relied on her.

She could handle most weapons and using plastic explosive was to her like modelling clay; she was at one with it. That was one thing the apartment did not possess: a supply of plastic explosive. There were a few more EP.22s but she would hate to go to war with them. But then it was never intended that this house be an arsenal. She had been here two days now, right in the heart of South Kensington, London.

There was a burglar alarm system. There were also other security refinements, and a fire ladder led to the flat roof which was in jumping distance of another although it would take a strong nerve to make the leap.

With no interest in TV or music, Ulla wondered for how long she could withstand the boredom of being alone and largely cooped up. She rose and slipped the pistol into her waistband. With her bright, very dark-brown eyes, there was more than a touch of the gypsy about her. There was much about her that was attractive, and much that was both challenging and forbidding. She was not a woman to be easily ignored and it could be a mistake to try. Ulla needed to be wanted.

The doorbell rang just as she put the kettle on to make coffee. She at once switched it off, drew her pistol and went to the front door to gaze through the spy-hole.

She saw Hans Steinbach standing there and smiled widely.

She called through the door in English, "Who is it?"

She saw that Steinbach was startled. He would have rung the bell as a precaution but she did not think he had expected anyone to be there.

"The gas man." Steinbach had recovered quickly. There was no gas in the apartment.

"May I see your identity, please?"

Steinbach put out his tongue and lifted two fingers, surprised that Ulla was already there.

Ulla unlocked the several locks and removed the chain and opened the door to throw her arms round his neck. She tried to bury her body in his, moving it sensually.

He broke away. Now speaking in German he said, "You want to give a public demonstration, Ulla? Let's go inside."

When they were in the hall and the door was closed and locked she asked, "Is Ingrid with you?" She had her arms round his neck again.

He pulled his head back. "You can see that she's not."

"I mean here in London."

"No. I'm alone." As she was still clinging to him he said, "It is good to see you, Ulla." Even Steinbach would not be so foolish as to rebuff Ulla openly when she was in this mood; she would take it as a personal insult and her reaction would be unpredictable.

"In that case we can go straight to bed." She fumbled with the buckle of her belt as she led the way inside the apartment. "It's ages since I had a man and I've been bored silly in this place. You arrived just in time to satisfy me."

And that is what he did. It took a long time but he knew he had to go through with it for they would get nowhere about real issues if he did not. Ulla took a lot of satisfying, her energy seemingly endless, but she roused him to a peak when he thought he could match her and almost did.

It took him time to recover and he dressed slowly while she put on the kettle for the coffee she had intended to have earlier.

Physically satisfied, she joined him in the kitchen and said, "You shouldn't dress like that in a posh place like this. You should smarten yourself up."

He spooned instant coffee into the mugs. "What about you?"

"I can get away with it. But the porter might think you're a tramp."

"Really?" He lifted the steaming kettle. "I make a point of entering when porters aren't looking or they're attending a call to nature. Let's go into the sitting-room and catch up on each other."

She took a mug from him and smiled wickedly. "I thought we had already done that; but if you want to start again . . ."

They sat at each end of a luxurious sofa and sipped their coffee. "Where is Ingrid?" Ulla asked.

"She was picked up near Berlin. We were all on the run. I hung around for a few days hoping I might get her out. But there was no Stasi to turn to. Those that weren't in jail themselves were on the run like me. I simply kept on the move. I did hear a rumour that Ingrid had died of a heart attack in jail. I ask you. At her age? That was when I decided to get out."

"Did you follow up the rumour?" Ulla gazed at Steinbach in a strange, disbelieving way.

He missed her expression because he did not want to look her in the eye just then; not as a matter of conscience, for that would not worry him, but because Ulla and Ingrid had been friends in spite of the infidelity.

"It wasn't easy to pick anything up. I was relying on other visitors and even that was risky. I believe the warders killed her, pushed her just too far. I don't think she died of a heart attack."

"Maybe she's still alive, Hans." Again that secret smile as if she knew something. "In which case I'll have to screw you dry while I've got you."

"And then I'd be having the heart attack." He tried to make it sound humorous, but it fell flat.

"So what are we going to do while we're here? We're cut off from the main crowd because they've either disappeared or been rounded up. We've got to rebuild."

"Or take a different turn. I need a gun, which is one reason I came here. I had to get rid of mine; it was too risky through customs. I don't think you should stay here too long."

76

"Only the three of us know about it. And as Ingrid is in jail that leaves you and me."

"There might be others we don't know about. Many of the safe houses will be blown. We are taking a risk all the time." She thought over what he said. "Are you saying you are not moving in?"

It was so easy to say the wrong thing with this girl. If they were planning something then there was no problem, her concentration would be solely on the job. But the moment discussion smacked of criticism her ears pricked up and she became touchy.

All the old gang knew of Ulla's inferiority complex, and that it could be dangerous if she felt slighted. They had developed an early warning system when there were signs of that happening, and they would change the course of dialogue to find room to compliment her in some way. This gave them an amusing exercise and kept Ulla satisfied at the same time.

With just the two of them there, Steinbach saw an additional problem. There was nobody to help head her off; he would have to humour her as best he could. "I didn't say that," he protested. "All I'm saying is that it can be dangerous."

She gazed at him as if he had gone soft; given the weapons, Hans Steinbach would blast anyone in sight he thought to be a threat; he could hold a complete armed police detachment at bay, and had done so, killing two of them and afterwards escaping. "Everywhere is dangerous until we've sorted things out. At least we can enjoy ourselves together here."

He hoped he could keep up with her lust; she was the only woman he knew who made him face his limitations. "I could move in for a couple of days. After that I think we should look around for somewhere else. If Ingrid is alive I hope she doesn't get to hear about it."

Ulla smiled widely. "She would approve. While you're with me you'll be getting into no mischief. But you think she's dead."

Steinbach detected that mysterious little attitude as if she knew something about Ingrid that he did not. And he was not prepared to ask.

8

On the drive down to London, Patterson and Daley had plenty of time to think. They took turns in driving. They pulled in at service stations for coffee and meals and were in no particular hurry.

At lunchtime, Patterson made his phone call again but was still unable to make contact with Monroe and he refused to speak to anyone else or give his name. This time, however, he said he would ring again at six that evening and would the operator make sure Monroe received the message; he would understand, name or no name. Afterwards he told Daley he was still unable to contact his mother who was at the hospital for an X-ray but was advised to ring again at six; she seemed to be all right.

Daley did not believe the story about the mother and thought Patterson was trying to contact a girlfriend which was a stupid thing to do. There was a lot he did not understand about Patterson. Now they were out of Ireland his doubts about him grew. He still preferred to have him by his side; Patterson offered a certain comfort at a time he needed it, but he was increasingly puzzled why Patterson stayed. It could not be just the money; there had to be another reason. The gun was no longer a deterrent because there was no gun.

Patterson was driving while Daley was reflecting. He glanced at his companion without learning anything except to see the strong lines of his face. He was beginning to take more interest in Patterson. And he wondered why a Protestant had linked up with him in the prison yard.

Prots and Catholics rarely mix; not in prison. It was true that Maghabery was not segregated like the Maze, or what he still thought of as Long Kesh. But there had been hardliners in Maghabery, too, who preferred it to the Maze for their own reasons. There had been some strange associations, though. But they had usually arisen from a mutual interest, like conditions, or some political slant, or sport, that happened to suit them both. There was something about Patterson that did not fit that particular bill. And yet he had been an ideal companion to escape with. Patterson had kept his nerve, and was at this very moment driving with skill and calm. He seemed to be used to driving on the English roads. Daley looked behind.

"Nobody's following," said Patterson. "Are you expecting someone to?"

"Don't be stupid. I'm just keeping a look-out for the fuzz."

"Balls," said Patterson easily. "You're scared of something and it's not the fuzz."

"And you've got no bloody mother in High Wycombe. I don't like these phone calls."

"I could have made them without you knowing once we were over here. I could have reversed the charge even though she's pretty short of money. I didn't have to be open about them. But I'm not screwing my bloody head off every few minutes to see who's behind us. There's been something on your mind ever since we escaped. And I don't mean being on the run."

Periodically, they tuned into the car radio news bulletins and found they barely merited a mention. Press and public interest had waned. Nobody cared any more. That was part of the problem of Northen Ireland, few in mainland Britain cared a toss what happened there.

The driving became difficult the moment they left the motorway. The nearer they got to London the worse it got. They were not used to this kind of traffic but Patterson was at the wheel again and drove well.

They found the Avis office with difficulty but eventually it was all over and the car was handed in and Daley paid the bill.

"Do you know what happens now?" asked Patterson.

"We go to a safe house. One of the specials. I could do with some more money, though."

As they searched for a taxi, Patterson said, "I might be able to help once I make contact with my mother."

"I thought she was short of cash," Daley snapped suspiciously as they climbed into a cab. They both found the noise of London almost unbearable after the quiet of prison, and the Irish countryside.

"She is. But there's someone else whose number she can give me."

"Jesus! Just how many more do you intend to tell?"

"Not nearly as many as those who are after you." Patterson thought Daley would be unable to control himself, but somehow he managed as Patterson desperately indicated the taxi-driver who might be listening.

"Kensington?" Patterson was intrigued. They had paid off the cab near the Albert Hall and were walking along Kensington High Street. It was late afternoon, rush-hour yet to begin, but traffic was still heavy and there were plenty of people on the streets. There was a faint drizzle which was caught by the street lights to form an intermittent glistening canopy.

"Can you think of anywhere better?" Daley was feeling pleased with himself. "Nobody sees you in a place like this. If you put up in a semi, or a doss house, you're noticed and people remember the accent."

They branched off and approached an imposing apartment block to stand on the lower step and look into the vestibule through heavy, double-glass doors. The porter was talking to someone at his small counter, and Daley signalled to Patterson to follow as he ran lightly up the steps. The porter looked up as they passed him heading for the lifts, but Daley's stride was confident; he obviously knew where he was going. Patterson kept alongside.

When they left the lift, they walked along a long carpeted corridor, turned left at the end, and faced an apartment door in a little dead-end. It was ideal.

Daley produced a bunch of keys to show Patterson. "This is something you didn't see me pick up at the still. It's a last line of defence, boyo." He inserted a key in the lock, turned it,

80

opened the door, and led the way inside. He made sure the door was closed behind them then crossed a small hall with Patterson following. He entered what was plainly a living-room and the next moment both he and Patterson had guns pressing at the base of their skulls.

"One move and we'll take your heads off."

German. Patterson and Daley had the thought at the same time. To some extent Daley was relieved; whoever had a gun at his head, it was not who he first thought it was. "Who the bloody hell are you?" he spat out with the outrage of fear.

"That should be our question."

The gun did not move and seemed to Daley to be screwing a hole in his head. "We can't tell you that until we know who you are."

"Talk more slowly. You are difficult to understand. Are you Northern Irish?"

A woman's voice this time, the English almost as good as the man's. There was no point in denying it. Patterson suddenly saw what should be an obvious answer. "Yes. Are you on the run? Like us?" What could he lose?

"First tell us how you got the key?"

"If you take the bloody gun from my head I'll tell you the whole history of the place." Daley was easing down. He was thinking as Patterson was thinking.

"All right. But first put your hands on your heads."

Steinbach and Ulla searched them from behind, surprised that they found no weapons, then Steinbach said, "Sit on the sofa and keep your hands where they are."

Patterson and Daley sat down on a two-seated sofa. They could now see who they were dealing with and were left with no doubts. But Daley was puzzled and angry. There were only three men who were supposed to know of this place; two were dead and he was the other.

"Go on," said Steinbach, his gun trained on Daley while Ulla levelled hers at Patterson.

The German looked huge from where Daley sat; and strong, and bloodless, eyes empty of feeling.

"This place was bought with money from Ghaddafi. I went

to Libya myself with another man. We were already being supplied with arms and cash but we needed something different in the way of safe houses. Our people had been picked up too often, and we'd had to desert other places as we got tipped off that the police knew about them, or we were being watched. Little of this reached the press because they are only interested in arrests.

"An emissary met us in London. The apartment was bought on a thirty-year lease by a Libyan in the presence of myself and a colleague. Arrangements were made for bills to be paid by a contact of the Libyan. And arrangements were also made for either myself or my colleague to take over the ownership in the event of the purchaser's death. It was all done under false names. Not long after that the Libyan was killed in a traffic accident and some time later my colleague was blown up on a mission. I found myself the owner and went through the legal process already mapped out. This place is mine and only two keys were ever cut."

Patterson felt the chill of truth but there were too many omissions. There was much more to Daley than he had realised.

The two Germans listened in silence and Steinbach inclined his head. "Was your colleague named Eugene Lynch?"

Daley was startled. "Yes. How did you know?"

"We worked with him. We helped him and two others kill off a few British soldiers in Germany. We supplied information and safe places for them. In return he showed me a duplicate to the key you have and told me that if anything happened to him I should take it off him and use it. He gave me the address which was of little use without the key. You didn't mention that his car was blown up in Germany. It's strange that some of us who use bombs are sometimes careless with them. We never expect anyone else might do it to us. He paid for the same negligence attributable to his enemies. Did you ever work in Germany?"

"No. No, I never did. He ran two units out there."

"I only knew of the one. He was good at his job." Steinbach paused, the gun still steadily pointing at Daley. "I think he had a premonition about dying. I think that was why he showed me the key which he kept on a chain round his neck."

Daley had now recovered his poise. "He had no right to give you the key. He broke a trust."

Steinbach smiled icily. "Perhaps he was not the only one."

"I don't know what that means. How did you manage to get it? I heard he had been blown to bits."

"He was. And it was not easy to get. I had to kill a morgue attendant and then go through the remains that had been scraped up off the street. Whoever planted the bomb had arranged an overkill. Only half the quantity was needed."

"Did you ever find out who did it?"

"No. We thought he must have been taking it somewhere but it went off. It happens. The police wouldn't kill him that way and the SAS would know just how much explosive to use, unless they were being clever. It's a mystery."

"Don't you think it time you put the gun down?"

Steinbach looked at Ulla. "Do you believe all that crap he has given us?"

Ulla was eyeing Patterson. "He has the key. It must mean something. They're cute."

"So you are IRA," said Steinbach.

"PIRA. The Provisionals. He's not. He's the enemy."

"Then why haven't you killed him?"

Daley could have bitten his tongue out. "We escaped from prison about three days ago. In Ulster. We got landed together. And we needed each other to survive."

"A strange combination. Okay, you are now safe. So kill him now."

"Here? In the flat? You're crazy. Anyway, we're both on the run. He's no danger. We're both in it up to our necks. For God's sake put those bloody guns away. They are not yours, they are mine. They were hidden here by me."

"And Eugene Lynch."

"And Eugie, sure. Just what the hell do you think you're playing at?"

Steinbach was smiling quietly as if enjoying a private joke. "We haven't heard of any escape." He laughed softly. "We've been too busy escaping ourselves." He turned to Ulla and she was laughing too.

Patterson considered his chances and decided there were none; he did not think Daley was handling it too well. Now he had been identified as the enemy there was little he could say. His arms were aching with his hands still clasped on top of his head.

Steinbach said, "Let us have your names first. Your real ones."

As they had been mentioned on TV and presumably in the press, Daley saw no problem in giving his. "Con Daley."

"And you?"

Patterson noticed that while the question was directed at him the gun remained pointing at Daley. These people lived by the gun. "Jamie Patterson."

Ulla said, "Yes, they are the two the police are looking for. They were mentioned on radio and television."

Steinbach grinned widely and put his gun in his waistband. "Ulla was here two days earlier than me, so she knows the news. We apologise for the rough welcome but you know as well as we do that we can't take chances."

Daley lowered his hands and said, "I'm still concerned about the key to this place. Just how many did you have cut?"

Steinbach was still smiling. "One for Ulla here. I have the original from Eugene, and we had one other cut but it will probably never be used as the holder was picked up in East Germany."

"Why have any cut at all?" Daley had risen and went straight to the refrigerator in the kitchen. He came back with two cans of Guinness and handed one to Patterson. "You've been bloody careless," he added as if he had never left the room.

Patterson wished Daley would shut up. The Germans would blow him away as soon as look at him and he had nothing to fight back with. And then he saw that he had. A pistol butt protruded from his back pocket and he was carrying another with the cans.

Daley tossed the spare pistol to Patterson as if to tell Steinbach that they were now all on equal footing. As a matter of routine Patterson made sure that there was a round in the breech.

Another thing worrying Patterson was that six o'clock was only twenty minutes away; he had arranged to ring Monroe at that time and he was wondering just how he was going to do it now that the Germans had complicated everything.

Steinbach took it all in his stride and showed no sign of anger, but Patterson considered he was not the type to show his feelings anyway. There would be no warning before this man fired, and he seemed to be totally relaxed about the sudden appearance of the guns. "Were they in the fridge?" he asked with amusement.

Daley did not reply; he saw no need to reveal a hiding place, but it was not the fridge although close to it. They had already found two of the more easily available pistols; let them be satisfied. "You still haven't told me why you had extra keys cut when the whole object of this place was its exclusivity. Now that's gone."

"Lynch made no mention of this to me. It was just a very special safe house and I gave keys only to very special people. They are not the sort who would talk about a place their lives could depend upon. You're upset because you thought you had it to yourself. Well, you have as far as the IRA are concerned. Be cool."

But Daley was seething, and not concealing it very well. Patterson could see trouble coming so to change course he said, "We've had no names from you two. Don't you think we should?"

Steinbach turned to Daley, handing back some authority to calm the Irishman. "Is he allowed to ask questions like that? Isn't he the enemy?"

"He's in the same bloody mess we're in. And the question is valid. You haven't volunteered your names."

"Ah, well." Steinbach sat on an upright chair and pulled one thick leg over the other. "We are disappointed. Our vanity pricked. We thought you might know." He swept out an arm to Ulla in an exaggerated gesture. "This is the beautiful, and remarkably clever, Ulla Geiger. And I am Hans Steinbach. I take it that none of us are travelling under our real names." He produced the laugh he intended and the atmosphere cooled down.

Patterson reflected that as German terrorists went they did not come any bigger than these two. Steinbach had good reason to think that they should be known by Daley and himself. Steinbach was a by-product of the Baader-Meinhof before they were broken up. In the terrorist world, they were in privileged company. The woman obviously liked being named to those she saw as fellow travellers; her self-importance was showing. She should get on well with Daley; they could bolster each other up every time there was a crisis.

Patterson could not see an opportunity to use the telephone with these people around until, totally unexpectedly, Daley said, "What about your mother? It's nearly six."

It was impossible to judge whether Daley had said it out of spite or genuine concern.

"God! Thanks, Con. I'd forgotten with so much happening. Is there a phone where it's more private?"

"In the bedroom. Second door on the right off the hall."

Steinbach and Ulla were immediately on the alert. "You want to phone your mother?" asked Steinbach in disbelief.

"She's sick. And she'll be worrying. I just want to let her know I'm okay."

Steinbach turned to Ulla. "You'd better go with him."

Again Daley bridled. He did not like the way the German was taking over. "Let him go on his own. He's not stupid enough to bring the police here."

"He's your enemy, yet you trust him?" Steinbach could not believe it. "How have you survived for so long?"

Daley did not like the gibe. "There are no enemies here. No Provos, no UVF, no Baader or Red Brigade. We're all on the bloody run from the same bloody enemy: the sodding police. We're not on operational service; we're in the shit. All of us. And I don't think this place is too safe any more. Too many people know about it and there is still one key missing. Don't try to tell me about security and enemies, you haven't shown much sense yourself. Now let him make his phone call."

Patteron was grateful but not fooled by the outburst; Daley was not protecting him but asserting his own authority which

86

he saw as being eroded. And he probably saw the Germans as a bigger enemy than himself. This was not the Daley he had set out with. Patterson said, "Thanks, Con," and headed for the hall.

He found the second door on the right and entered the bedroom. The bed had clothes strewn all over it as if there had been a fight, and Patterson was quick to grasp that is what there had been. Steinbach and Ulla must have had one hell of a romp and they had not been in a hurry to tidy up.

Patterson crossed to the bedside phone and picked up the receiver. He was dialling when he thought someone was in the room with him. He pushed down the cradle and turned to see Ulla standing by the partly opened door.

"What are you doing here? You'll upset Con Daley."

"Anyone could upset Con Daley. I take my cues from Hans."

Patterson gazed at the unmade bed and smiled. "I can see that. Are you going to make the bed for him?"

The dark eyes flashed and he realised that this girl was a powder keg and he would have to be careful.

"Aren't you going to make your call?"

"I'd rather do it alone."

"Are you afraid of what I might hear?"

"Not at all. Your boyfriend will be listening on the extension, anyway. I just don't like people around me while I'm on the phone."

"You're very calm; not like Daley." She suddenly smiled and her features changed dramatically. "Would you like to rough up the bed some more?"

Patterson was wary. "I wouldn't want to make an enemy of Hans."

"He wouldn't mind. He has his own girlfriend. She's in prison in East Germany; I am just a fill-in, but I do make my own choices."

"Of course you do. You could get as many men as you wanted."

Her gaze suddenly sharpened again. She was not sure whether or not he was making fun of her.

He followed up quickly, "You are very attractive, Ulla. I

87

meant what I said." And then, as though disappointed, "But I must make this phone call."

"Okay, I'll leave you to do it. We can talk later."

But he did not think it was talk she had on her mind. He waited until she left the room, leaving the door ajar, and picked up the receiver again. He was damned. He had to make a call because they expected it and would be highly suspicious if he suddenly changed his mind. Yet to make it could be suicidal. He had to hope he could get in the first word.

Patterson dialled, convinced that Steinbach would be listening in, and although Daley might be furious, seeing it as a personal slight, he would be equally curious and so do nothing about it.

Patterson was sweating as the RUC number rang out. He was on the point of hanging up when a girl's voice said, "Hello?"

He almost gave himself away as he replied too quickly, "I want to speak to Mrs Patterson, please. I believe she's back from hospital." None of it was rehearsed, it must be mumbo-jumbo to the police operator. He expected the voice to say he had made a mistake and that he was speaking to the Royal Ulster Constabulary, and he was ready to draw his gun and make a run for the door.

God, it could go hopelessly wrong. For a while there was nothing and he thought he had been cut off. What the bloody hell was happening? And then a man's voice came on and said, "Mrs Patterson is too ill to speak unless it's really urgent." The voice was broad Scottish. "Who's calling?"

"Who are you?"

"I'm her brother. I've come down from Glasgow. Is that who I think it is?"

"Aye. I just wanted her to know I'm okay. Tell her not to worry, Uncle Bob."

"You're a bloody disaster, young Jamie. Do you ken what damage you've done to her?"

"I know and I'm sorry. I can't tell you where I am but I'm safe. You tell her."

"I don't want to bloody well know where you are. I don't

88

want to know anything about you. I'll pass your message on."

"Wait. I want a telephone number of an old friend. He'll lend me some money. He lives in Birmingham but Mother knows where the number is. I can't remember them all. Will you ask her?"

There was a long pause and some heavy breathing, then Uncle Bob said, "I can't disturb her for something like that. I'll make arrangements for five hundred quid to be transferred to a bank for you. I'll put up the money, much against my will but in order to spare your mother. I don't want to hear from you again, Jamie. You're a little shit and a disgrace to the family. Where do you want it, Ireland or England?"

"Maybe we can reach England. I used to have an account with Barclays in Jermyn Street. If I can't get there it's too bad." And then for the benefit of Hans Steinbach on the extension, added, "By the way, who answered the phone?"

"You didn't recognise your cousin Mary? She's eighteen now."

"She only said one word. Anyway, thanks, Uncle . . ." But the phone went dead as the receiver was crashed down the other end.

When Patterson put down the phone he was wet through and hurried to the toilet to lock the door behind him. He sat on the seat and tried to cool off, wiping face and neck. Just how the hell had Monroe managed it? It did not matter how; the fact was there would be some money at Jermyn Street and he guessed it would be done at once.

He was shaking a little, it had been so close, and he owed Monroe a huge debt. He tore his mind away from what might have happened and bent over the wash basin to splash cold water over his face. Once calm he joined the others.

They were all drinking, Daley, still with his can of Guinness, and the other two had produced some Vodka as an alternative to Schnapps. Steinbach was standing near the telephone where Patterson expected him to be; the receiver was not quite straight on the cradle. He crossed the floor and picked up his own can.

Daley said, "How is she?"

"It doesn't sound good. I can't get near her. There's no point in trying to follow her up. Relatives don't seem keen for me to speak to her. But I might have some cash coming."

Patterson was not answering Daley but giving Steinbach what he hoped to hear. And Steinbach seemed satisfied. He raised his glass to Patterson, "Prosit!"

"Cheers!" Patterson replied. He hated drinking from cans. Everyone seemed to be content although there was much to decide. Or was it all a battle of wits with nobody trusting anyone?

9

Alec Monroe sat at his desk and felt much the same as had Patterson. He had taken a very risky step but it seemed to have worked. He had gone down to the telephone exchange and had tackled the operators separately. It had been immensely difficult because calls were coming in all the time and it meant putting some of them on hold while he made his point. But it had to be done in such a way that nobody slipped up. From 5.45 p.m. to 6.20 p.m. calls must be answered with an hello, and not the usual RUC greeting. It was not easy for women drilled to do the opposite. But to make sure it did not go wrong, Monroe stayed in the room so that he could remonstrate over the early mistakes. By 5.55 it was working well.

If he was asked for by rank and name by a caller who would not give his own name the chances were that it would be Jamie Patterson. But if someone came on with a mumbo-jumbo of which the operator could make no sense, then Monroe was to be advised on the spot. He was linked to a phone off the exchange so he did not have to leave the room. He accepted that Patterson had problems because he had already tried twice to contact Monroe. It had worked and Monroe told the operators to return to normal practice at 6.05.

The gamble had caused problems in the exchange, and had raised some brows, but it had paid off. Thank God. As by this time the banks were closed, Monroe made arrangements about the money as soon as they were open the next morning. He knew that what he had done would get around, it was impossible to hold the operators to secrecy, and in due course would probably reach the Chief Constable. It was a problem he would have to face when it happened. He was satisfied, though, that Patterson was still with Daley; it filled him with qualms but in any event it was obvious that he could not have discussed the matter on the phone. He would have to wait until Patterson found a way to communicate without someone else present. But he was certain that Patterson was in a tight spot, and would choose to remain in it rather than slip away; even if that were possible.

Commander Waring was not happy. In spite of a crackdown on interdepartmental differences over the last few years he was satisfied they still existed to the detriment of good police work, even if with the best intentions.

Since the Anti-terrorist Squad at Scotland Yard had taken over control of all investigations against the IRA in mainland Britain, including those of Special Branch, it would be thought that co-operation from other forces would be full-blooded and supportive.

The Anti-terrorist squad had been put in a position to co-ordinate all enquiries into the IRA, whereas before, too many manhunts had been bogged down by arguments among the regional squads. This should no longer happen although he was convinced that it did, albeit if only on a minor scale. But a minor slip-up was enough to let someone off the hook and he would not tolerate that sort of behaviour.

In spite of the fact that Squad officers were present at provincial CID offices, and Intelligence briefings were on a regular basis and had access to the central commuter database, nothing had been forthcoming on the whereabouts of Patterson and Daley. With the wide range of scouts and informers around the regions, he believed he should have received some sort of whisper.

The importance of these two missing men was a gut feeling. Nor was he satisfied about the part the RUC was playing in this; they had been remarkably reticent over this part of the escape. He knew he was batting on a much stickier wicket with them; they were touchy to criticism, and perhaps justifiably. It could be that they simply had no idea where the two men had gone, but he had the feeling that someone along the line was being less than forthcoming, possibly protective, and that would need some explaining. It was time to improve stake-outs on some of the lesser-used safe houses the computer listed. It was time to stir things up and get some results. He believed that Patterson and Daley were in the UK, and not in the more obvious areas around Dublin. He also believed that the two men were still together which might explain why they had become so difficult to pick up; they were co-operating, pooling resources, and he found that strangest of all; Prot and Catholic terrorists working together. There had to be a damned good reason. Knowing both their records, particularly Daley's in mainland Britain, and perhaps even in Europe, made him very uneasy.

Carmel Daley took the Larne-Stranraer service. It was the shortest sea crossing to the UK and meant a long train journey down to London, but for no particular reason she considered it the safest. It was illogical when compared to other sea routes, but fair appraisal if compared to air. It was too easy to pick people out at airport immigration.

She carried one heavy case with difficulty and encouraged no one to help her although there were many men willing. On the few occasions she had travelled via Stranraer the port had been misty and this October day was no exception. She boarded the train and resigned herself to the long trip south.

She kept an eye open for any of Mooney and Flynn's friends who represented the biggest danger; she believed she could deal with the police in her sleep. She dozed for long periods and wondered where Daley had gone to earth and why he had not contacted her.

She began to think what she would do on arrival in London. She should have considered it in Belfast, but Carmel could plan only a little at a time. She had friends in London who had their ears to the ground; they would help her. She stretched her long legs out and dozed again.

Mooney and Flynn flew to London. They knew they had been recognised at both Belfast and London Airports and obtained satisfaction from it. At Belfast in particular, they knew that the armed RUC would like nothing better than to empty their guns into them, but were bound to uphold the law. The police knew they were active members of the IRA but could do nothing about it without proof that would stand up in court. Going past controls like this was like cocking a snook at British authority, and they could do it with impunity even though another policeman or reservist might be murdered that very day.

Once in London the two Irishmen knew how to lose possible tails and to submerge into the London background. In such a hugely cosmopolitan city it was comparatively easy; they were, after all, British subjects when it suited them; for they carried dual Irish and British passports.

10

Patterson and Daley felt threatened by the Germans. They did not see it as a physical threat, although that could change, but a crass intrusion. Whatever they now decided to do they had to take the Germans into consideration.

They were all terrorists but their aims were quite different. Patterson and Daley were directly opposed to one another but at least they each understood what the other was about. The Germans followed a less definable outlook and were inclined to go for individuals whose way of life offended them. Certainly they had a political base, but to Patterson and Daley, it seemed less stable than their own. Daley could not see the similarity of his own indiscriminate killings which were all tied to the central theme of 'Brits out'; as if the killings would then stop if the Brits did get out. The two pairs were conditioned in their own separate ways but were just as illogical. Patterson was the odd man out but the moment he openly acted as if he was then he was dead.

"What the hell do we do about those two krauts?" asked Daley.

They were sitting on their beds; two singles with a bathroom en suite. They had already bathed but unlike the Germans, had no change of clothes.

"What *can* we do?" Patterson realised he was being unhelpful, but he was right. Just what the hell could they do? And then, "I'll go down to the bank in the morning and check if that money is through. If it is I'll get some clothes." He went to the window. The light was already poor but looking down into the street he could see the rows of parked cars like an assortment of multi-coloured matchboxes. The central gardens were screened by a line of plane trees, their dead leaves covering the street like layers of rust.

Daley was lying on the bed in his underwear, hands behind his head. It was warm in the room, the central heating covering the whole block from the basement, but adjustable in each room. "Those bloody krauts have caused problems. The porters are bound to notice the odd set-up; we can't avoid them for ever. The two of us could have got away with it but we've now halved our chances." He gazed at the lights on the pastel-coloured walls and added, "I'll come with you for some clothes."

Patterson wondered if Daley was still loath to let him out of his sight. Were all four going to become increasingly suspicious of one another? The evening was already closing in and it would soon be dark. The car roofs were merging into one muddy colour. He was thinking of the way his mother had died. He had to force himself to do it from time to time in order to sustain the impetus to carry on. He considered Daley to be right about the Germans who had staked out their towels and had no intention of moving. They did cause complications and he could see no way round it; they had taken the larger, double-bedded room.

Patterson gazed back into the room to watch the fading shape of Daley who was searching the ceiling for answers. He crossed to the door and switched on one of the lights. "We're going to have a job to sleep in these beds after prison and sleeping rough since."

"Yeah!" said Daley. He suddenly sat up on one elbow, and softened his voice. "We need some arms, Jamie."

"We've got some."

"No. I mean the heavier stuff." He paused thoughtfully. "It's out in the country. We'll need most of the day. We'll have to ditch those two. Hark at them. I thought Germans were supposed to be cool-blooded."

"Those two are," Patterson replied seriously. "And we'd best not forget it. I know something of their record; they could kill in their sleep."

"It sounds as if they're trying it now. Are you trying to scare me?" Daley was aggrieved. "They don't worry me a bit."

"Well they should. They're a couple of psychopaths. They'll kill anything they see as a threat."

"Oh, Jesus, don't we all!"

"Just a friendly warning. We'd better watch each other's backs."

"Do you think they have any money?"

"If they have, they won't share it with us. We've got to find our own. If the five hundred quid is waiting for me, it will be gone in no time."

"We'll find some," said Daley with quiet assurance. "Don't think about it. What about going out for a meal?"

Steinbach was exhausted. He should have remembered about the insatiable demands of Ulla Geiger. As he caressed her he could see that she was far from finished, and slowly, unnoticed he hoped, he took his hand away and moved back before she could be aroused again. But she was already aroused.

"Don't tell me you're tired," she said as he eased his body away from hers. "You've been too long with Ingrid; she was always easily satisfied." Ulla smiled wickedly and reached out a hand.

"I'm concerned about these Englanders. They are a problem."

"They are not Englanders, they're Irish. Then get rid of them."

"You know that's not so easy here. We would have to get them somewhere outside. They do not seem to be very intelligent but they must have the survival instinct or they would be back in prison."

"I think you are going soft, Hans." Ulla was still playing with words; she was annoyed that her attempts to rouse him were not working.

"Get your mind off it for a moment." Steinbach sat up. "We've got to work something out. They are not like us and that will cause problems."

"How do you mean?" Ulla snapped; she was not used to being rebuffed and it ruffled her. She too sat up, and swung her legs over the side of the bed to face away from him.

"They haven't arrived at their own conclusions. They've

97

been indoctrinated since they've been old enough to think. Daley follows a war chant, 'Brits out', as if that will solve all his problems. They are insular in their thinking, Ulla. I doubt that they have a university degree amongst the lot of them. They are not the brightest of people."

Steinbach had swivelled round towards her as he finished and saw her back go rigid just in time. "Of course," he added hurriedly, "I am not suggesting that a university degree is a prerequisite for intelligence. Of course not. Some of the most brilliant people hardly went to school at all. But the general standard of the Provos is low by our criteria. Wouldn't you agree?"

"I wouldn't know." Ulla was still tense but Steinbach seemed to have corrected himself in time. "I haven't met enough of them to judge."

"I mean, they have really achieved nothing." Steinbach continued to add to his misery.

"Neither have we. Someone always steps in to take the place of those we've killed. We are not killing enough."

Her assertion was a reflection of the mood he had created in her. She felt like killing, and, at this moment, him for preference. Steinbach recalled why he had slipped away from her advances earlier on in their association. She was not only too sexually demanding but was generally difficult to handle. He had been pleased when she had taken up with someone else and he had moved in with Ingrid. Ulla's man had been killed in a shoot-out in Frankfurt and since then she had taken anyone whose ego was big enough to believe he could cope with her.

Steinbach wanted to be rid of Patterson and Daley as much as Ulla did. But he did not want to be landed with her on his own. Life was suddenly complicated. There was also the question of raising money. The stocks in the apartment were now being divided by four and their time was halved. It was a crucial problem and one which he was not particularly keen on discussing with the Irishmen.

Daley tapped on Steinbach's bedroom door; it had been quiet in there for some time. He called out, "We're going round the corner for a meal. Be about an hour."

98

The door was opened by a ruffled Steinbach who was now dressed. "We'll come with you." He called back into the room, "Ulla, we're all eating out."

Daley was furious. He said, "Sod you. Jamie and I want to be on our own for a bit."

Steinbach switched on his charm. "You've been on your own in your room. I thought you would like the company. Come on now, you'll be on your own again when we get back. We would like a change, too, you know."

Steinbach sounded so reasonable that Daley was confused. He turned to Patterson who was standing behind him, but Patterson was grinning, knowing there was little they could do about it without creating a rift, and they all had enough problems without that.

They found a restaurant not far from the apartment. The wall lighting was subdued, a guitarist strummed out soothing Spanish music. The apartment was giving them the unaccustomed comfort of living, now they were enjoying the balm of good eating in pleasant surroundings. As they ate, in their different ways, they all decided that it was a lifestyle they would not want to relinquish.

They enjoyed their meal and for once found unrestrained harmony among themselves. By the time they were on coffee, laughter was softly flowing with the increasing standard of wit to which the two Irishmen largely contributed, a fact not lost on the Germans. And yet, below the goodwill ran an undercurrent of danger which would never leave them. They would always be looking over their shoulders, for the danger was real and from diverse sources. As they left the restaurant cold sober, for all four were far too experienced to fall into the gin trap, they knew more about each other and were slightly more attuned.

It was with relative ease that Patterson and Daley were able to detach themselves from the Germans the next morning. They travelled by underground to central London, feeling safer in the crowds. Patterson found that Monroe had transferred £750, which surprised him for, on a temporary basis at any rate, Monroe must have funded him from his own pocket.

They roamed London, sticking close together, bought some clothes, had a snack lunch in Oxford Street, then headed back to Kensington. They were almost like two boys on their first outing. London swallowed them and they felt secure. But never did they really believe that they were; the alarm was always switched on even in the middle of a laugh.

When they got back to the apartment the Germans were missing. They went round the rooms. They had made their own beds before leaving but were somehow surprised to find the bed made in the double-bedded room; Patterson was bearing in mind how it was when he first saw it. The whole place was tidied up and the Germans' kit was missing. It was as if no one had been in the place for some time.

Patterson said, "What are they playing at?"

"Maybe they've buggered off. Maybe we've got the place to ourselves."

But neither man was satisfied. There was something wrong. They dumped their new clothes in their room and were reluctant to unpack them until they had a better idea of what had happened.

Patterson prowled around as if he expected them to jump from behind the furniture. "Do you think they've done this deliberately to unnerve us? If we thought the place was blown we'd be out like a shot. And then they would return and have the place to themselves."

The gazed at each other uncertainly, each having the inclination to get out quick. They went round the windows, carefully looking down into the street. Neither located anyone who might be watching the place. And yet they were left with that strange feeling of unease as if something bad was about to happen.

"Do you think they were picked up here?" asked Daley.

"And tidied up before they went? Even their cups have been washed and dried."

"What do we do?"

They went back into the sitting-room and Patterson thoughtfully poured himself a drink before sitting down. "If the place was blown the police would have been waiting for us. If we run, where do we go? We stay and take our chances."

Daley said, "Have you got any money left?"

"Some. Not enough for tickets to South America."

"I thought we'd go to that little Spanish restaurant and have another meal. It will give us time to think." They left the apartment at seven-thirty and walked round to the restaurant. They sat down and ordered just half a bottle of wine between them, and selected from the English side of the menu. When they were eating Daley said, "We'd better hire a car to go out into the country tomorrow. There's a cache of arms in Hertfordshire and we should load up what we can because we are going to need them."

Patterson realised that Daley was speaking to him as if they were in the same para-military group, and belonged together. He said, "We're still on opposite sides of the fence, Con."

"Not in this we're not." Daley was not put out. "We've got to earn some money and we'll need some firepower. But you're right, it is a PIRA cache."

"Aren't you pushing your luck?"

"If we're caught. We'll have to be careful. But's what new?"

Daley had made odd references to arms before and Patterson did not like it. Something went from the meal. It was not like the previous evening when everyone was content. The food did not taste as good and something had gone from the atmosphere. The guitarist did not sound the same nor as good as before. The whole evening had gone flat.

From then on they ate in silence without really realising it until it was suddenly time to leave. And then came the thought of what might be waiting for them when they returned. Patterson paid and he could not say that he had really enjoyed himself. They had become morosely thoughtful ever since Daley had mentioned the arms cache.

They went for a short walk before going back to the apartment. It was a cold evening with a threat of rain and they had already walked quite a distance that day. Yet they kept going as if to avoid going back, not knowing what they might find.

Finally, they decided they had to face up to it and neither denied they were uneasy about the situation. They walked round the block until satisfied it was not under surveillance. Once they entered an empty corridor from the elevator they drew their pistols, keeping them out of sight at their sides. Temporarily, at any rate, they were on the same side.

They reached the door and crouched below the level of the spy-hole. The small cul-de-sac the apartment was in was a godsend just then. Patterson put his ear to the door and listened.

"There's someone in there. There seem to be several voices."

Daley reached up with the key, inserted it in the lock, then waited. He could hear the faint sound of voices himself without pressing his ear to the door.

Patterson nodded and Daley turned the key very slowly while Patterson put a faint pressure on the door, feeling it yield as the tumblers were released. Their guns now at the ready they pushed the door further open until they slipped into the hall one at a time, before carefully closing the door behind them.

They crept towards the closed sitting-room door and the voices were now clearer though subdued. Then there was loud laughter – Ulla. Patterson and Daley exchanged glances, took up positions as trained soldiers would, and then burst into the room, guns held out.

"Stay where you are."

A startled Steinbach and Ulla sat back in the sofa, for once at a disadvantage. The television was on and some form of debate was being transmitted. While Patterson covered the Germans Daley crossed over and switched off the set.

"What do you think you are doing?" snapped Steinbach, trying to recover. He had his arm round Ulla's shoulders and it was clear from the disarrangement of clothes that they had not been simply sitting there.

When Steinbach started to take his arm away, Daley snarled, "Leave it there." He was getting his own back for the way Steinbach had greeted them on first arriving at the apartment. "Where the hell have you been?" he continued.

"Put those stupid guns away and we'll tell you."

Ulla, who had said nothing, seemed to be getting some sort of satisfaction from it all and was eyeing the Irishmen with renewed interest.

Patterson tucked his gun into his waistband and said, "So tell us. You left no note, no indication that you would be back."

Steinbach removed his arm from Ulla to retrieve some self-respect. It had been a long time since he had been caught unawares and he was livid with himself. "Where we went is none of your business. We'll do as we please."

"We've already done that," added Ulla with a satisfied smile.

"And you'll do it once too often, you silly cow," Daley shouted. "And then we'll all be in it."

Steinbach grabbed Ulla as she dived at Daley, and Patterson had to help the German to restrain her. She fought madly but fortunately Steinbach was used to handling her and somehow got her hands behind her back with Patterson's help. But she had the strength of the demented and pulled them all over the room.

Seeing what he had unleashed, Daley tried to calm things down by saying, "I didn't mean it like that. I meant we're all in the same boat and had better be careful. If we can't do that then we'd better split up now. And as this is my bloody place Jamie and I stay here and you two piss off."

They got Ulla back on the sofa and Steinbach gasped, "We're making far too much noise."

Ulla began to calm down but stared at Daley balefully, conveying to him that it was far from over.

"Tell them where we've been," Steinbach said to Ulla in an attempt to bring her back into things.

"No. It's still none of their business. If you want them to know, then you tell them."

They settled down with drinks and the atmosphere improved a little as Steinbach leaned back on the sofa and said, "We reconnoitred the escape route over the roof."

The simple statement created an anti-climax. Whatever Patterson and Daley had expected, it had not been that.

"In daylight?" asked Patterson sceptically.

103

"Sure. Why not? Less noisy than at night when flashlights would have had to be used. We had a picnic up there. It was quite mild. Most enjoyable."

Ulla smiled again at that. "Most enjoyable." If she was trying to get even with Daley she failed for he showed no reaction. It was her way of getting back at people; she knew they hated and were afraid of her violent tantrums.

"Why couldn't you leave a note or something? You had tidied up and taken your kit as if you weren't coming back." Patterson wanted to keep the questioning away from the unpredictable Daley.

"If we go out for any length of time we always take our kit. It might not be possible to return; the police might be waiting. With us it's normal practice, which is one reason neither of us have been to jail. You should try it."

"It seems good advice. Why didn't you follow it when we went out last night?"

Steinbach shrugged. He resented the question and Ulla showed her contempt by flouncing from the room. "That was different. We were all together."

"What the bloody hell difference does that make? What else did you do up there?"

"You know what else. This has gone too far. What else we might have done has nothing to do with you. It does not affect our security one bit."

Patterson rose. He felt better on his feet and it was easier to get at his gun if he needed it. Steinbach was hiding something. "I'm not talking about your sex life. We all know what went on with Ulla and she'd better take several cold showers. You're lying through your teeth. What else happened up there, Hans?" Patterson slipped his hand into his waistband.

Daley, realising that Patterson was, after all, on his side, stopped sulking and moved back across the room so that he could see Ulla if she reappeared.

Daley's move was not lost on Steinbach who was still sitting down. He replied, "I've killed people for calling me a liar."

"Then don't put me into a position where I have to call you one. Okay, I'll retract. But something happened up there, other than the frantic amours of Ulla, that you are not telling us about. If it's so private that you can't tell Con and myself then you pick up your gear and you leave here and you don't come back."

"You are inviting a war." Steinbach was silent while he viewed his options. He did not want a fight; it would be crazy and could attract attention. And the Irishmen were not as stupid as he had supposed and there was something about both of them, in quite different ways, that needed explanation. If he was hiding something from them then they were certainly hiding something from him. But whatever their secrets might be they were prior to them all meeting in this apartment. "Okay," Steinbach agreed, "I'll tell you what happened." He leaned back on the sofa and Patterson thought he was almost too relaxed; a glance across the room informed him that Daley had picked up the same message. Steinbach was in a dangerous mood.

"We tried the fire escape to the roof. It worked very well. It was pleasant up there and we ate, drank very little and generally enjoyed ourselves. After lunch we roamed the roof; this is quite a large building. There are pipes up there and a kind of what you call a brick shed . . . an outhouse. There must be a way to it from a set of stairs from the top floor. But it was locked and we did not want to force the lock."

Patterson, listening intently, was satisfied that Steinbach was skating round the main issue. "That's the scenery. What was the action?"

"There is a very good view up there and we are surprisingly close to the building next door. Just a narrow gap, about six feet; an alley between the two blocks. The levels are almost the same. But only part of the next building is so close, a buttress? The rest goes back at right angles before running parallel again, but now some little distance away. It was possible to see into some of the rooms."

Steinbach stirred but made no effort to get up. He smiled up at Patterson without a trace of friendliness. "By this time the light was not all that good and some of the room lights came on. There was a couple getting ready to go out. We watched them through some opera glasses I always carry, until they left, marked the position of the rooms, jumped the gap which was quite easy to do, and went down that fire escape until we found an entry into one of the corridors.

"From then on it was easy. We found the apartment, opened the door, we are quite good at that sort of thing, and took what we wanted which included some money and jewels." He grinned widely. "It was quite a day out and well worth while."

"You burgled an apartment?" Patterson could not believe his ears.

"Sure. Why not? It was an open invitation and we needed the money."

Patterson was appalled but he noticed that Daley was grinning in approval as if to say that sooner or later they would all have to find ways of raising money outside the law. Patterson could see himself getting in too deep. But he was still not satisfied with Steinbach's account. "The golden rule is never do it on your own doorstep, and you do a break-in next door. You must be mad."

"Next building; not next door. It worked, so what are you complaining about?"

Patterson backed down. Ulla had returned to the room and he felt that they were all against him including Daley who kept chuckling as he saw the funny side. But it had been the sort of opportunist burglary that could be dangerous. Someone must have seen them. He supposed that they had become so bored that the temptation had been too great. He suddenly found himself grinning in spite of his reservations. He noted the expensive silk scarf Ulla had tied round her neck and said, "You'd better not wear that outside; it's too distinctive and someone might recognise it."

It was not until the local news after the main news at ten that he started to worry again. A woman had been murdered in Kensington at a luxury apartment which had been ransacked. Apparently, she and her husband had called on two other friends in the block and had a drink with them. Before all four went down to get a cab she had returned to the apartment to change her bag while the others waited. It was thought she surprised the burglars who callously shot her through the heart and head. The police stated that the killing was a cold-blooded professional job. Valuables worth several thousand pounds had been taken.

Patterson went cold and was further concerned when he saw that Daley gave no reaction, but he was quite sure Daley would have made the connection. Perhaps Daley had seen too many shootings, too many distraught wives of husbands killed on doorsteps or blown up in cars. Nothing had changed. The quick exchange of mute warning between Steinbach and Ulla was not missed by Patterson. He felt sick.

11

They met at Snow Hill Station and the four men greeted each other warmly. Flynn and Mooney had arrived in Birmingham the previous evening, found a small boarding house on the outskirts, and had over-slept. They had skipped breakfast and had lunch in a café before contacting Burke and Ross to arrange a meeting. As both the local men worked in car plants, Mooney had reluctantly left a message with Burke's wife. He did not leave an address or telephone number and if the meeting failed to take place he would have to start again.

Neither Flynn nor Mooney had any intention of making it easy for them to be located. So the system of contact was cumbersome and slow but, so far as they were concerned, safe. They believed they had been followed from their arrival in England but were satisfied that they had shaken off their tail.

It was seven in the evening when they met outside Snow Hill and, after the initial greetings, crossed over to Chad's Circus, entered the Gents toilet on the island and when they reappeared, crossed to the east side of the Circus to Chad's Cathedral. Traffic was still busy but to use the subway meant a detour.

There were a few people outside the cathedral and the four men detached themselves well clear of the rest. Although they had not seen each other for some time they had periodically maintained contact. Burke and Ross had Dublin accents, faded now by many years of living in Britain, but identifiable enough.

It was difficult to understand why these two men were members of the Provos; one of their wives was English and the two women were good friends, reasonably satisfied with their lot with other friends in the community. Perhaps the stark bloodiness was much too diluted this far from Ireland and the two men had been living elsewhere during the Birmingham pub bomb outrage when fifteen dead had been left behind in a tangled mess of horror. Sometimes it is impossible to know what motivates men like Burke and Ross who owed much to Britain in many ways. Perhaps it was simply an anomaly of human behaviour no one could explain, for in any other way they were honest, decent men. Right now they were terrorists by association.

"We're looking for Con Daley," Flynn said after the greetings. He wanted to get away from the other two as fast as he could in case they were being watched.

"Yer man who escaped? We've no idea," replied Burke, a tall man with a friendly face and watery eyes. "He hasn't been anywhere near us. Is that all you wanted to know?"

Mooney caught the remonstrance. "Believe me, it is important enough to call you out. All the time he's on the loose we're all in danger. Sure, he'd shop the bloody lot of us, and has already done some."

"Then how do you know he's not with the police now and they're keeping quiet about it?" Burke was feeling the chill and had shoved his hands in his pockets.

"He probably thinks he can get clear of the police and us. He's with a Prot killer called Patterson. At least we think he is. They were thought to take the same car."

As this made no impression on Burke and Ross, Mooney added, "Jamie Patterson is the UVF bastard who killed Daley's wife. Con doesn't know it. It's a piece of information we picked up from a Dublin contact who has a connection in the RUC. If we can find Daley we can kill two birds with one stone."

"We can't help you," Burke said flatly and Ross nodded in support. The Birmingham men were disappointed; this was not the kind of help they expected to give; this had nothing to do with the great fight for freedom. This was negative and pushed the cause not one step further.

Flynn and Mooney could not miss the indifference. Angrily, Flynn said, "What's the matter? Are you missing something on television? We're looking for a bloody traitor; it's important, for chrissake."

"Important to you, maybe. You keep your own house in order and we'll do the same." Those were the only words Ross had uttered and he was furious because Flynn was right about the television.

Flynn was too late in seeing he had been heavy-handed. "Well keep an ear to the ground, will you? Spread the word around the boys and see what comes up. We're going south to see what we can pick up there." He paused, unsure whether to continue, then said, "Do you know where the dumps are round here?"

"The tips?"

"No. The dumps. Arms."

Burke looked at Ross. "Sure, we wouldn't know that. You'd best speak to Tom Cagney. He might know."

"Tell him to keep an eye on them. It's just possible that Daley might get some ideas about some deals. They'll be worth a bit to anyone who can find them. Will you do that now?"

The two pairs parted less friendly than when they met. Burke and Ross headed towards West Bromwich, vaguely disillusioned at what they had been asked to do. They were being used as messenger boys and it had left them with no sense of importance, which perhaps gave part answer to why they followed such a bloody cause at all.

Meanwhile, Flynn and Mooney went down Snow Hill towards Colmore Circus thinking that the only people worth dealing with in their game were those who lived in Northern Ireland and did the real work. Just the same, if the word was passed around more people would be on the look-out; it was the only way, and there were lots of ears and eyes in England.

Carmel Daley had no problem getting accommodation in London. She went straight to her sister in Maida Vale, adjacent to Kilburn where there was quite an Irish community, and was offered a room straightaway.

Rose Simpson and Carmel had been born in the same house in Belfast and Rose, the elder girl by two years, had married a Scot while living in England and working as a waitress. She and her husband had laughingly agreed that in parts of Northern Ireland the accent was so similar to the Scots that they had no problems in communication.

It helped, in the present situation, that Jock Simpson was, at the moment, in India, trying to sell telecommunications for a Cambridge company. Jock knew his job which paid well and the apartment bordered on the luxurious.

The sisters sat down with Irish whiskey and white lemonade and swapped gossip until the main issue was raised. Rose knew all about the escape. She did not, nor ever had, liked Con Daley and she had been furious when Carmel had changed her name. A devout Catholic, Rose had strongly disapproved when Carmel had moved in with Con while his wife was still alive.

As they sat in comfort Carmel was not used to and the effects of whiskey eased her problems, Rose said, "I suppose you're out looking for him? Well you won't find him here."

Carmel saw an argument coming but she needed her sister's help so held her temper. "How can you know that? Nobody seems to know where he is."

Rose crossed her legs, one expensively clad foot tapping. The sisters were very alike physically, but Rose had the money to be better groomed and it not only showed in her clothes but in her attitude. She had grown used to comfortable living and with it had come confidence. Rose saw Carmel as she had once been herself and it distressed her; Carmel could have done much better than Con Daley and it remained a bone of contention between them. "Because he'd go to Dublin, where, if he's caught, he'll be released by the Irish courts on some legal technicality."

Carmel bridled in spite of her efforts to stop herself. "You've become more British than the British, so you have. That's a terrible thing to say."

"It's the truth. And I live here, Carmel. I like it here and people are decent to me. I don't like the way you go about things."

Somehow it always ended this way between them. They loved each other as much as any sisters can, yet their thinking was quite different. They were already distressed but Carmel needed somewhere to stay and the last thing she wanted was to be turned out. "Will you help me find him? Just that?"

Rose reached for her drink and almost drained the glass. "If I did find him I'd hand the little creep over to the police."

Carmel paled. She looked a slight, almost pathetic figure, curled up on a deep armchair, and her cheap clothes showed up against the costly Dralon. "Do you hate him that much?"

Rose caught the general image and felt sorry for her sister. "I'm worried about you, Carmel. Con is trouble. He always has been and always will be." She crossed to sit on the arm of Carmel's chair and put her arm round her sister. "Don't try to find him. If I know anything there will be plenty of people doing that right now. Don't be dragged in."

Carmel started to cry silently. Rose felt the shoulders gently heaving beneath her touch. "He's not worth it," said Rose. "Look at you."

"But will you help me?" The plea was almost a sob.

"Oh, God." Rose returned to her chair. "Even if I was willing just what do you think I can do?"

"You can talk to Billy Conner."

"You'd want me to do that?" The question was bitter. She could still feel his coarse hands fondling her, and the lust in his bloodshot eyes when he had had too much to drink. Billy Conner had once been Rose's lover for a brief time when she had first come to England. She had soon regretted it when she discovered that he was up to his neck in IRA affairs. He had turned out to be a brute of a man, cruel and sadistic, and she had left him after he had beaten her up and, with the help of a friend, had been forced to take out a court restraining order to stop him pestering and threatening her. She shivered at the recollection and realised once again just how desperate she must have been at the time.

He had left her alone after that but she had never believed that it was on account of the court order. Her belief was that he had been warned by his own crowd to keep away from that kind of trouble, and particularly from the courts. He had drawn attention to himself and they would not tolerate that.

Rose later discovered she was right in her assumption and for some time after that Billy Conner was out of favour with his crowd but had since gradually climbed back amongst the hierarchy.

"There's no way I can do that," added Rose. "No way. I have my pride."

"So it's your pride that's standing in the way?"

"That man's a monster. And you know it, Carmel. Even you don't know all the things he did to me." Rose shuddered at the recollection.

"He knows everything that's going on in the Provos in London. If anyone knows where Con is, then he will."

"No." Rose stood up, very shaken and afraid. The mere mention of Conner's name had brought back nightmares. She was appalled that Carmel could have asked. "If you're so worried, you ask him."

"I don't know him. Otherwise I would. I only met him the once."

"Then here's your chance to make it twice. I won't do it, Carmel. Not for you or anyone." With shaking hands Rose poured herself another drink and stood with it in her hand.

In one short visit, Carmel had destroyed her sister's sense of security and her happiness. In one short request she had put back the clock to an era Rose wanted desperately to forget.

Carmel obtained some satisfaction in seeing her sister crumble. She had envied her happiness and lifestyle and now she could see it was nothing more than a house of cards. Rose would never escape the past. "You mean you'll not do it to help your own sister?" Carmel turned the knife vindictively but maintained a reasonable tone.

"I don't intend to see that man again. I'll give you the last address I had for him and after that it's up to you." Rose turned to face Carmel. She was tearful but had recovered some composure. "It's a good job you haven't unpacked. Finish your drink and go. I've no intention of being pulled down into the mire with you. Go see Billy Conner; you might find him more suitable than Con Daley." She was sorry she had added that but felt she had been provoked beyond reason. For a moment she thought Carmel was going to come clawing at her but instead the younger girl glared undiluted

113

hatred. It had come to this between them and Rose felt shattered.

"I'll give Billy your love when I see him," said Carmel as she moved towards her luggage. "Perhaps he'll come round to find some," she added vindictively. "Now give me that address. And thanks for nothing. I'll pass the word around that you've crossed over. I'll make your life the misery mine has become."

12

Daley hired a car. It was safer because he still had his false driving licence for the paper work. The Germans were intrigued as to where the Irishmen were going but after their murderous escapade of the previous day were in no position to make demands.

By now the hall porters were used to them and one of them vaguely remembered Daley from the early days of his ownership, in spite of the dyed hair. Steinbach and Ulla had not been mentioned in the British press, let alone any photographs of them. Patterson generally kept in the background trying to avoid speaking to the porters at all. They did not think there was any suspicion attached to them but that could rapidly change and they had to be ready to leave at the first sign.

Once they were in the car Patterson and Daley spoke more openly, relieved that they did not have to worry about the Germans overhearing everything they said. They were all supposed to belong to the international brotherhood of freedom fighters, or what other name they chose as being relevant on the day. Yet there was a wide gulf between the two pairs. There was a gulf between Patterson and Daley too, but they could communicate on the same level even if arguing. They understood what each stood for, or they believed that they did.

The Irishmen left London early morning and enjoyed running against the traffic which tailed back for miles. Outward bound was almost a clear run and the weather was fine.

Once clear of London Daley took the M40. After a while, he said, "Things have changed a bit since we first did a runner, eh? They must be busting their guts wondering where we are."

They reached Buckinghamshire and eventually turned off for Chesham. It was a long way round for where Daley wanted to go but he was taking no risks and was constantly checking the traffic behind him. He found the car park and with Patterson went back into the town where they bought two spades and returned to the car and put them in the boot.

Just outside Chesham he took the country road to Wiggington and Tring in Hertfordshire. Now it was much easier to be sure they were on their own. The only car they saw for miles was going the other way and they had to pull over to let it through. Eleven miles later they entered Tring, a country town consisting virtually of one main street.

"We're back in the wild west," said Daley, laughing. "I know plenty of Irish towns like this." They passed John Bly's antique shop at the far end of the High Street and continued on into the country. At this stage Daley slowed right down and produced a rough sketch map. After a while he pulled into a passing bay to get his bearings. "It's been a long time," he muttered.

Patterson made no offer to decipher the sketch, and he doubted that Daley would let him look at it anyway. He was not sure whether Daley had picked the sketch up at the hideout in Ireland or had subsequently drawn it from memory.

While Daley studied the sketch, Patterson reflected that they were living in each other's pockets and were rarely on their own, as if each was afraid of what the other might do. The Germans at least knew each other but one of them was unstable. They were like four strangers living together, not knowing how much they could rely on each other. The alternative of splitting up was no more appealing than staying together. At least, as they were, they had mutual support of a kind, and someone to speak to. There was nothing worse than being on the run alone and unaided.

Patterson considered the situation while Daley tried to sort out his navigational problems. Patterson thought about cutting and running. He doubted if the other three would make a crusade of finding him once he was really clear. His

116

initial purpose of contacting Daley was now superfluous, and he wondered why he persevered. Monroe had left it to him. He hoped he would know when it was time to run.

"We turn left up here." Daley did not seem sure but he started the engine again and they edged up a little-used track. There was just enough crushed grass to suggest very old wheel marks. They were climbing slightly and disappeared into a maze of young saplings whose autumn shedding was almost complete.

"I hope you know what you're doing," said Patterson.

"So do I, boyo." Daley's grin was rather sickly as if he was now trusting to luck. "If I'm wrong we can back down again."

Patterson looked over his shoulder. "You'll be bloody lucky."

Suddenly they were in open space and long straggling grass with a clear view to some low hills almost due north. They were now on the outskirts of the copse and Daley pulled up and climbed out. He produced the spades and passed one to Patterson.

Daley was chuckling to himself, a self-satisfied smile on his face. He walked along the young tree line, brushing through the carpet of dead leaves, clearly highly satisfied with himself. He stopped at a young beech tree, the odd man out among the spruce.

"This is the easy part," said Daley. "You'd think it would be the hardest." He lifted his spade and rammed it into the earth. "The beech is the guide line but it's so obvious that we buried the cache five spruces along and between that and the next one behind it. It took most of the night so it's buried deep. Come on."

Daley pulled his spade out and the two men walked along the tree line with Daley counting. He then led the way just inside the tree line and took up a position roughly midway between the two marker trees. "Start digging," he said, and led by example.

The Land-Rover was below the summit of the rise and its two passengers were prone in damp bracken just below the ridge.

117

Their binoculars were trained across the dead ground to the line of young spruce across the shallow valley. The order to be there had come from high enough up the ladder for them not to ignore it.

They did not know precisely who they were looking for, or what. But they had been given an area of land to watch and so long as the weather held they would do it. Sod's law could work both ways; they were lucky to spot something unusual on the second day.

They saw the arrival of the car and two passengers get out. When the two men entered the fringe of the copse with spades, one of the watchers dashed back to the Land-Rover and used the car telephone. He gave precise positions and it was now up to others to deal with it. Meanwhile he returned to his colleague and continued to watch what was happening.

Commander 'Pongo' Waring received Detective Superintendent Ted Wallace that same morning just before noon. The two men shook hands and Waring indicated a chair. Wallace sat down, the two big men facing each other.

"It could be said that we look like a couple of coppers," Waring chaffed. "I remember you when you were on the beat in the East End."

"And I remember you when you weren't, sir."

Waring smiled. "You're making me feel old, Ted. Now what would Murder Squad want with me?"

"Probably nothing. But I'll give it to you anyway." Wallace eased his frame further into the chair and tried to find some comfort. "There was a murder last night. South Kensington. One of those posh blocks. Wealthy woman having left the place went back to change her bag because it probably clashed with her friend's, and she surprised some villains ransacking the place. She was shot dead. The first bullet killed her outright; straight through the heart. And the second, the follow-up shot, went straight through the centre of the forehead; unnecessary but accurate."

"I heard about it," said Waring. "Pro job."

Wallace agreed. "Pro shooting, but the robbery was anything but pro. The place was a shambles, inexpertly burgled, some stuff was left and some dropped. It had all the appearance of an opportunist break-in. The only thing was that they obviously wore gloves or had sprayed their hands with varnish. But even an amateur does that these days. So we have a professional killing and a kid's burglary."

"That should interest me?"

"The gun might. The pathologist and forensic worked late hours coming up with information. The bullet in the heart had missed the ribs and was almost perfect when it was extracted. Forensic came up with an EP.22, about 1964, German, of course. You don't see too many of those around these days. Thought it might interest you."

Waring was silent for some time before nodding his head slowly as if coming to a conclusion. "Thanks for thinking of us."

"We'll continue with the murder enquiry, of course. If anything else comes up I'll let you know. Didn't some of the terrorist groups use those?"

"They used anything they could lay their hands on in the early days. But once Ghaddafi took an interest the supply became more organised and the weapons sophisticated, more often than not, Russian. I don't suppose you know how many people were involved?"

"We're still working on it. But certainly no less than two because of the time factor and the speed with which they wrecked the place."

"Thanks, Ted. If anything comes of it I'll drop the word."

In Belfast, Detective Chief Superintendent Monroe felt he was at the crossroads. One of his many schemes, usually with the co-operation of the intelligence unit, was on the verge of collapse, and one of his men in extreme difficulty, which meant high danger in this black-hole war.

Monroe was treading hot coals and knew it but not which way to jump. What had started out as a simple prison contact with an inside informer had turned into something quite different. The unexpected bomb, unsuccessful in itself, had created an unforeseen situation. Patterson had stuck to Daley in a gut reaction move. It showed the dedication of the man, although he had every cause and incentive. But what the bloody hell had happened since?

Monroe could not warn the telephone operators to pull off the same trick every night; that had been a one-off and he supposed Patterson would be astute enough to realise it. But Monroe knew he could not let matters roam loose for much longer. The whole scenario had changed. Patterson's reasons for hanging on with Daley must have changed, but how?

Monroe recognised that very soon now he would have to confide in the Chief Constable, which meant involving him. There was an alternative which he thought over very carefully and decided he still needed a little more time before making a final decision. Meanwhile he was deeply worried by the fact that he had no real contact with Patterson.

Everything was packed tightly in waterproof covering. The detonators were in separate boxes so there was less risk of them sweating. And the Semtex was packed in small parcels and well separated from the rest. The arms were a different matter. There were half a dozen Skorpion VZ61 7.65mm machine-pistols packed tightly in two lots of three. There was an assortment of automatic pistols also bundled up in two lots. And there were some Command, remote-control detonators.

In a separate area were some mortar bombs but Daley did no more than establish what they were before repacking them. There was assorted ammunition, packed loosely and indiscriminately bundled together, and there was ample fuse wire and some standard plastic explosive.

Patterson and Daley had worked hard but had been helped by the softness of the soil and the fact that the burial of the arms was not as deep as Daley had believed. Nor had they uncovered the whole cache.

They sat in the bracken to recover some breath. It was broad daylight and they were open to observation although they believed it to be unlikely on an overcast mid-October day in a lonely spot. Just the same, both would be happier when the plot looked as it had before they started.

They took two machine-pistols to the car and Daley carried three packs of Semtex. They loaded fuse wire, and a limited number of detonators. Both of them carried a good supply of ammunition for the two extra pistols they now carried, and extra loaded magazines for the machine-pistols. When they were satisfied they set to work to cover the considerable quantity left. When finished they covered the whole sight with dead leaves and bracken until it appeared as if it had not been touched.

They wiped the spades as best they could and placed them carefully in the boot with the arms and explosive. After that they sat in the car for a while, recovering their breath and feeling the chill as they cooled down.

Patterson wiped his face. "Where are you going to put this stuff?"

"In the apartment."

"The apartment? You're crazy. How do you get it in and if you do how do you stop Steinbach and the lovable Ulla from getting their murderous hands on it?"

Daley switched on the ignition but still sat there panting slightly, now feeling the full effects of the work. "We'll buy a couple of grips on the way back to town. We have time. We keep the stuff under our beds and the bloody door locked at all times when we're not there."

"That's great. I can see a door lock stopping Steinbach. And if you catch him in the act he's just as likely to kill you."

"I know. That's why I'd make bloody sure I got him first."

Patterson groaned. "So it's war we're returning to. Don't you think you've already got a big enough one on your hands when your Provo chums find you've done the dirt on them? Now *there* you have a problem."

The car moved slowly and Daley did a series of movements so that he did not have to reverse down through the lines of spruce. "They already know I have. And you know I have. You've known all along."

Patterson glanced at Daley who was concentrating on avoiding a calamity as he slowed down. "What makes you say that?"

"Don't take me for a fool, Jamie. Hold on a minute." He eased through some spruce which brushed the sides of the car before it widened out. "I must have strayed from the track."

121

And then, as he picked up the route again, "You were my contact, weren't you? Why else would a bloody Prot be seen with the likes of me."

"It was chance. I didn't know the bloody bomb was going to go off."

"None of us did. But that was why you were there. You did it well, I'll say that for you. And it would have been better than some cooked up cock-up where the screws yanked me off on some pretext which would have fooled no one. Someone leaked it out that I had given information long before we did a runner."

"No one in the RUC would leak it out; they wouldn't be that stupid. Maybe one of your own crowd doesn't like you and spread the word that you gave a couple of your mates away."

"And maybe you're a Jewish rabbi. Anyway, why are you hanging on? You could have split." The wheels were slipping on the grass as they went down the slope and Daley was having more difficulty steering the car than on the way up.

Patterson laughed at Daley's effrontery. "You must be kidding. You almost cried your eyes out every time I suggested it. Anyway, once we were over the border I was in your hands. You had the hideout, and after that you had the gun and the hair-dye and the forged papers. I didn't stand a chance on my own, even if I wanted to be, and you were scared I'd give you away if I was caught." He watched Daley for a reaction and when there was none added, "And you didn't want to be alone, did you, Con? From the moment you heard the news that you'd been lost at sea you knew they were after you in a big way if they were willing to take a step like that."

Daley sat tight-lipped while he battled with the rough ground; the car was skidding now and again. His features were grim and drawn, eyes hardened as he had been forced to listen to what he did not want to hear.

Patterson pushed home his advantage. "Maybe there's something else they know about."

"Such as what?" snarled Daley.

"Such as how did you know there were *two* Provo units in Germany at the time Eugene Lynch was killed?"

The car swerved so violently that Patterson thought it was going to crash into a tree. Daley jammed on the brakes and above the roar of the engine and the snapping of young branches as they careered too close to them, Daley screamed abuse and Patterson realised he had gone too far.

The car juddered to a stop and Daley lowered his head on the wheel as he realised how close they had been to a serious crash. Without changing position he said in an ice-cold voice, "Don't ever say that again or I'll shoot your guts out. Eugie was a good friend of mine."

Patterson was about to say he had said nothing against Eugie when he decided to hold his tongue. He thought that maybe they had crossed wires and then realised the possible connection. Daley was in an unstable and murderous mood just then and it was the wrong time for both of them. "I'm sorry," he said. "I think you read too much into it."

It took Daley time to unwind. His body had been knotted and the tension eased out as if drawn. He relaxed enough to extricate them from the position they were in and Patterson climbed out to help as he reversed from the tree. It was Daley's opportunity to leave Patterson stranded had he wanted, but he braked and Patterson climbed back into the car. Again they had been tied by events. Had Daley left Patterson he knew it would be far too risky to return to the apartment.

So they continued on but their association was more strained than at any stage since escaping, yet they still had a need of each other.

In an attempt to ease the situation he had created, Patterson said, "Don't forget I'm just as much on the run as you are, Con. Contact or not, it would have made little difference to my sentence; you would have done much better out of the deal."

Daley did not reply but appeared satisfied and was doing a better job getting down the slope which seemed much longer than it had going up and he suspected that he had made a meal of the route. Eventually he did pick up the track again and when he did it was near the entry on to the narrow country road they had used on their approach. And blocking their way was another car drawn straight across the exit with three men waiting the other side of it, their heads just visible as were two of the guns they held.

Flynn and Mooney greeted Billy Conner like a lost brother. In fact Conner was remotely related to Mooney by marriage and they had once lived near each other in Armagh, before Conner came to England and Mooney moved to Belfast. Conner looked the bull of a man he was. Dark, tousled hair which gave the wrong impression of being permed, and thick brows above dark, strong, sometimes cruel, features. His eyes were deep sea blue, bright and penetrating and set into piggy surrounds.

Conner had a certain rough charm and could be very amusing. At base he had not moved far from being the school bully but had learned to acknowledge his match and with it a little discretion. He took the two visitors to a pub off the Kilburn High Road, and a nod to the chief barman across the crowded public bar received a move of the head and Conner led the way to a door at one side of the bar.

The small room had a table and six chairs round it and a frosted window along one side. It was spartan but clean, and was used for special occasions and meetings and sometimes for after-hours drinking. No one would be allowed in while the three men were there. A hatch opened and three pints of Guinness were thrust through with a plate of sandwiches. Conner gathered the drinks and plate. The hatch closed at once.

"You're well organised, Billy," observed Mooney with some admiration. "Sláinte."

They all drank deeply but, as Flynn put his glass down, he brought them back to earth. "The police must know you use this place. We would not want to be seen with you."

Conner wiped the froth from his mouth. "Be your age, Danny. There's no way to meet me without them knowing. I can't take evasive action every time I want to see someone, and if I did they'd know something was up."

Conner picked up a sandwich and took a huge bite.

124

Spraying crumbs everywhere he added almost indecipherably, "Let them see you openly. You're both on record, so what does it matter? They don't know what we are talking about and there's no way they'd be allowed in this room."

"You talk as if they're just outside," said Flynn in sudden alarm.

"Of course they're just outside. There's always an SB man, or MI5, or someone from C13 in the bar; sometimes all at the same time. We've come openly; they've nothing on us. And while they watch us it takes the pressure off the active service boys. Stop worrying."

Flynn and Mooney were not sure. They were uncomfortable because they had taken such pains to escape the attentions of the police once they had left Ireland. "You could have taken us somewhere less Irish," complained Flynn.

"Somewhere where we would stand out as Irish, you mean? Sure I could have done. But they knew you were here from the moment you telephoned me. So what's the problem that has caused this bullshit?"

"Okay." Flynn looked across the table to Mooney who gave him the nod to be today's spokesman. "We're looking for Con Daley."

Conner gave a little grin. "He's done well, hasn't he? Got the whole bloody lot of us scrambling in dark corners. I don't know where he is. I didn't need you two to come over to ask me to look for him. I've been doing that from Day One. He's avoiding all the usual haunts. If he's over here at all."

"He's here." Mooney was disgruntled. It was the same everywhere: Daley had disappeared from the face of the earth.

"How do you know? He could be in the Republic."

"Someone would have heard. No, he's here and he has that wife-killing Prot Jamie Patterson with him. That's what we can't understand. There's something fishy about it all."

"There was always something fishy about Con Daley. He was born into it but something went wrong along the line. Anyway I don't know where he is." Conner tapped the hatch for more drinks.

"Don't you think it strange that nobody, nobody at all, has heard a word? He's got to be somewhere, for God's sake."

"All that means is that you're looking in the wrong places. How do you know the police haven't got him and are keeping quiet about it to see what blows up?"

"Even those corrupt devils would have to go public some time. No, he's still on the loose. Maybe Patterson has holed him up somewhere."

The hatch closed again after Conner had taken the fresh drinks from the ledge. He pushed his empty glass to one side. "Well, that makes it easy. When you get back all you have to do is to have a word with the UVF."

"That's not funny, Billy." Flynn sat back, heavy features threatening. "You're not taking this seriously. We want Con Daley badly."

"Has he grassed on us?"

"That's not the only reason."

"Dipped in the till?"

"We think he's done that, too, but there's something far worse which only he will have the answers to."

Conner put down his drink with a bang. His eyes were narrowed, lips tight. "Do I get to know what it is you think he's done?"

"We're not sure. It's best to wait until we are. We don't want any injustice."

"Jesus." Conner burst out laughing and the sound must have carried to the public bar. "You come over here asking our help and you want to keep it all to yourselves. Well, find him yourselves."

Flynn said uneasily, "You're taking a dangerous line, Billy. You're not a separate organisation over here."

"Fancy. I was just beginning to believe we are; I thought you were making the point."

"Stop it, Billy. The control must come from Belfast. And you know it."

"So it's an appendage that we are. Well, we'll continue to look for Con but if we find him we want to know what it's all about. Just stop treating us like kids and yourselves as God Almighty."

13

Daley was quick to respond when he saw the car blocking the path. He braked hard and the rear wheels skidded on a carpet of needles and wet grass and it was sheer luck that the car swerved the way he wanted to go. He accelerated far too soon, for the skid was not complete, but they hurtled away from the other car and towards the lane.

Now off the track there seemed to be spruce everywhere blocking their path. It was something of a miracle that Daley avoided most of them, but to his credit he drove inspirationally and with the fear of another kind of death if a crash did not kill him. Patterson had disappeared from his thoughts altogether and it was a simple question of himself against the rest.

The car struck a couple of trees side on and there was a terrible screech of torn metal as they careered towards the lane in a crazy pattern of moves that could only end in disaster. Patterson grabbed both sides of his seat and hung on with his legs out to absorb the shock.

Each time a tree blocked them Daley managed to swerve round it by a combination of brilliant driving induced by stark fear, and sheer luck. They reached the lane but were going at such speed that they overshot it and entered another tortuous world of trees and loose undergrowth. But he managed to bring the car under control and swing back on to the lane before they entered a section of dense growth.

They swerved on to the lane as the rear window was smashed in a hail of bullets which fortunately struck it at an angle so that the shots hit the inside of the car or went straight out a side window. They shouted and ducked and hoped for the best.

Daley was driving dangerously fast. It was to their advantage that the lane was anything but straight and the constant curves kept them out of trouble for a while. But Daley could not afford to slow down. The car blocking the track had had to be reversed before it could get after them but that was small comfort. It was several miles to anything resembling a main road and even that was really a country road. The site for the burial of the cache had been carefully chosen for the very reason that now went against them: it was well out of the way of anywhere and difficult to get to.

Patterson looked back. He could see nothing much through the splinters of glass hanging from the rear window and there was just a constant blur of changing greenery as they raced round a never-ending series of bends. The rear seat was covered with glass and he could see that the rear nearside passenger window had been partially shattered from the exiting shots.

"Nice friends you have," he said bitterly to Daley who was too busy driving to answer. Because of the respite, the ridiculous thought entered his head that Daley had yet to return the car. He moved his body round so that he could get a better sight of their rear and thus shout early warning.

The speed Daley was doing on a lane little wider than the car was frightening in itself. If someone came the other way then that would be the end, for there was no way to stop in time while the bends were so constantly tight. And then he caught a glimpse of something other than the greenery behind them; just the barest sight of something dark. He glimpsed it again at the next bend. "They're catching up."

Daley swore. "That's impossible. They can't go faster than this."

"Someone is. Maybe you're not the world's best driver after all." It was a silly remark sprung from stretched nerves. Daley was doing his best; no, better than that, Daley was coping incredibly well. Yet so was someone else. "You'll have to go faster," yelled Patterson.

"If I go any faster I'll be in Formula One and we'll finish up a tree. I can't go any bloody faster. You couldn't have seen them." Daley shouted spasmodically, his concentration

128

wholly on trying to cope with what he was doing. "Jesus!"
It was a cry of despair as he tried to accelerate and hold a
steering wheel that was juddering at each bump.

Patterson drew out one of the two pistols he had, cocked it
awkwardly and twisted so that he could now kneel on the seat.
He thought he must be going crazy but the men in the
following car were out to kill.

For a couple of bends he saw nothing and passed this on to
reassure Daley. It was a mistake, for Daley, feeling that his
driving was getting dangerously out of control, eased down a
little.

Patterson saw a flash of dark colour again and a shaft of
light as the dipping sun caught a windscreen. It was so
momentary as to be almost subliminal. "Whoever's driving
must be a pro. How long before the lane straightens out?" He
did not expect Daley to reply, so added, "Is there any turn-off
we can take?" But even as he spoke he realised they could
place themselves in a trap if they took a turning which could
only be some sort of a track like the one they had left.

The sightings were becoming more frequent and for longer
periods, but Patterson still could not make out a whole car.
Daley went faster still until he felt he had no control over the
car at all. The steering wheel was spinning in his hands as if of
its own accord. He was almost tearful as he tried to cope, not
so much from fear, as from the frustration of knowing he was
coping incredibly well in the most difficult of situations, but
behind him someone was doing even better.

As well as Daley was doing Patterson thought he would
have the edge on him if he could get behind the wheel but it
was impossible to do. It would mean slowing and changing
places on a constantly snaking road at high speed. They were
stuck with what they had.

Patterson resorted to shouting out the sightings as they
came up while trying to keep the concern from his voice; he
tried to instil a matter-of-fact tone as a navigator would to a
pilot. A short burst of fire came from an automatic weapon as
the dark shape behind next appeared.

The burst did no damage to them, it was too hasty and they
still represented a fleeting target. A spray of foliage crashed on

to the car as a small branch was shot from a tree. A solitary round screeched off the car roof to leave a weird echo inside.

Patterson steadied himself on the seat, forearms resting on the seat back, pistol held out between both hands to steady the gun, his aim beyond the broken section of window. He waited.

The next bend almost caught him by surprise; he fired a little late but directly at the part of the car he could see and at what he reckoned to be driver level. He had no idea whether or not he hit anything.

Nothing happened for the next two bends as the distance between the two cars lengthened. Patterson yelled to Daley what had happened. Daley managed a quick nervous grin.

They must have travelled another mile and the bends were now almost casual. It could only be another two or three miles at the most before they reached the main country road which would surely make it more difficult for a gun battle with the risk of public view.

"Don't ease off," Patterson warned Daley. "Whatever you do, keep up the speed."

Daley needed no telling, but the driving was slightly less dangerous and the ground firmer under the wheels. The mad chase had taken it out of Daley, though, and from time to time he had trouble keeping his hands steady on the wheel. It was still too risky to slow sufficiently to change drivers and Daley seemed to realise this and made no complaint as he sped on. He was pale and shaken and knew, as Patterson did, that is was far from over.

"You must have got the driver," said Daley, as he quickly changed down for an S-bend.

"It would have been the luckiest shot in the world if I did. But it must have hit the car for them to know we can shoot back. I think they've changed their strategy. Just keep going and turn right when we reach the road instead of left."

Patterson held his position on the front seat and left Daley to get on with it while he watched the rear. "Here they come," he warned after a short break. "And they're moving." From the tunnelled canopy of greenery behind them, the dark shape of a car came fully into view for the first time. At the speed it travelled Patterson thought it must be super-charged. He steadied his position and yelled at Daley, "They're closing fast. Zig-zag or something."

Daley started a series of swerves which took him on to the rough verges both sides of the lane and did nothing to help Patterson's aim.

Patterson was thrown around on his seat and had difficulty in holding on to his pistol at all while behind him the car he could now see was dark blue, kept a straight course. A head appeared through the sun roof and a sub-machine gun was thrust out along the hard roof section. The man was in no hurry to fire and was waiting for the right opportunity. Patterson took a random shot but it could have gone anywhere. He managed to shout out, "Straighten out for a minute while I try to nail him."

Daley reacted so suddenly that the move almost had Patterson off his seat. He recovered quickly and fired through the gap of broken glass at the man who seemed to be returning the fire. When the front windscreen spiderwebbed between himself and Daley, Daley went into a crazy routine again and Patterson struggled to hold on to the seat back.

The boot half flew up and flapped away to block part of Patterson's vision. They must have hit it, he thought. And then he was really scared. The boot was full of ammunition, detonators, Semtex and plastic explosive. "We've got to leave the car," he yelled. "They've dropped back. They're trying to blow us to kingdom come."

"Holy Mother of Jesus." With his concentration on driving Daley had overlooked their cargo. He was driving a bomb large enough to destroy several tanks. He drove so wildly now that Patterson tried to swivel round so he could sit down beside him. There was really nothing either of them could do.

If the enemy had decided to go for the explosive it must have been a change of plan, for the earlier shots had been much higher as if they were deliberately trying to avoid it. Patterson guessed that they had wanted Daley alive but found it too difficult in the time left. They were going for an out-and-out kill.

There was nothing left to say to each other. Daley's face

was a mask, pale and drawn with eyes staring as if he knew he was driving to his own destruction. Patterson guessed he must look much the same. Before, there had been hope; now there was none. Daley could only keep up his mad driving for so long and those chasing them only had to have one lucky shot.

"Take that ridge," said Patterson lifelessly. The terrain had roughened up again and fell away steeply on one side. There was no point in staying on the lane; even with avoiding action it was too limited. It was true that the following car had fallen back but only to protect itself from the inevitable explosion. They were still within firing range and when Patterson glanced back again he could see a rifle poking from the roof. They had decided to go for accuracy and distance.

"The ridge, for chrissake," he yelled again.

Daley was reluctant. He could not see the extent of the drop the other side.

"What's it bloody matter, you silly bugger? They've got an AK 47 pointing at us. The ridge or smithereens and unlatch your door as we go over. *Now.*"

Daley held on for a while longer, then pulled hard on the wheel as he realised there was no alternative. The car hit the bank across a shallow gulley as if striking a ramp and was airborne as it cleared the ridge. There was a terrifying moment when there was no contact with earth and during which Patterson screamed, "*Jump!*"

But Daley was already flying through the air as the car dipped and crashed into bush which somehow managed to catapult it into another spectacular orbit before it hit the ground again, crushed the whole of its front and somersaulted down a steep slope at the bottom of which was a stream with a stretch of wire along one section and which incredibly steadied the car to a halt before it could enter the water.

The car was now on its side, its radiator steaming, body crushed, yet the contents in the rear had not exploded. Incredibly, too, the engine was still running.

On the road above, the pursuing car skidded to a halt and two men appeared on the ridge to gaze down at the damage. There was no sign of Patterson and Daley near the car and by unspoken consent both men took a prone position on the edge of the ridge and started to pump shots at the rear of the car where the lid flapped like a loose canopy.

Even then the explosive was resistant to the firepower, but the more sensitive detonators must have eventually been hit, for there was a sudden explosion like massive thunder, rolling on and on and the inevitable fireball mushroomed into the sky as bits of car flew out like shrapnel and the ammunition went off like firecrackers, almost lost in the general roar.

When they eventually considered it safe the two men climbed to their feet and were joined by the third. The flames were still belching into the sky but through them, swirling and writhing and forcing upwards high above the flames themselves, were thick, dark, ever-increasing palls of smoke which doused the orange brightness around them.

"A pity he had to fry. We needed him to talk."

"And how do you know he was still in it?"

The men appeared uneasy. The driver said, "That will be seen for miles. Let's get the hell out of this."

"We'd better make sure first. It won't take a minute. Come on."

Two of the men started to scramble down the slope, one complaining that they would never get near the car, as Daley shot the other one through the throat.

Daley jumped with eyes closed and head protected by his arms. He hit the ground and rolled a short distance. Momentary fear almost blacked him out.

He struggled to breathe, opened his eyes and saw that he had fallen just below the ridge. The sound of a car screeching to a halt above him made him move at once. He rolled into a hollow and tried to bury himself in the ground behind a pitifully small shrub, and then kept still once he had pulled out a pistol.

He could neither see nor hear Patterson, but the Prot was a survivor and without him Daley recognised that by now he would probably be dead.

Two men stood on the ridge above him. He dare not raise his head, but he heard them speaking quite clearly and the

Northern Irish accents surprised him into reflecting that an active service unit had been exposed to be used against him; there could be nothing more serious or dangerous.

When they started to fire he risked gazing up and saw their guns jutting out from the ridge as they aimed at the car down by the river. The explosion and the continuing reverberation nearly blew him from his shallow hollow. It was like an earthquake under his body which was being pounded by vibrations.

Daley flattened himself as best he could and during that time knew that he was still doomed unless he could get away. An explosion like this one, in so fairly remote a place, would bring out the police and fire brigade and a whole army of the curious. The only way out was on foot and three armed men were still making sure he and Patterson did not survive.

The rumbles and roars gradually subsided but he could still feel the heat from where he lay. When the two men left the ridge to make sure that he and Patterson were dead, Daley accepted that he would only get one chance. What could they expect to find amongst the scattered pieces that were left? And that only if they could get anywhere near the intense heat. Maybe they hoped to find dismembered limbs on the way down; the whole slope was covered with debris.

The two men approached near to him and he thought he must be seen. One was complaining and both were having difficulty in coping with the rough sloping ground. Daley made up his mind that if he was not seen then he would be when they returned. He raised himself on one knee and fired. As the man fell to his knees clutching his throat, the other one sprang round in panic, saw Daley, and raised his rifle to his hip.

Daley fired again, and again. The second man crumbled as Daley watched, the rifle slowly slipping down in reverse arms as if in a final farewell. And then the man collapsed. In sudden fear Daley glanced up at the ridge to see the third man staring down in horror before snapping from his stupor to raise a pistol in blind panic.

Daley, unable to swing round in time, threw himself flat

134

and rolled desperately. Two shots echoed out, the sound partially absorbed by the noise of the burning car. Daley kept rolling, trying to get as far out of range as possible. No more shots followed but he kept moving until Patterson shouted out, "Come back, you silly bugger."

Nothing had sounded so sweet. Daley lay on his back gazing up at the overcast sky. The evening was rapidly closing in. From where he lay the heat of the fire was considerable and he realised there was no way the men could have approached sufficiently close to what remained to examine it. He climbed to his feet and staggered up the slope to see a dishevelled Patterson standing over the man who had been shot in the throat.

"Is he dead?" Daley was panting as he climbed.

"He is now." Patterson bent down to feel the carotid artery in the neck, avoiding the blood. "He went the hard way."

As Daley drew nearer he noticed that Patterson's left arm was hanging straight down as though he was unable to move it. And he could see that Patterson seemed to have had a rougher landing than he had. Patterson's clothes were torn, one knee exposed and bleeding, and the sleeve of the arm which hung down was almost ripped off from the shoulder. But his right hand, the one that had searched for a pulse beat, was still holding a gun.

"I was thrown," Patterson explained to save Daley asking. He turned to use his gun as a pointer, "There's some dead ground the other side and I was dumped straight in it from a great height. When matey saw what had happened to his chums I was able to come up on his blind side." Patterson nodded at the rifle. "You were lucky he carried that instead of a pistol; too cumbersome for close range."

"I know. We can't leave them here."

"We can. But we had better get matey off the road first."

They dragged the body of the third man, whom they assumed to be the driver, off the road and rolled him down the slope to join the others.

The keys of the other car were still in the ignition and Daley took the wheel because Patterson could only use one arm. "Have you broken it?" asked Daley as he drove off.

135

"I don't think so. It's gone numb. Maybe a nerve; I don't know. I shall be happier when we're well away from here. Let's get home." Patterson sat back and closed his eyes.

Daley, still tense, drove as if they were still being chased until Patterson told him to ease down, the bad men were dead. And it might have been that fact that frightened Daley the most. They had removed a three-man active unit from the Provos who were notoriously unforgiving. He was compounding his problems with them. But at least Patterson was now directly involved and it gave him a degree of comfort.

They reached the turn-off and decided to take the same route as before; there was no longer any point in changing it. Traffic gradually increased and suddenly they were back in the land of the living. An ambulance raced past in the direction they had just left, followed by two fire-engines. Someone must have reported the explosion.

It did not matter now; they were in the clear except that they were in a stolen car, and one which they would not wish to leave too close to the apartment.

Patterson said listlessly, "We've lost the lot. A whole day's work and we've nothing to show for it but the two extra pistols we have with us. And three dead bodies and a murder hunt to follow." He gave Daley a glance. "C13 will be brought into this as soon as it's discovered who the dead are. We could do without that complication."

"And the loss of a hire car. Lucky I used a false name and address." After a while Daley added, "We'll have to go back."

"Back where?"

"The cache. They won't expect us to do that. We still need the stuff and there's plenty left."

"Then you take Steinbach and Ulla with you. My arm is not going to get better." Patterson turned round awkwardly, "That place is going to be crawling with cops for days. You're crazy."

But Daley was still feverishly scheming. Their successful escape had acted like a drug and he was on a high. "I'd better drop you at the apartment first because of the state of you. And then I'll ditch the car out of town and come back by train or taxi or anyway I can."

Patterson could not argue with that but he was worried about Daley's sudden euphoria. He hoped he would return to earth without a fatal bang.

Carmel Daley called on Billy Conner the day after seeing her sister. She had stayed the night in a cheap boarding house cursing what she saw as the self-satisfied callousness of Rose. Her sister had always kept clear of the cause and it annoyed her, the more so because she had actually come to live amongst the enemy and was enjoying it. And of all people, she had married a Scot whom they had been trying to get rid of from Ireland for the last four hundred years.

The door was opened by a big, powerful, smiling man who immediately saw some resemblance to Rose, for he said, "Where have I seen you before?" It was not the usual come-on but a sincere question; Carmel knew it at once. This man had charm and was gentle in his manner in spite of his size and piratical looks.

"You knew my sister Rose. She sent me to see you."

Conner's expression fleetingly changed but he opened the door wider and said, "Then you'd better come in."

Carmel followed him down a passage, narrow stairs to one side, his frame blocking the view ahead, and into a pleasant, chintzy room with several modes of furnishings attributable to the varied tastes of a series of girlfriends.

"Drink?"

"G&T, please. Nice place."

Conner opened a cupboard and produced some bottles and glasses. He poured the gin and tonic and put a bottled slice of lemon in it, then poured himself a large Scotch. He handed her the gin and raised his glass. "Here's to you. Have a seat."

They sat down, Conner eyeing Carmel suspiciously. He could certainly see the likeness of the sisters but Rose had a style this one seemed to lack. "What's your name?"

"Carmel. Didn't Rose mention me?"

"She might have. I haven't seen her for some time." Conner was wondering just how much this younger girl knew about what had happened. If she did know it had not stopped her coming. "You've nice legs, Carmel. Better than your

137

sister." Shock treatment, see how she stood up to it. Conner was still suspicious, though attracted. Safety first. It had been a long hard lesson.

"Thank you." Carmel well knew her skirt was too high. She wanted his interest and his sympathy. "You're much nicer than Rose said you are."

Conner smiled. Carmel was not very good at it but she had plenty in her favour. "Rose might have said a lot of things. We didn't always see eye to eye."

"Then she's a fool." Carmel found the drink very strong but would not let him see what she felt. She took another defiant gulp.

Conner said with a smile, "Have you just come to offer your services to me, or have you some other reason? Although it's nice to see you, so it is."

Carmel at last recognised that she had placed herself in a slightly compromising position. She had set out to please him and he was poised to take advantage. It was going to be difficult to back down. There was no compromise in what she said next. "Have you seen anything of Con Daley?"

Conner was surprised. "Is that why you're here? Looking for that little shit?"

Carmel felt she had made an awful mistake. "I know you know everything and everyone. I thought you might help."

"Who told you I know everything and everyone? Who told someone like you?" His anger was partly feigned but he was annoyed that someone like Carmel should carry this sort of knowledge.

Carmel squirmed and tried to pull down the hem of her skirt. "Danny Flynn and Mike Mooney." She wondered desperately if she had said the right thing.

"They told you that about me?" Within the space of twenty-four hours this was the second time he had been asked about Daley. He could perhaps understand the girl wanting to know; Daley had probably put up a black-out on her, which showed he had some sense. But there was much more going on about Daley than he knew about.

Carmel could only nod and raise her drink to cover her mistake.

"Did they give you that black eye while they told you?"

Carmel instinctively touched the tender puffing round the eye. She thought she had covered it with foundation cream.

"I'll give you one to match if you come out with any more of that bullshit. Just what do you think I am, Carmel? Go find him yourself and don't you mention my name to anyone ever again. Understand?"

Carmel drained her glass and almost immediately felt muzzy. "Don't be like that. I'm no danger to you. All I want to do is to find Con." She tried to stop slurring her words. God, the drink must have been strong.

With some compassion he said, "Have you eaten at all? You're acting as if you're drinking on an empty stomach. Can't you hold your booze?"

"Of course I can. I changed my name for him." He was wavering in front of her.

"Did you now?" Conner was puzzled and suddenly thought that she might hold more information than she herself realised. He tried to draw her out. "I knew his wife. Long before she was shot by some gun-happy Prot. Were you living with him at the time?"

Carmel hung on to the chair. "He had already left her." She hardly knew what she was saying but was aware that she must try to get it right if she was to get anywhere.

"I heard you were the cause of her leaving. Some say she set herself up to be killed because she was heartbroken."

Carmel looked to her drink but the glass was empty. She shook her head in futile denial. "They didn't get on. He loved me not her."

Conner gazed thoughtfully at Carmel, then left the room and came back with a scotch egg on a plate. "Get that down you. It might help you sober up." He handed her the plate and added, "You say you're no danger to me; let me tell you that like that you are a danger to everyone you know."

Carmel attacked the egg so ravenously that Conner went to the kitchen to make her a sandwich. When he returned the egg had gone and she looked as if she was going to be sick. But she held on and ate the sandwich more slowly.

139

"Did they ever get the guy who killed her?" He knew the answer but wanted to see how much she actually knew.

She stopped chewing for a moment. "There were all sorts of rumours but I don't think anyone knows. Some say the Brits know but are covering it up."

Conner nodded as if in agreement. "What made you come to England, Carmel? What makes you think Con is here?"

She still felt woozy but the food had helped her and she did not feel so sick. Her head was pounding though, and she wished he would stop asking her questions. Yet something within her made her stick at it, perhaps knowing he was her only chance. The question surprised her. She had not seriously considered why she had crossed the water to mainland Britain. It had been an instinctive thing to do and she had wanted to get as far away from Flynn and Mooney and their crowd as she could.

"Don't you know?" Conner prompted.

"I hadn't thought about it."

"Yet you came. That's a strange thing to do without good reason. You must have thought he was here."

She was in no condition to think straight. Why had she come? She had just come and that was that. "I don't know why. He and the other man hadn't been picked up and I just thought they must be here."

"Why not the Republic?"

"I think we would have heard something. Don't you?"

"You're not as dumb as I thought you were. But why here? Why London? You must have had a reason."

Carmel groped in her memory and wished she was in better shape to do it. Yet the way Conner had spoken made her think that he believed she had a reason which she must have overlooked. God, it was so difficult to think at all.

When he saw her struggling for an answer he tried to help her. "You reacted instinctively. But you would not come to England on spec. That costs money and you don't seem to have enough for regular meals. He must have said something sometime to give you an impression that if he were ever in trouble he would come here."

She did not argue with that but nor could she supply an

140

answer. She had not really considered why she had come to London but it had seemed the right thing to do at the time. But Conner made her think. There had to be some reason.

"Look," Conner said at his gentlest, "you're not feeling too good. Sleep it off, there's a spare room. And when you feel up to it we'll talk it over again." He stood up and smiled down at her, the complete image of reliability. He offered a hand to help her up. "Con's whereabouts may be inside your own head and just needs a little drawing out. If I'm right, then I can certainly help you, Carmel. Meanwhile stay here for a few days. We might even find time for a little fun."

14

When Patterson was dropped off by Daley outside the apartment block, he did not at once go in. As soon as Daley disappeared Patterson searched for a telephone. It was the only time he had been alone and the two previous calls he had made had been anything but satisfactory.

When he found a callbox he sorted out his change and rang the Belfast number. His luck was no better, Monroe was out, but a message had been left that any insistent callers were to be put through to Monroe's private house. He could not use the name of Patterson to the switchboard in case it leaked out and once that happened the whole press would have it and he might as well give himself up.

He rang Monroe at his home and his wife answered the phone to say her husband was out but was expected back any moment. Patterson felt it was a conspiracy to stop him communicating. The only thing he could do was to give the pay-phone number and stress the urgency. When Daley returned, one way or the other he would check on the time Patterson entered the apartment, so he could wait only so long.

And it was a difficult time of day. Rush-hour brought out the home-scurrying crowds, and Patterson was in despair that someone would use the phone while he was waiting for the call. Because his clothes were torn and dishevelled, he did his best to keep out of sight by skulking near the kiosk. His arm was still stiff, the sleeve still half off and he tried to pull it up. It was ten minutes later and he was on the point of returning to the apartment when the phone rang.

Patterson was in such a nervous state by then that he had difficulty in opening the door of the cubicle and then almost dropped the phone as he picked it up. "Yes?" He was still reluctant to give his name.

"Alec Monroe. That you, Jamie?"

"Thank God. I thought I'd never get you." Patterson was annoyed that he was so shaken.

"It's my call so we won't be cut off. Give it to me as fast as you can."

When Patterson returned to the apartment he had to hang around the entrance before making safe entry, and then rushed for the elevator. When he unlocked the apartment door with Daley's key, he bore the routine of Steinbach and Ulla being ready to blow his head off, and was slightly surprised to find them there. They wore new clothes, formal for them, so they had certainly been out.

They took one look at his condition, and Ulla poured him a stiff drink while Steinbach wanted to know what happened.

Detective Chief Superintendent Alec Monroe landed at London Airport on the last flight from Belfast. He was met in person by Commander 'Pongo' Waring who shook hands warmly and led the way to his chauffeur-driven Jaguar. When the two men were seated in the back Waring said, "Have you eaten?"

"No, sir. My wife was on the point of killing me as I left home. I didn't have time to explain to her why I had to go."

"I haven't eaten either. I'll take you to my club. It's not as posh as some but the food isn't bad."

They spoke only of generalities on the way into London. When they were eventually ushered into the dining-room of a club off Victoria Street, they were shown to a corner table where they would not be disturbed. It was a situation they were used to and serious conversation always died at the approach of a waiter.

"Right, let's have it," said Waring after they had ordered.

Monroe had thought it over on the plane but it never seemed to come right and he knew that it would not now, however he put it. He had a great respect for Waring. He saw him as one of the few mainland coppers who really understood the Northern Irish problem from within. Monroe did not have to explain any of the background. Waring knew why things happened, right or wrong. And he wondered how he would see this one.

"Con Daley is a 'grass' who lost his nerve with good reason. We'd already had a few names from him but the judicial system fouled up everything. He was arrested and put up for trial before he could be extricated. It was a case where secrecy did not pay. The officers who pulled him in had no idea what some of the rest of us were up to. Unfortunately the report came through very late and due process was in operation before I could do anything about it.

"Once inside, Daley clammed up immediately and any attempt to pull him out would have spoken volumes to those who wanted to know who had fingered them. As it was, suspicions had been aroused and he received threats shortly after beginning his sentence."

"Your food's getting cold," Waring pointed out. "I'll fill in. You decided to plant someone inside to pick up the pieces. Someone who would not raise eyebrows. And then the bomb went off." Waring smiled. "They do say that when it starts to go wrong it goes all the way."

Monroe gazed round the dining-room while he ate, surprised how empty it was. "It was worse than that. Jamie Patterson was planted because he is the namesake of someone nobody would suspect. It's not an uncommon name. The fact that he is a Prot actually made it easier. We could not put up another Catholic; it would by no means be easy to find one willing in the circumstances, but this particular Prot would have been acceptable had he been allowed to get going. It was to be an in-and-out job, no more than three days."

Waring ate slowly, and thought carefully. "Whose place was he taking?"

"James Patterson who is at the moment in the prison hospital at Hull. He is not a member of the UVF, or any of those, nor ever has been. He's a loner pure and simple and little is known about him at all, particularly about his state of mind. Something of a nutter. A psychopath, if you like. He simply killed as many IRA and associates as he could. Sometimes the wrong person."

144

Waring picked up the warning. "Is there something you are not telling me?"

Monroe knew he had eaten too quickly. He rubbed his chest. "As I said, the real Patterson is known only to the groups by reputation and result. He shunned the groups like mad. He kept himself to himself so effectively that nobody knew who was doing certain killings. He fled to Britain and was picked up quite by accident: driving without a licence, insurance and road tax. His accent placed him as Northern Irish, his reluctance to answer any questions at all called for a run-down. A few things came to light, but not too many." Monroe sighed, looked at Waring in an apologetic way, and continued: "Patterson fell ill, and started confessing to virtually everything he had done. The staff in Hull were so confused that they contacted us and we had to send someone over. Most of what he said checked out. It seemed that we had found the maverick killer. It appears that he has some brain disease; he's already partially blind and he's unlikely to live long enough to stand trial. They've put him in isolation."

Monroe held out his hands as though his gesture explained everything. "It was an opportunity too good to miss. We slipped in the other Jamie Patterson with the agreement of the prison authority, and the other inmates could draw their own conclusions. Our man made contact with Daley in the sort of accusing, aggressive manner the other one might have done, and before he could identify himself as a contact, probably the next day, the bloody bomb went off."

"It was all a bit risky, wasn't it?" suggested Waring. "- Supposing someone knew what the other Patterson looked like?"

"All implants are risky. No claim was made that he was the other Patterson. By the way he would have acted it might have been assumed that he was. Risk of recognition was minute; we never managed a photofit of the real man. But the moment Daley handed the rest of the stuff over, during a fight or whichever way they might have planned it, Patterson would have been lugged off to another prison as a potential trouble-maker. It would have worked all right."

145

They sat back, plates empty, expressions thoughtful, until Waring said, "You should have warned me."

"I didn't know which way Patterson would jump. He rang me this evening which is why I came over straightaway. He and Daley have taken out a three-man IRA active service unit today. Hertfordshire. They've done you a favour.

Waring looked annoyed. "I've had no notice of this. What the hell is going on?"

Monroe could not resist a small grin. "Maybe it's waiting on your desk. It would take the locals a little time to establish identity. All the papers would be false and dead men don't speak with Northern Irish accents."

"Anything else?"

"They're holed up with Hans Steinbach and Ulla Geiger."

"What?" Waring had difficulty in keeping his voice down. "We've had a fax about them from Bonn. They thought they might come our way. They apparently have a place here but we haven't run it down. And now you say you *know* they're here."

"Before you say anything more, sir, I caught the first available plane over to give you this information in person. I couldn't have done more."

"Where are they?" Waring demanded.

"He wouldn't tell me." Monroe quickly held up a hand to ward off Waring's explosive protest. "His life is on the line. With killers like those he wouldn't last a second if they got a whiff of who he is. He'll let me know when he believes that he cannot produce more than these three. He thinks there is more to Daley than a straight grass. Daley has other secrets. Meanwhile, with the IRA still after Daley, he thinks he can do better. Daley now knows he was a plant, and seems to need him as support. It appears that Daley won't cough any more while he's on the run with a chance of not returning to jail. He's keeping quiet now so that he can use his information as a bargaining factor if he needs to later on. That's Patterson's assessment. We'll have to wait for the full story from him. But there is another grave danger."

Monroe toyed with his coffee spoon and was clearly worried. "Daley hasn't connected him with the other

146

Patterson. They simply were not in prison long enough together for that impression to form. If he ever makes that connection, I have to say I am deeply concerned by the fact that, shortly before I caught the flight, I was advised by our intelligence unit that the Provos are spreading the word that it was Jamie Patterson who killed Daley's wife. I see it as a tactic to separate the two. Although Daley was not living with her when she was shot, he would not take kindly to her killer, even if only from a guilt complex."

"Oh dear. Is there any truth in the allegation?"

"It is not one of the crimes James Patterson has confessed to. If word reaches Daley he might kill Patterson which would not worry the Provos, but might bring Daley into the open. That is what they would hope for."

"Then let's pray he doesn't find out. Is there any way of warning Patterson?"

"No. He has to find ways of contacting me. We have now arranged a simple code to make things easier. The big problem is Daley's instability. Even the Provos couldn't handle him but they have certainly given him every priority now. I don't like this any more than you. But what can I do?"

Waring thought it over and heaved his huge shoulders in a sigh. "I suppose you had something to do with no press photographs appearing, although I must admit that from a public point of view they don't warrant it. This is a Fred Karno's, Alec. Why is Patterson being so bloody awkward?"

"His sister and mother were killed by the Provos. He saw what was left of his mother and was at her bedside when she died. It is not something he is likely to forget."

Waring nodded in understanding. "I hope, for his sake, that his hatred doesn't colour his judgement. This really is a bloody mess. If you make contact insist on the address and bring him in."

"I'll certainly insist and I'll certainly order him to report in. But I can't make him unless I can lay my hands on him."

"Then he might lay himself wide open to charges along with the rest of them. As it is his chances of survival are three to one against, plus a network of Provos."

"That, sir, worries me more than anything else."

147

15

Jamie Patterson hid behind his weariness and his injury to talk as little as possible to Ulla and Steinbach. He really wanted to go to bed but would not be happy until Daley returned. When he finished his drink and had given the Germans a vague outline of what had happened he bathed and changed and felt better but still desperately tired.

The bath had been too hot but it had eased his arm a little. The events of a very long day now got to him. He wanted to be alone yet he needed company for reassurance. He began to see something of how Daley had been feeling ever since they escaped. Loneliness brought problems of the imagination and both pairs were now guilty of killing in a very short space of time. It was best not to think of it, yet it could not be ignored.

Sitting with Ulla and Steinbach with the television turned off was a strain because he knew he had only skimmed the surface of what had happened that day, and what happened to one affected them all in this critical situation. They knew he was waiting for Daley and accepted that but they would stay with him until that happened. And they could not avoid noticing the frequency with which he looked at the watch he had bought on the shopping spree.

It was as well that they thought he was worried about Daley rather than his phone call to Monroe. He had misled Monroe about the cache, telling him that it had been quite small, that they had taken the lot and that there was no point in giving the location of an emptied dump. So when the car blew up everything went with it. But he could not satisfy himself why he had said that. He could have given the position away and he had not. What was he playing at? It was a question he asked himself repeatedly but still could not answer.

"Would you like me to get you something to eat? I don't mind."

Patterson gazed across at Ulla. He sometimes felt sorry for her because he could see no future of any kind for her. "No, thanks, Ulla. It's kind of you to offer. But I'd rather wait for Con to get back. You go ahead if you want to."

"We'll wait, too." When she was not thinking of murder, revolution or sex, Ulla could be soft-natured, but the mood could change in a flash.

Steinbach was sitting on the settee with his long legs drawn up under his chin, his arms around them. He had not said much at all and was eyeing Patterson moodily. Freshly shaven and with his hair shorter, Steinbach looked quite different, clean-cut and respectable.

"I cut it," said Ulla with satisfaction. "I prefer it long around his shoulders but this way he is not so noticeable."

"It's very good." Patterson smiled although he noticed that Steinbach did not. "What's on your mind?" he asked the German.

"We can't stay here indefinitely. Sooner or later people will notice, the porters might begin to find us strange. There is a limit."

So that was why they were dressed more soberly and Steinbach's hair had been cut. Even Ulla appeared almost traditional. "I agree. Who decides when it is time to move?"

"We must make some money first and then split up."

They had obviously discussed the matter. "I thought you had made quite a bit last night."

"Don't believe the media. That was from the bereaved husband for the benefit of the insurance company. And we can't cash in the jewellery until we know of a safe fence."

Patterson went cold. It was easy to do in this company but now Steinbach was making no pretence about the murder across the street. He had not been accused of it, yet he was virtually confessing as if it made no difference to anybody. Patterson took a chance. "I hadn't connected you with the death across the street," he said quietly.

"Did you not," Steinbach answered icily. "I saw you and Daley exchange glances last night during the television news."

"That could have meant anything. You don't seem to mind that you killed a woman."

"I don't mind and she didn't have time to mind. She wasn't a woman; she was a bourgeoise floozie. Changing her bag because her friend had one similar; I ask you. She was not important."

Ulla kept out of this exchange but was watching the two closely. She understood Steinbach perfectly, but Patterson puzzled her. He was not ruthless enough on some issues, but was far more intelligent than she expected him to be. She understood something of the Irish problem and accepted that the aims were different from her own, but they still had much in common and she could not see exactly where Patterson fitted in. She also found the combination of Patterson and Daley, sworn enemies with totally different ideas, puzzling; she had from the beginning. But Patterson was standing up to Steinbach without visible effort and few would do that. Steinbach could make most people shiver by just looking at them as he now looked at Patterson who returned the look with one that challenged, 'Try something'. It was interesting, and she knew that both Steinbach and Patterson were holding gun butts in their waistbands.

Daley came in before that particular mood had evaporated and it perhaps saved a nasty scene. Daley rapped out a prearranged signal, which Patterson had forgotten to do, before unlocking the door. When he entered he failed to pick up the tension because he was tired and untidy and had been travelling for too long after what he had suffered. He gave them all a cursory greeting and went straight to the bathroom. It eased the situation.

When Daley eventually reappeared Ulla went to the kitchen and put some prepared meals she had bought that day, in the microwave. A few minutes later they all sat down to eat.

They talked, but for Patterson the mood was heavy. It was as though they had all gone back to the deep suspicions of the first day. Something must have happened between Ulla and Steinbach while the other two were away. It reminded

150

Patterson of Daley always wanting him to be there. Today had been the first time they had been separated for any length of time since escaping from prison. Neither pair seemed prepared to trust what the others had been up to. After the callous and unnecessary murder across the street it was understandable.

Steinbach said, "So you crashed and the car blew up and you lost the lot?" It was the story Daley had given them and was close enough to the one already told by Patterson. Neither man had mentioned the three dead men; explanation would have been too complicated and the Germans would have wanted to know why Daley was being chased by his own crowd.

Daley pushed away his empty plate. "The ground was rough, and the detonators might have been sweating; they're always dodgy. And Semtex is not as stable as most people think." He gave a sheepish smile, "I suppose I was driving too fast. Jamie will have to answer that. But we wanted to get back as soon as possible."

"So you then stole a car and dropped Jamie off here?"

"Is this an inquisition?" asked Daley, suddenly annoyed. "I had to take the car well away from here, and coming back by train was a sweat. What's your problem, Hans?" he said, glaring at Steinbach.

Steinbach smiled to himself. "I just find that as much a load of bullshit as we gave you last night."

It could have turned into an awkward situation, Steinbach had been in a strange mood all evening. But Patterson suddenly burst out laughing and it fortunately caught on. Soon they were all laughing, Daley as loud as any of them. But it could not last like this and perhaps they all felt it. Something had to go unless they could find a common task. It was Steinbach who provided the answer although Daley had suggested it to Patterson much earlier.

"Let's rob a bank. We need a lot of ready cash and it is the best way of getting some." Steinbach looked at each one in turn. "Yes? It would be fun, would it not, and would keep us going for a while." He smiled as if he had been holding back for this very moment. "We might even get to like it."

Daley nodded slowly. "Jamie will tell you that I've had the same idea in mind for some time. That's one of the reasons I

151

wanted the Semtex; there's nothing like it for putting on the frighteners."

Steinbach leaned back in his chair now that he knew he had all their attention. He pulled one leg across the other and the chair creaked as it went back on two legs and he gently rocked it. "In Frankfurt once, an art thief told me that he never went for the main galleries because they were too complicated and unpredictable. Security was good and an immense amount of research was necessary. He told me he always went for the solitary valuable painting. Local councils who did not know what to do with public money would often invest in a valuable painting and hang it in the town hall or somewhere like that.

"Few ever looked at it, but what was important to him was the general lack of security. From a professional thief's point of view they were relatively easy to steal."

"What the hell has this got to do with robbing a bank?" It was a safe question from Patterson and showed he was interested.

"I'm merely pointing out that it is no use us trying to rob one of the big London banks. The research on escape would take considerable time and the alarm system would be very sophisticated. We would be unlikely to get away if for no other reason than the traffic would stop us." Steinbach spread his hands. "So we go for a much smaller, more isolated bank, where the avenues of escape are numerous and the police force small. Does anyone know of such a place?"

Patterson pushed back his chair and took his plate to the dishwasher. He wanted time to think. He had been expecting something like this to happen but was not sure just how far he could go with it. But he must show interest. As he pulled down the door of the machine he said, "It needs researching unless someone has a quick answer."

"I have," said Daley, bringing his own plate across and then returning for the cup. "I've had a place in mind for a long time."

Patterson collected the other plates. "What were you going to do? Collect for the Provos or for yourself?"

The question caught Daley off balance and raised a doubt in the minds of the other two. It was one thing robbing a bank for survival but quite another for personal gain against the interests of the 'cause'.

"You know damn well we rob banks to feed the kitty," Daley snapped. He glared at Patterson who had so easily found him out.

But Steinbach and Ulla were anything but fools. Daley's motives meant nothing to them so far as a robbery was concerned, but it spoke volumes for his disloyalty to a cause he claimed to follow, and it was something they noted.

"I've always thought ahead," Daley explained. "None of us know what's round the corner. And I was right, wasn't I?" he added triumphantly. "Look at us now!" He gave Patterson a venomous look and continued, "While I was on active service over here I kept my eyes open for this sort of day. There are one or two possibilities, one is in Stoneham near Winchester."

'Pongo' Waring viewed the newspapers spread across his desk. The three men shot dead in Hertfordshire had made the headlines in all but one of the dailies. There was some solid speculation and the consensus of press opinion suggested that the men had IRA connections. Their arms-laden car had been blown to bits, which posed the problem of why the occupants had been shot outside it. It was a misleading deduction which suited Waring very well. Two dailies suggested the SAS had taken out an IRA active service unit which would annoy the Regiment because the appeasers would exploit that and wring it out to dry and raise the old issue of shoot to kill. Had it been Patterson or Daley or both? Even Alec Monroe had been obscure on that point. Perhaps deliberately so, in order to protect his man.

Waring rang his counterpart in Bonn. After the personal exchange he said, "Max, have you heard any more about the movement of Hans Steinbach and Ulla Geiger?"

Max Kranz sounded surprised. "Only what you've been advised. We believe Steinbach went your way."

"Have you any idea where they might be here?"

"Not specifically. Steinbach's girlfriend Ingrid Lotz was picked up in East Berlin some days ago. She's now been transferred to Frankfurt. She was sent a box of poisoned chocolates. She did not believe they were poisoned and tried to swallow the lot. Her stomach was pumped out and she was lucky to survive. But she was then convinced and we had to convince her further that it was her great lover Hans Steinbach who sent them. She thinks he would go to London. But she does not know as much as we hoped."

"Steinbach must have had a reason to send her the chocolates. Like thinking she knew where he might go next and not trusting her to keep quiet?'

"Right. But all we got was London. Maybe she didn't know or had forgotten. She knew he had access to a place in London but they had never used it. She believes it was an apartment used by PIRA. She still has a hang-up for Steinbach despite his trying to kill her. But I don't think she's holding back too much. You'll remember Eugene Lynch who ran one of the PIRA groups over here? Well, apparently, Steinbach and Lotz helped Lynch quite a bit while he was in Germany. He promised Steinbach the legacy of a safe house in London if anything happened to him. He kept his word; Steinbach took the key from the neck of what was left of the corpse after shooting the morgue keeper."

Waring was excited by the link with the IRA and wished he had been told this detail before. "Anything else?"

"She was there when Lynch showed the key to Steinbach but it meant little to her at the time. She had not been listening as carefully as Steinbach imagined she had. Whether the address was attached to the key she cannot remember but the incident remained with her. And she seems to remember Lynch saying it was posh; which she interpreted as meaning upper bourgeois. Nobody would suspect terrorists of staying there."

"Posh? They usually go for the average digs that attract no attention. Were you satisfied how Lynch died?"

"He was certainly blown up in his own car. And he had certainly used explosives against your own army HQ over here, as you well know. Whether it was an accident or not we were not convinced. It remains open."

Waring said, "You didn't find the second group you thought were operating at that time; do you think they are still there?"

154

"The pattern has changed as we discussed when you were last over here. The killings are becoming more indiscriminate and the wrong people. No, I think that particular group disbanded soon after the Lynch killing and another one took its place. I can't be absolutely sure."

"Thanks, Max. I'll try to run down that report. And if Ingrid Lotz has a sudden attack of memory, could you contact me personally?"

"Of course."

When Waring put the phone down he made a few notes, then buzzed for Detective Inspector Gaunt.

"Don't sit down, Peter, you won't have time." Waring took the edge off his words with a smile. "DCS Monroe flew over from Belfast late yesterday and brought me up-to-date on the Patterson–Daley escape. Nothing is as it appears. It's a bit of a cock-up really due partly to a lack of communication, and partly fate. I can't see how it will turn out. It could be in our favour or become a disaster. Patterson isn't the Patterson we thought he was, and Daley's a bigger shit than we ever realised, wanted by us and PIRA. That's as much as I intend to tell you at the moment. Meanwhile, check on all luxury apartment blocks in central London and see if you can track down Patterson, Daley, Hans Steinbach and Ulla Geiger."

"Together?" Gaunt stared in disbelief.

"Together." Waring beamed at his subordinate's discomfort. "Interesting, ain't it?" When Gaunt failed to reply quickly enough, Waring added, "When you've found those four put a solid team on them but don't pull them in until I say so."

"Luxury apartments?" Gaunt queried as if still unable to grasp the order.

"Yes. Anything you would deem as being posh. Start with estate agents. The Met might even have a register."

"I might need some of their manpower."

"I'll fix that for you. You're wasting time, Peter."

"That's good Irish bacon. Eat it." Conner slapped the plate down in front of Carmel Daley. "And fresh eggs. You look like a stick insect."

He had come to her room before turning in the previous

155

night but had merely stood in the doorway leering at her as she pulled the blankets up around her. After a while he went, closing the door firmly, but he had left an unspoken message if she was to stay here. She had felt just a fraction of what her sister used to feel. Conner only had to be there to be intimidating.

She had not slept well and found it cold in the house. She was glad to get up next morning although he had not troubled her again. And now she sat in the kitchen-diner with the breakfast he had cooked before her. She tried to put him out of her mind while she ate, for she was ravenous and had not eaten properly for days.

He sat across the table and watched her, much to her embarrassment. "Are you having nothing yourself?" she asked, trying to break his concentration.

"I had mine early. Always do. Just toast. Never eat a big breakfast myself. Coffee or tea?"

"Tea."

"Okay." He put the kettle on and slipped a tea bag in a mug. It was basic-living with Conner but his food was wholesome and he personally cooked most of what he ate. He pushed the mug of steaming tea across to her knowing she was wondering which way he would jump. When she had finished eating he said, "Now think hard about where Con might have gone."

"I have. And I don't know." She felt better after the breakfast, more ready to resist him. But as she gazed at him now she realised it would make no difference; he would break her arms if he thought it would prod her memory. So she added, "I've really wracked my brains."

"That wouldn't have taken too long. There must have been a time when he discussed with you what would happen if he was really in trouble. He must have talked about where he would go if he had to split suddenly. Think, for God's sake. You're not going to tell me the two of you never talked about leaving Ireland sometime, if things got tough. Did he mention America, for instance?"

"America? Sure we never discussed America."

"Well, then, Libya?"

"He hated Libya. When he went there that time with Eugie he couldn't get back fast enough."

"I remember that, too. They raised some money and a promise of arms. He did well that time. I'm surprised he talked to you about it, though."

"It was a long time after and didn't matter any more." With surprising spirit she added, "You can't have it both ways. You want to know what we talked about and then criticise it."

"You're right. I'm sorry. Did anything else come out of the Libya trip?"

"They stayed with this wealthy Arab in London while they sorted out the details. That left an impression."

Conner rose from the table and switched the kettle on again. "You want another cup?"

"Yes please."

He kept his back to her. She saw no connection but he thought he did. Just possibly. "Did he mention his name?"

"No, he wouldn't do that, now. And if he had I would have forgotten."

"Did he see him again any time?"

"I don't know. He worked in England for a while so might have done. I think he died."

Conner reached across for Carmel's mug as the kettle boiled. "Are you sure?"

"I seem to remember Con telling me sometime, but I wouldn't swear to it. Does it matter?"

"No." Conner handed over a fresh cup of tea. "I don't suppose you know where he lived, this Libyan?"

"This is my first trip to London. If Con told me it wouldn't have meant anything. I don't know where it was but I know Con was very impressed. Very posh, it was. Something special. But that's all I know."

"And it was in London?"

"I suppose so. He didn't say it wasn't. I think Con lived in London while he worked here."

"Tea all right?" Conner was thinking rapidly, calculating the amount of help he might expect from Irish apartment porters, and there were a good number of them. Most would

157

not sympathise with what he stood for, but, just the same, there were ways of doing things and the Irish like to communicate with each other, and approaches could be ostensibly innocent. Conner was a past master of the game. It could take time, though, and he had the strong impression that time was vital.

He turned back to the table and sat down while she drank her tea. He was satisfied that he had already obtained from her more than Flynn and Mooney who had little subtlety. "How are you off for money?"

Her reaction gave her away, and she cringed back in the chair. "I haven't much. But I can get by."

"What will you do? Go on the streets? It's tough out there, Carmel." He delved into the depths of his pockets and pulled out a screwed-up bundle of notes, peeled some off and tossed them across the table. "There y'are. That will keep you going for a bit."

She stared at the money; most of the notes were dirty, fivers and tenners all mixed up. She wanted to take them and she could see he was waiting for her to do so. "Why are you offering me this?"

"You suspicious little bitch." He laughed unpleasantly. "You can push off without them and take your chances with the mixed bag out there. At least here you know what you're getting. Go on, take it. You've got to doss down somewhere." There was a time when he would not have been so crude, but age was creeping up and his cavalier looks were disappearing all too soon, and a whore could more easily be kicked out.

Carmel reached across and took the notes, blaming her sister Rose for being placed in this position; Carmel would never blame herself. "What happens when Con finds out?"

"Why? Are you going to tell him?" Conner burst out laughing. She seemed unaware that she had given him a starting point to find Daley. And when he did she would no longer have to worry about her old lover. He must start the rounds at once.

158

16

They split up, Ulla with Patterson and Daley and Steinbach together. The idea was that any bulletins circulated by the police would most probably have them in their original grouping: the two Irishmen together, and the two Germans.

This time Steinbach hired a car with his false papers and paid a cash deposit, as Daley had previously, while Patterson and Ulla took a train from Waterloo to Andover from where they could get a taxi to take them the twelve miles to Stoneham.

As this was a reconnaissance they were in no particular hurry and the two pairs were to operate independently of each other. Ulla, concerned about safety, did not show her desire for Patterson whom she found increasingly attractive; but at odd moments she did display a coquettishness which both intrigued and worried Patterson. He had enough complications without Ulla upsetting Steinbach.

Patterson quickly realised that Ulla fed on being on public view. She loved the risk of it without being careless. The gun in the bag slung over her shoulder would ensure that she would shoot her way out rather than be captured. And yet she could be a lively and interesting companion and the time went quickly on the hour or so's journey. Ulla had committed too many murders to have any future. On the other hand, he was convinced that she was tough, and ingenious enough to somehow survive as some had.

At Andover they found the taxi rank right outside the small station and they were soon on their way to check over the bank they intended to rob.

Meanwhile, Daley and Steinbach had a much longer journey. The car hire formalities held them up and getting out of London by road was slow. And the two men were not comfortable together.

It had been Steinbach's idea to change partners in this way and he was probably right from a security angle; also he wanted a break from Ulla. But Daley preferred to be with Patterson whom he had come to understand and trust in their daily relationship if not their ultimate destiny.

Steinbach felt much the same. He did not trust Daley, or really anyone, but preferred to be with those he knew best. He would rather have Patterson at his side. He trusted him no more than the others but he thought he understood him better and he had respect for him. Patterson did not back down and it sometimes made him wonder why.

Steinbach found similarities between Ulla and Daley. Not in personality – Ulla could be vivacious and interesting – but in unpredictability. There was an uncertainty about Daley that Steinbach could not determine. Daley could also stand his ground but it would not be on a matter of principle or pride but usually pique. As Steinbach coped with the London traffic and drove, on what to him was the wrong side of the street, he tried to puzzle Daley out without being too successful except to acknowledge that he was not a man to turn his back on. He smiled to himself; nor was he.

They spoke little. Daley studied a map and gave instructions from time to time, although he seemed to be familiar with the road anyway. It started to rain about half-way there and the obscured vision did not help their relationship. They fell into a silence which was rarely broken and a strange tension built up between them.

It was a bizarre situation. They had only known each other for a few days; both were on the run for terrorist crimes committed under different banners; both were murderers although neither would have seen it that way, believing they could make their own laws and get rid of anyone who did not agree with them; yet both could talk endlessly, and with deep hatred about oppressors.

It was little wonder that the mood in the car was strange. Neither would have needed much conviction to kill the other, given the right circumstances, and yet they knew they must

160

stick together, at least until the bank job was over. Once they had enough money they could all go their own ways and leave the apartment to be used only for fall-back.

A few miles from Stoneham, Steinbach said, "I don't like these roads. I prefer the Autobahnen where we can get a move on."

"And fall asleep from monotony and bloody well kill each other," said Daley in the unlikely tones of a loyal Brit. "If you don't like it here, why don't you piss off?"

It had been the same, more or less, all the way down and Steinbach was now so used to it that he merely laughed because he had deliberately provoked the response. To get back at Daley he asked, "Why do you trust Patterson so much? He's an Orangeman, your sworn enemy."

"Who said I trusted him? At the moment we're in the same boat together. Like you and Ulla; she's a nutter yet you trust her."

Steinbach shook his head. He delayed his reply while he tried to get round a truck, finding it difficult with the windscreen smeared by the rain. "We're on the same side, though. Our objectives are the same. Yours and Patterson's are quite the opposite."

It was difficult to answer. Patterson had saved his life. He had thought about it a good deal. Patterson could easily have let the third man shoot him before firing himself. It would have been easier for Patterson to have done it that way; kill the PIRA man just after he had killed Daley. And yet he had not.

"I see I've hit a nerve," Steinbach goaded as he fell back behind another car.

Daley was annoyed for showing too much of his feelings. "It's your driving that worries me."

"Well, at least we haven't had a crash and been burned out yet."

And so it went on until they reached the outskirts of Stoneham and professionalism took over and they began to co-operate. They drove slowly into the small town, which really comprised one wide main street with angled-off street parking.

Daley knew it to be a tourist attraction with antique shops

and old pubs and coaching houses. It was a delightful rural setting, surrounded by the Hampshire countryside.

"There's a gap. Pull over," instructed Daley, and Steinbach did not hesitate. It was lunchtime and most of the shops were closed. They parked opposite the tiny bank.

"We'd better have something to eat first," Daley said. "The place will liven up more after lunchtime and give better cover. He led the way down the street towards the George Hotel, the biggest in the place. The bars were crowded, even though it was a weekday, and they had trouble finding somewhere to sit.

Steinbach went to the bar to order from the bar menu because his faint German accent was much less noticeable than Daley's Northern Irish one. They sat with pints of ale and ploughman's lunches were brought to them and it was all very pleasant and friendly; the noise level was high with talk and laughter and the prospect of a bank raid in this pleasant little town seemed to be incredibly remote.

Steinbach suddenly spotted Patterson and Ulla through a glass door leading to a secondary lounge. He gave no sign of recognition but whispered the news to Daley who did not glance over until some time later. Not one of the four gave acknowledgement.

Steinbach and Daley left the lounge bar at one forty-five when the place had noticeably thinned. The street was still fairly empty and they walked away from the bank, towards the big roundabout at the far end of the street.

They took their time as tourists might, and when they reached the end of the street stood outside an antique shop with its blinds halfway down. The big roundabout was close to them.

"Take a look," said Daley. "A choice of four turn-offs. About a hundred yards along the second turning is a small hotel lying well back from the road; we must check that it's still as I remember. You'll never get a better place for escape routes. They're all over the bloody place."

Steinbach took his time. Everything depended on good reconnaissance. He was happy with what he saw. "We'll have to drive round to make sure. There might be road works."

"Sure. It's some time since I've been here." The rain had

stopped and the sun was trying to lighten the clouds. Daley gazed round. "I think we should do that next and then look at the bank. That will give the other two a chance to see the bank first."

Ulla and Patterson left the hotel after Steinbach and Daley. They saw them go but although they had noticed them inside no mention was made until they had gone.

"As if there aren't enough inns in the place, they have to choose the one we did." Ulla seemed unreasonably angry.

Patterson smiled. "Probably because it's the biggest. Come on." He took her arm. "Let's take a look at this bank."

"It looks like a toy town bank, hardly a real bank at all. Are you sure there is any money in it?"

"I haven't a clue, Ulla. It's not my nomination."

"Nomination? You use strange words for an Orangeman."

Patterson burst out laughing. It was partly a nervous reaction for, more and more, he wondered what he was doing there. "I'm not an Orangeman. And if I was why would that be a strange word for them? I meant it is not my choice. I don't know anything about it."

As they approached the bank he could see her point. It was joined to a house on one side and a hairdresser's on the other. He had to admit the bank did stand out like a small model. "You might be surprised what some of these country banks handle. There are probably a lot of traders around here, many dealing in cash, and farmers. Come on, let's go in."

They went in and Ulla went up to a till to ask for change for a five-pound note. The tills were protected by bullet-proof glass and the note had to be dropped into a swivel trough. A girl came in, passing close to Patterson who was just inside the main door while he waited for Ulla. The girl went to a door at the side of the counter, pressed a bell, and someone opened the side door for her after a short wait. He heard the door being locked behind her; one of the staff returning from lunch. Ulla got her change and went out with Patterson who held the door open for her.

"Well, if you're not an Orangeman you are certainly a gentleman, Jamie. Hans wouldn't have done that for me. Did you get what you wanted?"

163

Patterson had not cased a bank before but supposed he should not have been surprised by the question. "I think so. As long as we're not worried by alarms, television scanners, police and so on, I think we can cope." His banter hid his deep concern; this was not going to be a refined job and there were too many hot-heads in the team.

There was little else they could do but amble round the town waiting for the return of Daley and Steinbach, and when they gave the signal, they would get a taxi and go back by train from Andover while the others motored back. They did not want to make visible contact with the other two for it to be remembered. Two hours later they were on the train.

"Any one of us could do it," said Steinbach in contempt. "They would only have stage money in a place like that." He turned to Daley. "Just how much do you expect to get from the place?"

"One of us couldn't do it," Daley retaliated. "We need a driver. And that had better be Jamie; he's good. And we need at least two inside. But three would be better. If you don't like the idea then find your own bloody bank."

They were back in the apartment, Daley and Steinbach had arrived late, because of the traffic delays, and had then had to hand the car back and they were tired and irritable yet eager to get the job done, to do anything to relieve the mounting boredom. Ulla had served up a scratch meal which had been a near disaster, and nerves were stretched.

In a quieter tone Daley added, "I don't know how much they handle. Whatever it is will be more than we have now and it will be cash which we need. I never suggested it would be enough for us to retire to the Bahamas. Now do we do it or not?"

"No hire cars," Steinbach insisted. "Nothing that can be traced back to description or even false papers."

"We'll need two cars. Jamie can nick one and I'll nick the other. We'll pick them up on location. That will take the weight of the Met off our backs."

Patterson could see no way out apart from deserting them and that would not be easy. Everyone was stretched; to try to run would bring a bullet in the head. "Why two?" he asked, but he knew why.

"The usual reason. One for outside the bank and to ditch quickly. The other for the ride out of town. You drive both times. The rest of us will do the real work. A piece of cake." Daley gazed round at them and no one disagreed.

They sat around the lounge with drinks, and discussed some of the problems that might arise. When the doorbell suddenly rang there was immediate and astounded silence. They sat rooted. The bell rang again.

Patterson rose quickly. He must head off disaster. For on the second ring, the glasses were placed on table tops and guns appeared in hands. He put down his drink and moved out of the room and noiselessly to the front door. The hall light was not on and he approached the door at one side.

Patterson peered through the spy-hole. A man and a woman stood before the door, each holding a bunch of leaflets. They wore the weary expression of those used to waiting and to being rebuffed. They were talking quietly to each other, and then the woman turned more squarely to the door and Patterson was almost sick. He knew her to be far more attractive than she appeared at present. To him it was as though she had purposely set out to make herself dowdy, and he fearfully realised that could be the case. But it was hard to hide her kind of attraction and when she moved her head again her features were more difficult to define in the indifferent corridor lighting.

Patterson felt someone tug at him and turned to see Steinbach wanting to take a look. Neither spoke but there was little Patterson could do but to give way. Steinbach squinted through the hole and while he did so the woman reached out and rang the bell a third time. The bell was so close it made them all jump. Daley looked and then Ulla, who held up a hand to the rest while she was still looking and which the others failed to understand.

"They've gone," she said, and slipped her pistol into a large skirt pocket. But they remained in the hall taking turns to peer out into the now empty corridor. It was the first intrusion they had had and it created an unsettling effect.

165

Patterson led the way back to the lounge. "Jehovah's Witnesses," he pronounced as he picked up his drink again and turned towards the window so the others would not see his hand shaking.

"At this time of night? It's after eight." Steinbach checked his watch and the others did the same from habit. Suspicion dripped from Steinbach's tone.

"Those people work all hours. They have to get so many hours a week in to convert people like us." Patterson tried to make light of it but he knew it had not worked.

"They managed to shake you up, boyo." But it was clear that Daley too was unsettled; they all were.

"Cops," said Steinbach after giving it more thought. "I could smell them right through the door. Cops."

The possibility was at the back of all their minds except Patterson's, and he knew for certain. Donna Smith had been transferred from Ulster almost a year ago now. After receiving one threat too many, for the sake of her safety she had been hustled out one night and he had not seen her since. He was furious that she was now being used in this way when she might be recognised by someone like Daley.

There was tension in the room mainly because they had been disturbed at all, and at a time when they felt so secure. Suspicion of the callers was inevitable, but so far as Patterson could judge Daley had not recognised the girl.

They were all concerned for one reason or another. They had no post, no milk was delivered, no groceries, not even a telephone call. They were shut off from the world, in a luxury prison which allowed them to visit outside. But no one visited them. Until now.

Ulla had made no comment at all and in the end they turned to her for direction because she had clearly been assessing the situation.

"Well?" Steinbach demanded of her. "What do you think?"

"I think we keep the kitchen window unlatched ready to hit the fire escape. And I think we take it in turns to keep awake. Tomorrow we can do a little careful checking outside. But we must be ready to move."

It was a sensible conclusion, one that provoked no argument. And it spoiled the rest of the evening.

For the sake of appearances, and just in case the word got round, Donna Smith and Detective Inspector Peter Gaunt called on some of the remaining apartments, getting short shrift from almost all of them. Some, like the one they had just visited, where three men and a woman lived according to the porters, offered no response at all. There was nothing unusual about that. Most routine work was boring and found little result. Nor, these days, was there anything unusual about four young people living in the same apartment. They gathered that it was one of those places where a wealthy owner, seldom there, let it out to friends. But it remained one of the possibles and might turn out to be a lucky call.

What Donna had forlornly hoped was that the apartment contained the terrorists they were searching for and that Jamie Patterson opened the door. But life was never so simple. She had no idea how close she was to being right and how much he put into quelling the urge to warn her.

They left the block and decided to call it a day. This was the third block that day and the work was tiring. C13 had really pulled out the stops in tracing apartment blocks of this nature and putting teams on to them to reduce the numbers to the possibles only.

As Donna Smith said goodnight to Peter Gaunt and went back to her not-nearly-so luxurious apartment as some of those she had visited that day, she thought of Jamie Patterson, of the love they had once had and of the tragedy that had ripped into it; they had been torn apart by a series of incidents over which they had had no control. She wondered just how badly he had been affected and whether the scars were still there. For the first time in almost a year she cried that night, at last unable to shut out the pain she had managed to hide. Why, oh why, had he come to England?

Patterson too could not sleep that night. He twisted and turned, aware that Daley was just a few feet away. But

167

fortunately Daley had found the day exhausting and was soon fast asleep.

Patterson finally lay on his back staring at the darkened ceiling and finding it difficult to keep down his hatred of the man in the next bed and all he and his kind stood for. He was willing to admit now that his hatred had coloured his judgement and that he should have opted out of this connection at the first opportunity.

He had only agreed to the original mission in the fervent hope of putting more terrorists away. But once he and Daley had escaped he wanted more than that and could find no compasson for the three who had been killed. He could have killed Daley too, at that moment, and wondered why he had saved him. Because he might lead to another three to kill? And another?

He was still awake at two a.m. when Steinbach crept in to rouse him. He was out of bed before the German could shake him. He went into the lounge to sit in a chair facing the open door leading to the small hall so that he could hear anyone who might tamper with the front door. He was glad to be alone.

Seeing Donna had been a great shock. The last he heard was that she was leaving the service to assume a new identity. When his mother and sister had been blown up Donna had thrown herself into finding out who had done it to such an extent that she had become marked and had twice found bombs in her car and once had been shot at while out; a schoolgirl had been maimed by the wild firing.

Donna had taken risks he should have taken for she had done it on his behalf. But he had become so emotionally disturbed after his double loss that it was considered his judgement was too faulty to allow him to continue in that line. Donna had taken on the fight for him and had almost lost her own life. When she was transferred to the mainland it was at a time they were both on a low and perhaps it was fortuitous that they split up just when they were feeding on their own failures. He still did not know who had killed his mother and sister.

When he thought like this, Patterson could see more clearly

why he had stayed. He wanted to hit out blindly at anyone on the other side in an effort to make up for his own frustration and for losing sight of Donna. He had not corresponded because her whereabouts was secret and he was in no state to carry such a secret at that time. He had hoped to get letters from her but for whatever reason they had not come. If they had, then they had been intercepted.

For some time he stared blankly at the open door. The night noises surrounded him: odd creaks as the central heating eased off; the air cooling until it was almost chilly; the wind blowing leaves against the windows. The curtains were drawn across to make any kind of surveillance difficult. It was almost like putting the clock back a year and the old frustrations were returning.

They must be mad to use Donna, yet when he thought it out perhaps not. Had they come face to face he wondered if either of them would have had the presence of mind to cope with the others looking on. Ifs and buts, it was always the same, and he sometimes yearned to be doing something else.

He rose to pull the curtain back a fraction. There was a whole row of cars below. Doorways were dark and seemingly empty. Then he saw a couple, arm in arm, walking in the middle of the road, staggering a little as if drunk. Their faint laughter reached him. It all seemed so normal. Yet he was surrounded by violence; it was in the rooms around him, automatic pistols tucked under pillows of people who would think nothing of using them.

And if he was to win this particular battle, if he was to stand any chance at all, he would have to be just as willing and just as good. And it would still be three to one against. Yet it did not cross his mind at that point to leave. He was trapped by circumstances and his own foolish obstinacy. He did not believe he could win against these people but must continue to try. And tomorrow they were to raid a bank. It was almost as if he had crossed the bounds of reason to become one of them in every sense.

17

They left the block one at a time with well-spaced intervals. And they were right to be cautious. After leaving Donna Smith, Detective Inspector Gaunt had radioed instructions to have the building watched. At this stage it could only be a containment operation. Nobody was sure of anything and the move was precautionary. There was a limit to how many teams could be put out, for there were other blocks to watch. And it would be impossible to have each of the four suspects followed round the clock; that would take twenty-four men per person. What they were looking for was anything to make them suspicious enough to justify increasing the manpower.

Ulla had shaved Steinbach's head down to his scalp and darkened his brows. Daley's dyed hair still held good. Patterson was given a close clip, a false moustache and a pair of plain glasses. Ulla herself changed to a startling short-skirted outfit and wore a wig.

The wigs and disguises, like beards and moustaches, were part of the Germans' basic needs; they always carried them. Disguise was an essential part of their equipment. The change in all four was startling.

When they left the building one by one, the police team watching them did not raise too much interest because they had descriptions of all four, and police file mug-shots. There was no way they could tell if the four were, in fact, those living in the same apartment. All sorts of people came and went from the building between the four departures. Only Ulla raised an immediate interest and that came in the form of muted wolf-whistles. In her modern outfit she might have been a model or an actress. Even the porter on duty did not recognise her as she crossed the lobby.

There had not yet been time to find an empty room in the offices opposite the apartments so a video camera was not in use, but a police officer managed some long-range shots with a telescopic lens from a car parked further down the street. The routine of surveillance went on, the four being recorded only amongst the others.

They caught the same train to Andover but travelled in different compartments with Ulla going first-class. At Andover they took separate cabs to the centre of town.

From the covered shopping centre Patterson made his way through to the multi-storey car park, aware that Daley was close behind. Only now did they begin to close up. It was late morning, most of the early shoppers had gone but the car park was still quite full.

Patterson climbed the incline, reached the Waitrose level, and stopped when he saw two empty slots well spaced apart. A car drove in behind him and he walked across as if going through the doors to the main precinct. The car parked. A stout woman got out, oh, so slowly, opened the boot, took out a mobile shopping trolley, closed the boot and locked the car doors.

Patterson hung around, dangling a set of keys in his hand as if waiting for a companion, opened the precinct door for the woman who did not thank him, and went straight to her car.

A family came through the door with laden bags, complaining of the slippery floor of the arcade, and went to a car across the bay. Patterson wasted no time; he opened the offside door with a gadget supplied by Steinbach, climbed in and fiddled with the wires under the dash. This was the awkward, time-absorbing part, and he began to sweat. When the engine was finally going he could not get out fast enough.

He drove down to the barrier which lifted, and eased his way out. He drove the short distance to the bus station and there was Ulla standing by the kerb looking like a superior tart. The analogy was not lost on him. He leaned across to open the door, she climbed in, and almost before she had closed the door he was driving off. His relief came out in a long sigh. Ulla patted his knee and gave a sweet, understanding smile. It was no time for new relationships, but Ulla

171

always managed to give the impression that she could fill in the gaps. She gave no inkling at all that she was as taut as he.

Patterson followed the route which Daley had graphically outlined for him. It was countryside and farms all the way and very little traffic. He followed the signs and drove at a reasonable speed and at last began to relax.

"You get too wound up," Ulla observed, "but you drive well. You're at home behind the wheel."

He supposed that she was right. Being behind the wheel of a car soothed away his worries where it might add to many others. But to relax with Ulla beside him was quite another matter.

When he reached the turn-off for Stoneham he cruised down the High Street and slipped into the first empty parking slot. While they waited Ulla opened her copious shoulder bag and removed four assorted plastic shopping bags and spent the time in trying to unfold them.

After a while Patterson wondered if he had missed Daley and Steinbach but at last he saw them in a Ford Fiesta as they slowly went past. He pulled out and followed.

They went to the end of the street, turned right at the roundabout, and then left on to the second turn-off. Shortly after, they took another left turn up a steep, sloping shingle drive and swung right, under some trees. They repositioned the cars one at a time so that they were ready to speed out.

At the far end of the drive was a small residential hotel. It was a quiet, ideal position for stopping. Daley, who had donned a cap, and Steinbach, climbed out to join Patterson and Ulla. They made a few nervous jokes about the way they looked and then Patterson drove off to enter Stoneham from the opposite end to the one they had entered by. It was one forty-five. The town would soon come to life again.

Patterson pulled in opposite the bank, waited for a gap to appear outside it, then swung over to park facing the way they had just come. He could feel his face muscles pulling. Daley tapped him on the shoulder, "I've left the wires on the Fiesta just apart. All you have to do is to make a quick connection."

Patterson acknowledged. It was all he could do. He kept his engine running and tried to keep his face averted from passers-by. The others climbed out, Ulla having rammed the unravelled plastic bags back in her shoulder bag, and chose their moment to move.

The three entered the bank. There was only one till operating and two customers were waiting behind the one being served. Daley got on the end of the short queue, Ulla stood just to one side of the main door and Steinbach lounged by the staff door. The customer at the counter finished her business and moved to one side to tidy her papers as the next person moved up.

The girl they were waiting for to return from lunch was either late or was not coming at all. The group began to get fidgety. If Daley reached the counter he could cope for only a limited period. Another person went which left Daley the next but one.

The main door opened and another customer came in, an elderly woman with heavy make-up. Daley insisted she take his place in the queue as she had only a cheque to cash. He took a quick look at his colleagues who stood wooden-faced but he guessed they were feeling as desperate as he.

It was after two when the girl returned from lunch. She shouted a laughing apology across the counter to someone who was out of sight, hurried to the side door where Steinbach gave her a smile, and rang the bell, turning her back pointedly on Steinbach. As the door opened he pushed her hard in the back, and followed her with a drawn pistol. "One move and I'll blow a hole through her head." He held the girl by her tinted hair. "Don't anyone try to touch an alarm or she dies. Hands on heads, all of you."

Steinbach kept his voice remarkably low but the mixed staff behind the counter heard him clearly enough. The very lack of panic in his voice was sufficient to scare them. There were four people seated in a small general office: two men and two women. They had all put their hands on their heads and the younger girls looked petrified. The girl he was holding by the hair was on the verge of collapse and he was half holding her up. He whispered viciously in her ear, "You shouldn't have turned your back on me, you stuck-up bitch."

At the main door Ulla slipped one of the catches; it was

sufficient to discourage anyone else coming in, and she stood with her back to the door making it difficult for anyone outside to see through. She held her gun close to her body but straight at those in the queue. She said in a heavily accented voice, "Don't move and if you scream it will be your last." She had set out to be dramatic and it instilled terror into the two waiting customers.

Meanwhile Daley had stepped from the queue, taken the bags from Ulla, and followed Steinbach through the staff door. He threw one bag to the cashier and told her to fill it up, and placed the others on one of the desks. "I want these filled from the vault."

One of the men stammered out that the manager was still at lunch and only he had the key to the small vault until Steinbach, with the luxury of a fitted silencer, fired and blew the telephone off his desk. The girl Steinbach was holding started to scream until he hit her on the head with his pistol. He let her fall and stepped over her. "Fill them," he snarled. He did not like the idea of the manager still being out.

In the stolen car outside, Patterson waited with the engine quietly running, and watching the small town liven up after the lunchtime sessions in the variety of pubs in the High Street. Everyone was so amiable, unaware of the drama taking place so close to them. The gun-happy trio inside the bank worried him. Life was so cheap to any one of them and it made him sick with anxiety.

A police patrol car approached and Patterson tried to sink into his seat. The running engine outside a bank was a clear signal to any policeman but he was facing them and they probably could not see the tiny puffs from his exhaust.

The patrol car continued on and he watched it in his mirror until it was out of sight. He guessed that the area they had to cover in the country was vast with so many scattered villages. But they had a radio and could quickly return.

Nothing seemed to be happening in the bank. He could see Ulla's back and then tried to slip down in his seat again as a middle-aged couple came along and tried to open the bank door. They pushed with no success and could not understand why Ulla did not respond as she was standing so close. They peered through the glass with cupped hands and complained bitterly in cultured tones. For the bank to have its doors locked at this time was a major event and they would complain. They were on the point of moving on when their world suddenly turned upside down.

Ulla spun round to release the catch in a movement so quick that it took the couple by surprise. They had just moved away from the door, and started to turn back, when it flew open, Ulla rushed out, thrusting them aside with a sweep of arm and bag, followed by a running Steinbach and Daley carrying the bags. The middle-aged couple went crashing to the pavement, people stopped and stared, astounded by what they saw. A girl was the first to realise what was happening and started to scream. Steinbach pistol-whipped her round the face as he passed and the screaming stopped.

At first sight of Ulla moving, Patterson flung open the nearside front door, almost knocking someone down, leaned back to open the offside rear door, put the car in gear, keeping the clutch down, waited until the others had scrambled in, and while the doors were still being closed drove off as fast as he could, while angry car horns blared out behind him as he cut across the on-coming traffic.

In his rear-view mirror Patterson could see the crowd swell around the bank, gazes fixed on the disappearing car. Someone would be ringing the police and he recalled the proximity of the patrol car.

Fortunately there was little in the way of traffic ahead of him and he took the roundabout on two wheels with a clear run. There were angry shouts from his passengers as he took the Winchester turn and the centrifugal force sent them crashing against the inside of the car. In the short distance to the hotel turn-off he had to slow right down and as he braked smoke flew from the tyres.

He took the actual turn much more sedately and as he swung round under the trees to stop beside the other car, knowing they were safely out of sight of the main road, relief oozed out of him. But it was not over, had barely even begun. They climbed out quickly. There was a rising green bank with trees which stretched back some distance between them and the building and it offered reasonable cover.

They spread the bags on to the rear floor of the other car and Ulla and Daley, as they were the smallest, climbed in and placed their feet on the bags. Steinbach climbed in with Patterson who bent down to make the connection. When the engine was running he gazed round to make a last-minute check on everyone. Ulla had removed her wig and jacket and already appeared different. Daley had taken off the cap he had worn in the bank and Steinbach had put one on to cover his baldness. Patterson took off his glasses and moustache.

Under Daly's directions Patterson kept to the country road and found the going easy. Suddenly, after the frenetic events at the bank, they suffered an anti-climax. There was no joy in pulling the job off; it had been a purely professional caper induced by the need to ease their cash-flow problems. And they did not know yet just how much or little they had stolen.

The mood was sombre as they drove on. It was important to keep a look-out for the police who might, by now, be searching for the car number. The nearer they could get to an urban area the better; car thefts were so numerous that it was a policeman's nightmare looking for them.

They drove to Basingstoke, a big thriving town on the Hampshire fringes, and from where there were frequent trains to London. They were content to leave the car in one of the town's main car parks to give the impression that the journey had ended there. They separated as they had before, each carrying a shopping bag, and they stuck to their previous pairings. They would return to London on different trains.

To avoid arriving back in daylight they had afternoon tea in separate restaurants. As he sat drinking tea with Ulla, Patterson was almost afraid to ask the question, "Was anyone hurt?" He meant in the bank. By her expression he at once saw that someone had been. Steinbach had hit the bank girl on the head and she had not looked too good when they left.

It meant little to her; she was more concerned about the effect it might have on Steinbach. As she talked on Patterson could see that this warped thinking made him wonder what her reaction would be if she knew his own part in all this.

They went to a cinema to pass the time and saw only part of the film before going back to the station to catch a London train. It was quite late by the time they reached Waterloo where they split up. Patterson allowed her to go first while he sat on one of the station seats to watch the diminishing number of passengers and trains. While he sat there he considered ringing Alec Monroe in Belfast, it was the best opportunity he had had. But he knew Monroe would order him to return to Belfast if he told him about the bank raid. And he did not want to do that just yet. He could judge his own dangers and decide the time to quit.

It was eleven-thirty when he caught a cab from Waterloo to the apartments, once again wearing moustache and glasses. He paid off the cab, keeping his head down, and went straight into the lobby and headed for the elevators with just a grunt and a nod to the porter who glanced up to say good evening. He felt better once he was riding up.

Patterson went one floor above the apartment level and then walked down carefully to make sure the corridor was empty. He approached the corner slowly, peered round to find the little dead-end empty. He whipped off the moustache and glasses, gave the signal on the bell and was let in straightaway. Steinbach locked the door behind him and Patterson threw his bag on to the sofa where Ulla, now back in her usual voluminous skirt, emptied it on to the seat.

Patterson was the last one back. He noticed that, on a central marble table, ornaments had been pushed aside and bundles of notes lay in neat piles. He went straight to the bathroom to wash thoroughly, feeling that he would like to scrub away the whole of the day's events. When he returned to the lounge, Ulla was still counting a mixture of notes, most of them fivers and tenners.

Steinbach and Daley did no more than glance up when he entered then continued to watch Ulla who was working as deftly as any bank teller. Finally the job was done and the table was almost covered in little stacks. She did one last check of the stacks themselves, made a note on a pad, and said, "Thirty-two thousand, two hundred and five pounds."

The silence was drawn out. None of them had known what

to expect and it was difficult to judge whether they were pleased or disappointed. They exchanged thoughtful glances until Daley said soberly, "Not bad. More than I expected."

Steinbach remained thoughtful and Ulla simply tidied up the piles. Patterson said, "I agree with Con. It was easy money." Easy? He recalled the short but mad escape outside the bank. It was not something he wanted to repeat.

"Not good, not bad," said Steinbach at last, inclining his head in a qualified acknowledgement of Daley's appraisal.

"We didn't have to spend months planning it," Daley followed up. "A quick in-and-out job."

"£8051.25 each," Ulla pronounced and promptly started to divide the money up.

Split up, it did not sound so much, so Daley continued to justify the raid, "Instant cash. About two grand an hour."

Nobody argued how he arrived at his figures. It did not matter. The point was they all had instant cash and at the moment the amount was irrelevant. They had breathing space; enough to go where they wanted.

Ulla handed the four separate piles round and because the notes were largely small denomination the bundles were difficult to handle. Daley supplied the change for the four 25ps so the amount to each was exact.

The remarkable thing, Patterson noted, was the degree of trust between them. Since he had returned nobody had suggested that anyone might have dipped into the kitty. Each with a bag they had all had their opportunity including himself. The money had been loose in the bags. It was a peculiarity that did not escape him; they did not see themselves as common criminals; there was no such connection in their minds. This was merely survival money before they could get the cause going again. Daley was probably the exception, but even he would not be stupid enough to cross the two Germans.

"Has anyone listened to the news bulletins?" Patterson asked before pouring himself a drink and sitting down. The others were beginning to smile now as the realisation at last struck home that their immediate cash-flow problem had ended.

"They claimed we got away with over fifty thousand," Steinbach said, accepting that the lie came from the media or the bank. "And the girl died."

"Which girl?" Patterson wondered at his own control; he was churning again.

Steinbach looked over, the ceiling light reflecting on his shaven head. "I had to hit a girl to stop her screaming. She must have had a soft skull. Had she not panicked it would not have happened."

There had been the farmer in Ireland, the woman in the next block, and now a girl in the bank, plus the three he and Daley had shot. He did not know about the old lady Steinbach had killed in Germany. None of these deaths touched them. "What about the girl you pistol-whipped in the street? And the elderly couple Ulla sent flying?"

"You are so concerned?" Steinbach raised his touched-up brows and appeared rather ridiculous; but his eyes were ice cold.

"Yes, I am concerned. It adds to the weight of the police enquiry."

Steinbach conceded with a slight nod. "Sometimes it can't be helped. Nobody really wants it but when it becomes a question of our safety then it has to be done. I don't think they were badly hurt." He was not talking of warm-blooded people, nor of animals, but of objects, something in the way to be destroyed.

18

Donna Smith was on the late shift. They had now managed to get the temporary use of a small office opposite the main entrance to the apartment block. They had rigged up the camera and had the latest in directional microphones which was useless because the apartment that interested them was on the other side of the building where they could not get access. So they were left with covering the main entrance. But it was a start.

She and Peter Gaunt, who had teamed up for this exercise, missed Steinbach because he arrived home while the previous shift was on duty. But they were there when the remaining three entered the block. Daley was next. She did not recognise him because she did not know him. Ulla followed some time later in her tight skirt. Other tenants interspersed these arrivals and some guests left. Again there was no pattern of movement that could link the four except that they all carried plastic shopping bags, but then, so did others; they could well have been in separate apartments.

Three main blocks were at present under surveillance taking up a large number of officers. As soon as one was considered negative the team would move on to another luxury block where reports might indicate a further interest. It was routine but there could be no lack of concentration.

Both Donna Smith and Gaunt checked the notes and the hastily developed mug-shots taken earlier by previous shifts, including the daylight car detail further down the street. Not all of those who had left that day had returned and the mixture covered most age groups. All Donna and Gaunt knew for certain was that there were four people, a woman and three men, living in one of the apartments. Those they

180

had seen so far did not match the descriptions put out by the RUC and Interpol. The mug-shots faxed over were like lifeless wax models and would only help if the subjects still looked like that. Identification was a delicate game, even for experts.

When Donna saw Jamie Patterson approach she almost dropped her night glasses. Gaunt, sitting on a stool to ease his wounded leg, was beside her with a mounted image intensifier, said, "You recognise him?"

Donna needed time to think. "I'm not sure." But she was thinking that Jamie never wore glasses or had never grown a moustache. It was not so much that she recognised him as that she knew it was he. Her heart leaped with excitement then quickly became leaden as she realised the implications. Nobody had told her that the Patterson involved was her Jamie; she understood that the Patterson they were looking for had been in Hull prison and was a crazy maverick. Perhaps there was no connection.

She needed time but Gaunt was not going to give her any. He noticed her reaction. "You seem agitated," he observed. "You sure about him?"

"He reminded me of someone I used to know." Why was she being so protective? They should have warned her.

"Who was he?"

"Someone I knew in Northern Ireland. A long time ago."

"What is his name?"

"Oh, I forget, sir. It's not important."

"It is if it's Jamie Patterson."

Donna felt the cold creeping over her. She was both afraid and furious, convinced now that she had been used. When she had first been detailed to work with a detective inspector who was so close to the 'chief', she had been flattered and delighted. Now she began to see why. "There are plenty of Jamie Pattersons."

"I'm sure there are." Gaunt was still peering through the huge image intensifier. "But only one that we know of who is working closely with three well-known terrorists."

Oh God, no. Surely his family deaths had not done that to him.

"You're wearing your heart on your sleeve, Donna."

But when she turned to Gaunt he was not even looking at her. Suddenly she was in turmoil. She had received a shock and now another as she realised that she had been set up by her own employers.

Gaunt, still at the image intensifier, glanced at Donna. She had lowered her glasses, her head averted slightly away from him. "Came as a shock, did it?"

"It was a dirty trick to play." Under stress her accent became more pronounced; she had lost something of it since coming to England as part of an identity change, which had, in the event, become farcical. She had been too good to lose so they had watered down her direct contact with the enemy as a compromise towards her safety.

"You are the only one we know outside Ulster who can positively identify him. And I think we were right to use you."

Donna was still shaken. "Why didn't you come straight out with it?"

Gaunt smiled understandingly in the darkness. "Because you would probably have cried off sick. We are told he meant a lot to you at one time."

Donna swallowed awkwardly. "He still does. Perhaps I didn't realise it until just now. Just what the hell is going on?"

Gaunt shrugged. "We think he is still working for the RUC police intelligence. If so he's in a very dangerous position. But he's getting too involved. If he goes on like this, soon he won't know which side of the line he is."

Donna was finding it difficult to assimilate. Jamie had suddenly been thrust back at her and in circumstances she could not at the moment fully comprehend. "Just how did he get in this position?"

Gaunt told her as much as Waring had told him. "DCS Monroe flew over to fill us in but apparently our Jamie is holding out on him too. It is difficult to understand exactly what game he is playing. We think he should pull out and hand over what he's got. We think, though we're far from knowing, that he and Daley have already taken out a PIRA active service unit."

"The shootings in Hertfordshire the other day?"

"It could be them."

"If you are right, I'll tell you what he's playing at. He's intending to take out as many PIRA as he can and he's using Daley to get at them."

"We considered that too, but the PIRA are after Daley for reasons only part of which we think we know. I'm sorry, Donna. I really am. But it worked, didn't it? You recognised him although you haven't yet said so."

Donna was drained. She had no idea Jamie Patterson was an object of the surveillance and what Gaunt had now told her did nothing but scare her. There was no longer any point in avoiding the issue. Disconsolately she said, "So far as I could see, it was Jamie. He'll need protection."

"There's nothing we can do. We can't get near him without giving him away. And how long do you think it would take someone like Steinbach or Ulla Geiger, or Con Daley for that matter, to fire a shot? The first sign of intrusion from us and Jamie Patterson has had it."

Please don't talk like that, Donna wanted to say. But she could not. She wanted to race across the street to catch up with him and implore him to pull out. But he had gone long since and, anyway, her legs seemed too weak to move. "You should have told me," she said again, but her despair only confirmed that they had been right not to do so. She was drained and disillusioned and could see no point in staying. She sat on a wooden chair by the window. "We're wasting our time, sir. They won't come out again now."

"They? You know the others are inside?"

Of course she did not. She just felt that was so and did not reply. It did not matter what she did at the moment nor what discipline Gaunt might apply. Nothing mattered. She had enough problems in trying to cope with her own reaction on seeing Jamie after so long. It made her face up to what extent she had been stifling her feelings. Would fate never let him be free from danger? Or was he just seeking it in the hope it might bring satisfaction and a final solution at the same time? Donna shivered; she felt sick. But Gaunt was speaking again.

183

"If you're right, if they are all home, and Jamie Patterson was the last, you will understand the degree to which they now trust him. Otherwise they would not give him the opportunity to telephone Belfast. That's either a considerable achievement on his part or they are completely right to trust him."

Donna lifted her head. "There's no way he would go over. None."

"It's some time since you have seen him, Donna. You may not know the changes."

"If that's the official line of thinking then I want off this case as from now."

"You do what you're told to do. You are in no position to back down."

Donna stood up and tossed her binoculars to Gaunt who just managed to catch them after fumbling. "Stuff your orders, Inspector. I've just resigned."

When Donna was half-way across the room, Gaunt called out, "Bravo." He laughed quietly in the darkness. "Just testing. Wanted to see how deep your feelings are. Really. I wish someone thought as much of me as that. We'll need you to help get him out, Donna."

Donna stopped in her tracks and turned to face him. She quite liked Gaunt; he had always been straight up to now, and could be very gentle. "Then why don't we get an armed team and go across to bust them?"

Gaunt picked up a telephone on a desk that had been cleared for them. "It's not so simple. They're not holed up in a town house. We'd have to empty the block and that's impossible to do without them knowing. And we must be absolutely sure which apartment they're in, so we'll have to rig a mike next door."

"I thought we were already sure. The porters have told us; one of the apartments we called on."

"We have to make sure they are the right ones. The only one positively identified is Jamie Patterson. If it is them, and it looks like it, we have to empty the whole of their wing. It will be easier to wait for them to come out singly as they seem to have done today. And it will give us more time to get

184

organised. These people are not easy to take; the Germans have escaped before and left a trail of dead."

Billy Conner moved away from Carmel and complained, "You're pretty frigid. I can't see you staying long at this rate."

"I'm Con's girl." Carmel was not far from tears. She could not bring herself to admit that her sister was right about this man beside her. He was rough and coarse and surly and full of lust when he had been drinking, as now. In her petulant, unforgiving way she blamed Rose for her being here at all; it was all her sister's fault that she had been forced to become a whore in order to find out where Con Daley was. And she was no wiser now.

Conner thought he was. And it was the only reason he was satisfied this evening. "Con's for the long drop; sure, get used to the idea, you little slut. And then what will you have?" From one of his networks of Irish porters he had heard that afternoon where two Irishmen with northern accents were staying and it confirmed what he had been told about the style of accommodation. The snag was there was another man and a woman staying with them. Dutch or Germans it seemed. It did not make sense but it certainly needed to be followed up and he intended to do that early the next morning. To call at this time of night was to invite a bullet through the door. It was time to bring out the dog-collar and the dark suit. When Carmel started to snivel beside him he promptly kicked her out of bed and told her to sleep somewhere else.

185

19

Perhaps for the first time, Patterson was seriously considering breaking away. The best chance he had ever had he had not even considered – when Ulla had left him alone at Waterloo Station. There would not be another opportunity like that. It seemed to him that the only occasions he considered doing it were those when he felt it would be a mistake to follow up the idea.

He faced the fact that he had been conning himself. He had not really wanted to leave at all but had given his conscience an outing each time he knew it to be impossible. But now it was different. He had no qualms about the shooting of the PIRA men, he had only to think of his sister and mother to quell anything like that, but the other death toll was mounting, and those victims had been innocent of any IRA involvement. The girl in the bank was the final straw.

He tried to justify staying but the taking of innocent lives could not be defended by his hatred and need for revenge. His objective had never been to kill off as many Provos as possible at the expense of others. The fact that all those who had died would still have done so whether or not he was involved did nothing to help. It was getting out of hand. Somehow he must plan his escape in such a way that the other three got caught.

It was Patterson's turn to do the pre-dawn shift and it was Ulla who came to wake him. Daley was out to the world and snoring heavily when Patterson climbed out of bed.

Ulla had woken Patterson skilfully, made sure he was on the move, and then left the room leaving the bedroom door open so that the light from the lounge filtered through. When Patterson wandered into the lounge he carried his pistol in his waistband, and wore an unbuttoned jacket. He was yawning when he entered the room to find Ulla still there.

She smiled up at him, noted his surprise, and said, "I must admit I've seen more enthusiasm."

"I'm sorry. I thought you'd gone. You've done your shift."

"I thought I'd sit yours out with you. Keep you company." She had been on the verge of promising something like this all the previous day. "You flatter me, Ulla. You really do. Right now I haven't the energy of a dead battery."

"Then I'll recharge you, Jamie." She smiled as only Ulla could, with a mixture of pleasure, coquettishness and the suggestion of eternal ecstasy.

Patterson was far from tempted, not because she could not deliver but because of the complications that would inevitably follow from Steinbach and from Ulla herself. Ulla was far too demanding.

"Ulla, I simply haven't your capability. I'm no good in bed; you'd kick me out."

"Only when I'd finished with you. I can teach you."

"That would only spoil it for me for there would never be another like you." The shock of seeing and trying to cope with her had removed all dregs of sleep. He could see he had said the right thing but that would not appease her.

"Hans never says things like that. He would not know how. You're a gentleman, Jamie. I did not think there was such a thing." She patted the seat beside her. "Come, sit down. I won't eat you."

"Yes you will." Patterson managed a smile but felt like death. He had to get rid of her. "You'll eat me and spit me out."

"Like a female spider? I'm sure you'll taste delicious."

"I'd make you ill, Ulla. But it was kind of you to offer. I know you are choosy." He at once knew that he had made a mistake. By her sudden change of expression it was obvious she had taken it the wrong way.

Her dark eyes began to smoulder angrily. Her complex nature had presumed a ridicule, a coarse piece of sarcasm.

As if nothing had happened Patterson continued smoothly, "Though you must be slipping to invite someone like me. I'm

187

really not up to your high standard. I wish that I were. Hans is a lucky man."

"Hans is a pig. He should learn from your manners. You English can be so gentle."

"Irish," said Patterson with a smile. "I'm Irish."

"Of course, darling. But you're all from the same wet and windy islands. We're wasting time."

"What about a raincheck? Tomorrow? When we've all recovered from today."

"It took so much out of you? A run in the country? We'll need another one soon. That money won't last us long."

He decided then, to get out now. Having no front door key, he would have to climb over the roofs. Just how could he get rid of this woman? "Come on, Ulla, I'll see you to your room."

"I don't want to go to my room. The pig snores and it is impossible to get to sleep. I want to stay with you."

His frustration was mounting and valuable time was passing. He could knock her out but he already knew that her reflexes were incredibly sharp and she would fight and scream and, if it came to the point, shoot him. When he considered shooting her first he knew he would be unable to do it in cold blood and it would rouse the others before he could get anywhere. He was becoming angry from frustration because he could see the opportunity slipping away.

He rose, walked slowly towards her and just as slowly past to come round the back of her behind the settee. He leaned over the back, his face close to hers and drew his right hand back behind her head. She turned swiftly to kiss him and in moving ruined his opportunity of bringing down a crushing rabbit punch on the nape of her neck. She moved again and had an arm round his head and tried to pull him over the settee.

Patterson was furious with himself because his effort had been half-baked. He tried to pull himself away but Ulla clung on, more than half-way to a conquest. It was the sudden sound of someone moving in her bedroom that made her stop. As Patterson straightened he saw that she already had a gun in her hand and it must have been on the settee covered by the folds of her skirt.

Both realised it could only be Steinbach. Ulla quickly switched on the television and turned down the sound until it was barely audible. A few seconds later a dishevelled Steinbach wandered into the room to see Ulla and Patterson sitting well separated on the same settee watching an old western.

He was at once suspicious. He offered Ulla an icy smile and said, "Your absence woke me." It was a strange thing to say but believable. Steinbach had survived on instincts and gut feelings for most of his life. His mental auto-alarm had warned him that Ulla should be back.

"I was watching this when my time was up. I wanted to see the end."

"Then it must be good." Steinbach rubbed his face vigorously. "So I'll watch it with you."

Patterson knew his chance had gone. Steinbach would stay will Ulla for the rest of his shift because Ulla was so mad at being interrupted that she had no intention of going back to bed with him.

Whenever Billy Conner dressed as a Catholic priest his transformation was impressive. He wore a charcoal-grey suit and his large, rotund figure somehow gave extra dignity to his appearance and the dog-collar. He also wore a hat and carried a well-used bible. He left his home before eight the next morning and, because of his attire, Carmel assumed correctly that he had received news about Daley which he had no intention of passing on.

She tried to scratch his eyes out in order to make him tell her but he simply laughed and punched her once on the jaw and she took no further interest. He left her lying on the kitchen floor, her face swollen on one side. What happened to her now was of no consequence to him. He double-locked the front door and went in search of a taxi.

The mood was strange at breakfast. Patterson was tired out and disconsolate and was trying to hide both. Steinbach and Ulla seemed not to be speaking to one another, and Ulla was shooting Patterson strange glances which contained a

189

continuing invitation. Patterson was embarrassed because she made no attempt to hide it from the others although only Steinbach noticed. Daley seemed to be in an introspective mood, hardly speaking to the others. In spite of their successful bank raid an air of discontent was creeping into the atmosphere.

The bell rang and they looked at each other in turn, all asking the same unspoken question. Guns suddenly appeared and they took turns at the spy-hole.

When it was Daley's turn he took time in scanning the caller who had not made it easy because he wore a hat and his head was down and he was looking at a sheaf of papers supported by a well-worn bible.

Daley stood back. In the light of the small hall it was difficult to be certain but he appeared to have lost colour. He turned to Ulla. "Let him in."

At once the others knew something was wrong. The bell rang again. Steinbach and Patterson returned to the lounge, to take up positions each side of the door. And Daley hid behind the front door. Ulla undid the top two buttons on her blouse and turned to make sure the others were out of sight.

Ulla opened the door on the chain and peered through the gap. She could now see that it was a billboard the priest held, with papers clipped to it; the bible was held on top of the board as an identifiable object. "Yes?" She did not intend to make it easy; if she did he might smell a rat.

"Good morning. I apologise for the hour but I have a lot of ground to cover. I'm taking over St Mary's Church in Hackock Street, not far from here." Conner smiled. "And I'm trying to do a survey of the possibly more transient parishioners living in accommodation where records might change more often." His smile widened. "I am chasing up Catholics, Madam." His gaze slipped to her cleavage as she had intended. "I hope I haven't alarmed you in any way; you are quite right to use a chain. One cannot be too careful."

"Catholics? I think there might be one or two in here. Do come in, Father." Ulla slipped off the chain and opened the door wide.

Conner was not sure. He did not know what to make of this

foreign girl who spoke good English with a heavy accent; Dutch or German, he had been advised. He said, "I really don't want to take up your time. All I need are some names and whether they will be staying long enough in the district. Of course, even if they are here for only a day or two . . ."

Ulla offered a smile that put the fear of the God Conner purported to support into him. Something was far from right. If only he could get a hint that it was Daley staying there. "Have you any Irishmen staying? Their names will do."

"You can ask them yourself, Father. Do come in."

Conner's instinct was to disappear fast. The woman looked like a tart and was playing with him. "It is kind of you but I really haven't the time just now. I'll come back again, perhaps tomorrow."

"You are not trying very hard to save their souls, Father, and believe me they need a prayer or two. I insist that you come in."

He was about to turn away when he realised with horror that she was holding a silenced gun and it was pointing at his middle. Her expression had not changed but her eyes were now full of humour. He tried one last bluff. "How amusing. Those toy replicas are very convincing." He raised his hat. "Good day, Madam. Thank you for your time."

"Come in, Father, or you won't reach the main corridor."

The tone had changed completely but her expression remained the same. And he had heard tones like that before. She was right, he would not reach the corner and she gave the impression that she wanted him to try. He smiled, "Well, put like that how can I refuse?" He stepped smartly towards her and she stepped back towards the lounge making it impossible for him to make contact.

When he was half-way down the short hall the front door closed and he realised that someone had been standing behind it all the time. Ulla, who was walking backwards while facing him, said, "Just keep your eyes on me, Father. That shouldn't be too difficult, should it?"

But as she backed into the lounge he knew someone was coming up behind him and that he had made a big mistake in coming here in this way. These people were pros.

191

At last they were in the lounge and everything he saw was the complete opposite of all he knew about Con Daley. This was a rich man's apartment block, the interior confirmed it.

Apart from Ulla, who had taken up a position behind a damask settee, the room appeared to be empty but he could feel that it was not. "Do you always invite people in at gunpoint?" he asked, playing for time. Conner knew he was in a jam as grave as any he had known. His own gun was inches away inside his jacket. He might just as well not have brought it.

"Only bogus priests." Ulla was back to toying with him.

"So it's bogus I am? Well, that's a new one, I must say. There is a limit to the time I can stay. May I see the others, or shall I just go?" Conner heard soft laughter behind him and was tempted to turn but could see that it might annoy the woman if he tried.

"When did you take Holy Orders, Billy? Did you suddenly see the light? If you did it must have been a red one."

Con Daley came into sight and Conner continued his act because if ever there was a time his life depended on his ability to deceive, then this was it. He showed his recognition slowly. "Con? Con Daley? Jesus, man, the whole bloody country is out looking for you."

"What's happened to your priesthood, Billy?"

"Oh, bugger the priesthood, I'm going round on a scam to try to raise money. I had no idea you were in the country."

"Raise money for the cause?"

Conner offered a guilty little smile. "And a bit for myself to keep body and soul together. When did you come over?"

"When did Flynn and Mooney say I came over?"

"Just what the hell have they got to do with it? I haven't seen them for ages. The last I heard they were still in Belfast."

"Put the bible and the papers down on the table there, Billy."

Conner did as told, but he moved slowly and Daley knew he was looking for the half chance.

"Take his gun, Jamie."

Patterson came forward and removed Conner's gun from behind.

"Jamie? Jamie Patterson? You two escaped together? I

192

wonder if you would have done if you'd known Patterson was the one who killed your wife?"

Daley's face tightened as though he had just received an injection for a tooth.

"He's trying to stir it up between us," Patterson said easily. "I wouldn't know what your wife looked like."

"I don't suppose you did, you Prot bastard. You hit the wrong bloody woman. You killed her."

"Don't be stupid. You weren't there so how would you know?" Patterson felt he should have done better than that so added, "Unless Flynn and Mooney told you. They were always good at disinformation. Con, take no notice. It's all he's got left. Ask him how he knew you are here."

"I know what to ask him."

Before Daley could speak again Conner said, "I had no idea you were here. It was sheer chance. Don't listen to this Prot bastard."

"This Prot bastard is going to smash you straight in your lying mouth if you continue to say things like that. You're a slippery sod, Conner. You must get a kick out of abusing the hospitality they give you here. Answer the question."

"I don't answer questions from you."

"Then you'd better answer it from me, Billy. You're in the shit. You've got over-confident."

Steinbach had come further into the room and stood beside Ulla behind the damask settee. The Germans were fascinated by the exchange and wondered how it would end, knowing how they would deal with it.

Conner was beginning to lose confidence. His gaze darted around, his expression increasingly desperate. He had been so used to getting his own way and controlling everything he touched that he had become careless at a crucial time. It was too late to realise it. Nor did he like the look of the Germans or understand their presence.

"Do you mind if I sit down?" he asked as a distraction. "My feet are killing me."

"It won't be your feet that will kill you, Billy. You shouldn't eat so much. You look more like a pig than the last time I saw you. You'd better answer the question."

"I swear to you that it was pure chance. I did not know you were here."

"You mean you didn't know for certain but had to be sure. So who pointed you towards us?"

"It was no more than a rumour that you might be staying in grander digs than usual. Look, when the boys hear of this they'll be after you, Con. I can sort this out with them given the chance."

"They're already after me. There's nothing you can do and nothing I'd trust you to do. I'm going to ask you one more time and if you don't answer I'll use the gun. Okay? Was it Flynn and Mooney who tipped you off?"

"It was them who asked me to find you." Conner smiled nervously, "I've a network you'd never believe."

"Did they say why?" Daley appeared to be weary of his own questions though the tension in the room was high.

"No. But I think they wanted to help you. They realise you are on the run and were upset by your being with a black-hearted Prot."

"Okay, Billy, you can sit down now. I've got to think out what to do. Is anyone else involved?"

Conner hesitated fractionally before saying, No. It's their call. They won't give up, you know."

"The three in Hertfordshire did." Daley was slowly pacing the room, tapping his gun against his thigh.

Conner went very white. There was no answer and it showed him more than anything else just how far Daley was prepared to go. He looked towards the door. The way was clear but there were still four of them in the room. He had the feeling that the Germans might keep out of it. They had not said a word since Ulla had ushered him in and it seemed they recognised a private fight. He half-rose from the chair as Daley raised his gun and shot him through the back of the head.

Conner fell forward, his head hitting the table to spill its contents across the surface.

Even Steinbach and Ulla were stunned. Nobody moved. Nobody expressed horror at the ghastly sight of Conner with a small entry and a huge exit hole in a head which lay sideways on the table among unfinished breakfasts. Crockery had been scattered but no one said or did anything.

If there was obvious reaction at all it was from Steinbach who gazed at Daley with new respect. Then the implications of the murder set in and they started to think what might happen next.

"We'll have to move out," said Patterson finding it difficult to feel sympathy for Conner whose own bloody exploits he had heard about in Ireland, and who may have roused Daley's feelings against him. So far as he was concerned they could kill each other off as often as possible. But he was shocked by the way it had happened.

"We have to move out anyway," Daley snapped. "We're washed up here and you all know it."

Steinbach nodded towards Conner. "You are right. If he knew we are here then so might others. What do we do with him?"

"Leave him here. What difference does it make? Better than trying to get him out."

"And where do we go?" asked Ulla, raising the real problem. "Do we split up now?"

They had had their problems yet somehow they had got on and had proved that between them they had the capability of successful bank robbers. It could extend to other parts of Britain or even abroad. And between them they had the capability of pulling off far bigger jobs than the one at Stoneham.

Daley said, "There's one place we can try for tonight, anyway." He searched Conner's pockets without qualm and produced a wallet, and a pack of credit cards signed in Conner's own name. There were two hundred and fifty pounds in the wallet, a driving licence and a small pack of business cards in the name of Sykes, all purporting different occupations but with the same private address and telephone number. And some keys. Daley stuffed them in his pocket after withdrawing one of the cards and promising the others that he would share the cash.

He rang the number on the card and held on so long that he gave up. On impulse he rang again. After a while a shaky, female voice said, "Yes?" Daley had only to hear the one word. He put down the phone awkwardly. "The bitch," he said softly to himself. For a while he stared at the telephone, oblivious of the others and said, "We'll leave it until after dark. Conner won't have told anyone where he was going; he was too bloody secretive. We wait until then."

Across the street various shifts came and went and nobody recorded a sign of Jamie Patterson nor of the other three they had seen the previous day. Others who had come and gone that day were seen again, but not all, so real information was sketchy. They now had full descriptions of Patterson and some mug-shots plus Donna Smith's own description of how he had last looked. Patterson was the key and he had not reappeared.

They had seen a priest enter the building during the early morning and he had not yet come out again. One or two other strangers had entered and one of those had yet to reappear by the time Gaunt and Donna Smith were back on the late shift.

They had brought the usual refreshments. At half-past nine nothing of interest had happened but a few minutes later Gaunt received a radio call from the mobile patrol. He listened, then said to Donna who was still at the window:

"That's strange. Jim Barlow has just been round the block; there are no lights on in the apartment where the four are staying. He's staying that side for a while and will give another call if anything changes."

Donna was immediately concerned for Patterson. "Perhaps they've gone."

"That's the obvious conclusion but no one has seen them or anyone remotely resembling them."

"What about the fire escape?"

"That's been covered since we were satisfied that this is where they are. I think we had better take a look. Have we still got that Jehovah stuff?"

"Not here. I'll call Phil to bring some over at once."

Daley followed up the rear. They went up the escape to the roof with Steinbach and Ulla leading as they had already made the journey, and Patterson just in front of Daley who

196

was showing less friendliness to him now. Conner had implanted suspicion in Daley's mind. Patterson wondered if his namesake in Hull prison had killed Daley's wife. But nobody had an idea so far as Patterson knew, and the man in Hull had been unsure of all those he had killed over the course of time; the man was a nutter and had executed anyone he had considered to be an enemy.

As they climbed into the darkness Patterson thought these things over quickly should they become important. He began to think what he had said to Conner was true; the PIRA were tring to split them up and sow seeds in Daley's mind to unsettle and to isolate him. Meanwhile Daley was in a dangerous mood. The hostility he was showing was new, worse than when they had first escaped.

They reached the roof and Steinbach led the way over pipes and projections and blockhouses until they reached the parapet and looked across a deep black chasm to the next building which was slightly below. It appeared highly dangerous in the dark but if Ulla had done it the others could not refuse.

They threw their gear over first then jumped in turn, Steinbach first, so that he could help the others land, then Ulla, followed by Patterson and Daley. Once landed they brushed themselves down and continued over the new roof, still led by Steinbach. It occurred to Patterson that, at the moment, Daley had the ace card of the knowledge of safe accommodation, which was sufficient inducement for the Germans to stay. But new moods were creeping in, old suspicions returning.

20

"What did he tell you?"

"Nothing. He went out dressed as a priest." Carmel crossed herself.

Flynn and Mooney exchanged glances and Flynn took the questioning. "Now listen, you stupid bitch. We know you're not too bright. It looks as if Conner has already busted your jaw but that is nothing to what we'll do to you if you don't start remembering. So start from the beginning. How did you know where to find Billy Conner?"

Carmel wanted to sit down but they would not let her. Her legs were shaking and the side of her face where Conner had struck her was swollen and painful and it was difficult for her to speak at all. She began to regret ever having met Con Daley. But, apart from the pain, it was easy to recount how she had come here.

"So you whored yourself off on to Billy and he showed you how rough he liked it?" Flynn could not resist a grin. "How did Con ever get mixed up with you? Okay, so then he heard where Con was and went off to get him."

"I don't know." Carmel grasped the edge of the table as she swayed. For a moment it appeared that she might faint. "I think he had learned something but he did not tell me and it might not have been about Con. He wouldn't tell me anything."

"So you whored for nothing?"

"I stayed for Con's sake."

"When will you learn that if he cared about you he would have been in touch? Has he been in touch?"

"Would I be here if he had? Can I sit down? I feel terrible."

"Not as terrible as you will if you don't come clean. You

see, Mike and I don't believe you. You lied to us in Belfast and you're at it again here."

The two men sat on chairs the other side of the table. Carmel was on the point of collapse and but for clinging to the edge of the table would have done. She was afraid, disillusioned and in a good deal of pain. And she knew there was more to come because she simply did not have the answers they wanted. Suddenly everything spun round, the two men gyrated in a haze as she slipped to the floor pulling the table-cloth and crockery down with her. Carmel cracked her head on the edge of the table as she fell and a long gash appeared above her brow. She lay still, facing the door, eyes closed.

Flynn and Mooney searched the apartment and, in the kitchen, near an extension telephone, found the impression of a hastily written address on the blank edge of a newspaper. They shaded it in and decided it was worth following up. They left Carmel, as Conner had done before them, on the floor; it did not matter to them whether she was alive or dead.

Forty-five minutes later they entered the apartment block and took the elevator to the sixth floor.

Donna Smith was taking delivery of the Jehovah's Witness leaflets when Flynn and Mooney approached the block, having paid off their cab at the corner. With the bundle of leaflets still in her hands she turned back to the mounted image intensifier as a matter of routine, and almost dropped the bundle as she peered through the lens.

"Flynn and Mooney," she said in disbelief. "What the hell are they doing here?"

"You know them?" Gaunt held the night binoculars for a change.

"Everyone in the business in Ulster knows them. They still do occasional field jobs but are mainly link men with the Sinn Fein, and troubleshooters when necessary."

Gaunt said, "Perhaps we had better wait to see what happens." He raised his two-way radio. "Get an armed team round the front as quick as you can. Two well-known PIRA.

When they come out arrest them on my signal and hold them under the Anti-terrorist Act. They are dangerous, so bloody well keep out of sight."

Flynn and Mooney found the apartment and approached cautiously. Because they were in such a small, out-of-sight, dead-end passage, they drew guns, keeping them at their sides, and stood each side of the spy-hole with their backs slightly turned so that identification would be difficult. Mooney rang the bell.

No light appeared in the hall so when a prolonged ring produced no result, Mooney worked away at the lock with one of his gadgets. There was no indication that anyone was in. He got the door open to find the chain on.

They stood back, puzzled. Either someone was in and waiting or they had gone out by another exit, a ploy well known to both men. They waited, listened carefully, then made up their minds. There was no sound from the main corridor so Mooney, the heavier, drew back and hurled his weight at the door, breaking the chain away at the first attempt. He braked half-way into the hall then waited for Flynn to join him before continuing to the lounge door.

They were on hands and knees when they opened the door and, as no shots came, Flynn reached up to switch on the light before throwing himself flat. When they tentatively looked up to see a man with his head resting on the table, food and crockery all over the floor, they accepted then that the place was free of the living. They climbed to their feet to see the horrible mess of Billy Conner and they silently backed towards the front door. Once out they closed it quickly and headed breathlessly for the elevator. They had seen death often enough but suddenly it was far too near to home. They could not get out of the building fast enough.

Donna Smith and Peter Gaunt saw Flynn and Mooney leave the building to stand on the main steps looking extremely agitated. Gaunt said into his radio, "That's them. Get them. They'll be armed."

Mooney had gone to the edge of the pavement to search

forlornly for a cab when a series of shadows came out of the darkness and before he had any idea of what was happening four men grabbed him. He struggled powerfully while an unmarked police car came gliding in, doors flung wide before it stopped.

Flynn had the advantage of still being in the shadows when Mooney had wandered off. The fight Mooney put up helped him. He saw a gap, drew his gun, and raced for it, firing twice over his shoulder as he hurtled for the corner of the street.

He could have been picked off easily enough, but a taxi came round the corner just as Flynn reached it, and it blocked off the main line of police fire. Once on the busier street the chase became more difficult for Flynn was as fast as he was desperate.

There were few people on the streets at this time, which did nothing to help him and he guessed there would be other police on the far side of the block, so he raced across the road, just missing being knocked down by a late bus, and took the next turning. He doubted that the police would fire blindly but he knew a car would be despatched to block him off at the other end.

There were rows of parked cars each side of the street. He heard running footsteps turning the corner behind him and he suddenly dived into a gap between the cars and flattened himself to crawl under the nearest vehicle. He lay quite still, breathing heavily and cursing his condition while he listened to the approaching footsteps. Something plopped on his face and he was so startled that he almost gave himself away. Oil. He let it trickle down his face.

Three sets of footsteps raced past and he gradually pulled himself back to the corner he had left, car by car. It was a slow painful process and sometimes he thought there was no room, but by wriggling, feeling his way, accepting the tightness and the scratches, and the sometimes almost impossible lack of space, he worked his way back towards the corner. It was a gamble. Whatever he did would be a gamble. He was gambling that the search would widen away from its original starting place. In the process he ripped his clothes in several places and it was impossible to

201

judge just how far he had gone. His only source of information was the sound of the police.

Gaunt, with Donna Smith and four other armed policemen, crossed to the apartment block while the chase for Flynn still went on. Mooney had already been whisked away in a police car. The apartment door had been closed and Gaunt rang the bell and did not wait long before instructing one of his colleagues to open the door.

They found what Flynn and Mooney had found. Conner had not been moved nor had anything else. "The priest," Gaunt observed. "Nobody had recognised Billy Conner, the bloody fools." He turned to Donna, "Find out whose shift it was when Conner arrived."

Donna made a note but thought Gaunt was being wise after the event. Conner's attire was quite convincing but, to somebody, evidently not convincing enough. She turned away from the ghastly sight. They went through the apartment carefully but Gaunt had meanwhile put in a call for a forensic team. There was ample evidence in the form of discarded clothing, as though whoever had been staying here did not care what the clothing might provide in the way of evidence.

When they had finished and teams of police were getting in each other's way trying to rake through the evidence, room by room, Gaunt said to Donna, "I'm pushing off to interview Mooney. You want to come?"

"Sure. Any news of Flynn, yet?"

Gaunt raised his radio and spoke for a while. "None. A slippery eel."

"He was that in Ulster. Used to be a sprinter in spite of his shape."

"Well, it's down to you and Flynn, Michael. What happened, did thieves fall out?" Gaunt sat on the edge of the table to ease his leg while Donna stood with her back to the door. Both knew they were being watched by Commander Waring and two other officers through the one-way glass window set into a wall.

Mooney, depressed and frustrated, sat smoking a cigarette

despite the no-smoking sign. "He was already dead when we got there. Long before." He had given up the idea of denying that they had ever been to the apartment; their fingerprints would be all over the front door. "Don't try pinning it on us."

"Why not? You were in there long enough. And you came out agitated. We'll have no problem at all in pinning it on you. We know you did it anyway. You were both armed."

Mooney said, "If your forensic aren't as bent as usual, they'll find neither of our guns were used."

"Come now, Mike. That gag's wearing thin; discarding the murder weapon and being found with another. What did you do with it? Flynn has convinced us that it was down to you."

"Don't try that stuff, copper. Danny wouldn't do that; there's no need. Anyway, I don't suppose you caught him, he can move when he wants to."

"Faster than a bullet?"

"You're not very good at this," Mooney sneered. "You must have a lot of men on leave for them to let a rookie loose on me."

Gaunt was unruffled. Men like Mooney were well-practised with police interrogations. "It was a classic PIRA execution. Straight through the back of the head from close range. Why did he have to die?"

"You'd better ask the bloke who did it."

"Billy Conner was a big mouth but hardly a traitor, so why, Michael? What do you think?"

"I think you are stupid."

"Stupid enough to wonder what the hell you were doing there in the first place? What did you want with Conner and how did you know he was staying there?"

This was much more dangerous ground. Mooney crushed out his cigarette in a tin lid. "Is this the best ashtray you can provide?"

"It's a non-smoking area. We made an exception in your case, as you've very little future left. Why were you and Flynn there and why was Conner?"

Mooney was having to think more carefully. He could simply refuse to answer all questions but had decided he did not want to be tucked away for ten years, or possibly the rest of his natural life, for something he had not done. "We had no idea that Conner was there. As soon as we saw him we beat it. You were looking, you must know the truth of it."

"You were there longer than you think. Plenty of time to commit a murder. If you didn't go to see Conner who did you go to see?"

"No comment. Anyway, we waited a long time for someone to answer the door. No one did. I want my solicitor flown over from Belfast."

"That will take time. Was it Con Daley? And if it was, would you have blown his head off?"

"Don't be stupid."

"The word is that he ripped off some of your funds. Isn't that why you want him? And how did he come to know this plush nest he's just flown? Was that another rip-off? Did he do a deal with the Libyans to provide a safe house for the boyos and somehow work it for himself? You got the arms he negotiated and he got the apartment without your knowing? He did go to Libya for PIRA, didn't he? And didn't he give one or two names away to the RUC? A bad lot, our Con. I can understand why you want him so badly. We think he might have killed three of your colleagues in Hertfordshire the other day. You are really in deep trouble, Michael, whether or not you killed Conner. Co-operation with us might help a little. We could believe your story."

"Get stuffed," Mooney snarled. "I'm not saying another word until I've seen my solicitor."

Gaunt rose and limped away from the table. "Actually, you've said quite a lot." He stared at Mooney for some time. "It would be quite easy for us to pin the Conner murder on you."

"That would be your usual form, wouldn't it? You've had plenty of practice convicting innocent men."

"They are all innocent, Mike. We never convict a guilty one. Makes you wonder how these murders come about, doesn't it? Anyway, think over anything you can tell us about where Con Daley might have gone."

"And Jamie Patterson," said Donna from the door.

Mooney had not been interested in Donna but now he gazed at her and memory came back. "I remember you, you bitch. Patterson is it? The one who killed Con Daley's wife." "Is that what you are putting about?" Donna was horrified.

Mooney grinned. "Well, it's at least as true as me and Danny knocking off poor old Billy Conner."

Gaunt gave Donna a warning glance. "Come on, let's go and see what Flynn has to say."

"He'll say no more than me, you bastards," Mooney bawled at them as they left him and two plain-clothes policemen slipped into the room to take him to a cell.

21

Once they were on the streets they were so noticeable as a group that they broke up into pairs. Steinbach wanted them to separate completely but Daley did not want to lose touch with Patterson who, knowing the dangers of staying, now decided to hang on. Keeping Daley in sight had again become important to him.

So that the Germans would eventually meet up with them again, Daley had given them the address to which he was going. Short of booking into a small hotel or boarding house, obvious places for police searches, there was little any of them could do but trust in Daley at this point. It was impossible for Daley to use any of the safe houses used by PIRA, and the Germans were forced to take the view that the few addresses open to them in England could well be suspect and under police surveillance, due to the numbers of their colleagues arrested in Germany and the mass of information obtained from the East German Stasi. So far Daley had served them well even if their stay had been fairly brief. They were used to moving on.

It was too far to walk but it was some time before Patterson and Daley could find a cab. They had no idea of the drama being played by C13 and Flynn and Mooney, and had been well clear of the whole district by the time Flynn fired shots at the police. Nor had Daley any idea that Flynn was now on the run like himself and that Mooney was in custody. And Patterson had no inkling that Smithy had seen him enter the building complete with false moustache.

They were silent for most of the journey. They knew that, as soon as Billy Conner was found, the search for them would be intensified. Neither realised that the balance had already swung against them.

They were aware, though, that something had gone from the association of all four. It was difficult to place but part of it lay in Daley's sudden lack of trust for Patterson. He had never liked him, had in fact hated him at first, but he had come to trust him in tight situations. That, however, was no longer clear.

Patterson felt some of that resentment in the back of the cab so he took a chance and said, "I did not kill your wife. If you can't see that they are trying to prise us apart then you are stupid. I helped you against the three in Hertfordshire; they are trying to make sure that I'm not there next time so they can get you." And when Daley did not reply, added angrily, "Use your common sense if you've got any. Do you think for one moment I'd have strung along if I'd killed your wife?"

Daley seemed partly convinced but the doubt would return, the damage was too deep. Patterson felt like jumping the cab but would not put it past Daley, in his present mood, to shoot him in the back as he had shot Conner. Besides, since Conner's murder, events had changed and he again felt strongly that he had unfinished business to complete.

When Daley told the cabbie to stop he paid him off and said to Patterson, "This way," and waited as if expecting Patterson to make a run for it.

Patterson noticed that Daley had one hand in his pocket but even if he was not holding a gun he would still have accompanied him. As they walked side by side Daley said, "It's a fair distance but I didn't want the cab to stop too close. It's quiet round here."

Patterson did not argue with that. He did not know London very well but thought they might be somewhere in Fulham. It was quiet simply because it was late at night, but the nearby main streets were still busy enough. Daley took a turn and then another, and they were walking unhurriedly when he said, "I know you helped me when we went for the cache but if I thought you killed Jean I would kill you."

It took Patterson by surprise. "You don't seem too sure that I didn't." And when Daley hesitated, he added, "Your wife had left you long before she was killed. You were living with

Carmel what's-her-name. Why would it be so important to you?"

"She was my wife, for God's sake."

"Once. But the word is that you didn't get on, were always rowing and you had a roving eye which she didn't care for."

Daley stopped and pulled Patterson round to face him. "What are you bloody well talking about? Who told you all this crap?"

Patterson forced Daley's clutching hands away from his jacket. "It was common knowledge. Everyone who knew you, knew. You were glad when your wife left. Maybe it's your bloody conscience getting to you at last; maybe that's why you're so bloody morose about her death. Well, I'm not answering to your conscience, Con. I've heard it said that whoever killed her did you a favour. And I wonder who started that one?"

Daley flung himself at Patterson but did not draw his gun. They fought silently, two shadows merging in the shadows of a short, lifeless street with the occasional window showing light through drawn curtains.

They fell against parked cars and rolled along the row. Patterson found little difficulty in restraining the wiry Daley who was striking out wildly, gasping for breath, his effort desperate.

"I loved her, you bastard, you wouldn't understand." There was a sob in Daley's voice and his blows were becoming more frantic, losing a good deal of power as Patterson dealt with them competently, closing in and generally tying him up.

"You must have had a bloody funny way of showing it," Patterson panted. "Or she wouldn't have left you."

Daley was working off his aggression, slowing down and running out of steam. "It was that bastard Danny Flynn who told her about Carmel. And then everyone knew; even you, a Prot." He was resting against Patterson now, his blows no more than token.

Patterson knew it was over and held on to Daley merely to keep him upright. He sensed that Daley had not finished explaining and waited for him to recover.

"I wouldn't have gone off with Carmel. But Flynn had put

208

the boot in and there was nowhere else for me to go once Jean left. I always had the feeling that Flynn wanted her for himself, but he's a slippery sod."

It was too much for Daley to apologise and his naturally suspicious nature was not entirely satisfied. It would take little to rekindle his distrust of Patterson. But he had gone some way to exorcise his guilt about his wife whom he felt would not have died had she stayed with him. It was the kind of hypocrisy or self-delusion he lived by; seeing only what he wanted to see.

They continued on down the street swaying like a couple of drunks until Daley suddenly veered into a doorway and fiddled with the keys he had taken from Conner's pocket. They went in to find Carmel still spread on the living-room floor, blood having run from her forehead and down her face, and congealed round her mouth like freakishly applied lipstick.

"God Almighty!" Daley, with tears in his eyes, lifted her head and cradled it. He looked up at Patterson and said, "I'm glad I shot that bastard. We've got to get her to hospital."

Patterson could not help reflecting that, had the girl been conscious, Daley would probably have beaten her to her present state for betraying him. He said, "You can't have an ambulance come here. The best you can do is to take her to the nearest hospital casualty and walk out damned quick."

As he spoke there was a hammering on the front door.

They went to the front door, one each side. There was no spy-hole and they wondered how Conner had ever coped with visitors. Daley reached forward and undid the latch, pulling the door ajar. Nothing happened. Patterson was behind the door and could no longer see Daley.

"Anyone there?"

It was Ulla's voice and Patterson pulled the door right back for her to enter. As she came through Steinbach said behind her, "We arrived about twenty minutes ago. There was no reply so we waited across the street. We saw you arrive."

They crowded into the living-room and Carmel was the immediate focus of attention. Steinbach knelt down to search

209

for a pulse. "Who did this?" he asked looking up at the two
Irishmen. He was not concerned with the state of Carmel but
how it would affect them.

"Billy Conner must have done it," said Daley bitterly.
"The guy I shot. May he be in hell. We must get her to a hospital."

Steinbach straightened. "How? You can't bring an ambulance here." He did not realise he was echoing Patterson's
words.

"I have to drive her there."

"You mean steal a car? While the heat is on? It would be
better if we keep low for a while, I think."

"She's my girl, I have to do something." Daley was hoping
one of them would make a suggestion. He did not know what
to do. But there was nothing that could be done without
endangering them all. "I can't leave her like this." He turned
to them one by one. "She's dying."

"She's almost dead," said Steinbach coldly. "It would be
foolish to compromise us for someone who cannot be saved."

The words came out like a death sentence. The logic was
sound, the delivery totally unfeeling.

There was utter silence. They looked down at the battered
face of Carmel as if she herself might provide an answer.
Without expressing the thought Steinbach hoped that she
would, simply by dying.

Daley, having expunged all responsibility for his wife's
death, now found himself in another, similar, situation. He
seemed to be on the point of tears. His emotional stress had
increased considerably over the last few days, and his
unpredictability was on the verge of overflowing.

Ulla felt for him because she was just as unstable, guided
too often by senseless feeling that could produce a killing
mood. "Let's get her to bed," she said, putting a protective
arm round Daley's thin shoulders. "Hans and Jamie can carry
her." She glared at the other two.

Leaving Ulla and Daley in the hall, Patterson and Steinbach
carried Carmel upstairs as gently as they could and laid her on
the unmade bed she and Conner had obviously used. Once she
was prone, Steinbach again searched for a pulse beat and gazed

210

across at Patterson and shook his head. They pulled the blankets up to give her some warmth.

Making sure the curtains were drawn, Steinbach switched on the light and closed the door. He signalled to Patterson and they sat side by side on the edge of the bed, their backs turned towards Carmel.

"This is a complication," said Steinbach. He did not really mean to state the obvious, but was looking for a solution which he preferred to discuss with Patterson rather than Daley or Ulla. "Will someone come looking for her?"

"It's unlikely." Patterson was quite agreeable to see PIRA killing each other off, but people like Carmel really knew little of motivation, and she was on the fringe only through being besotted with one of the actual members. She was too far gone to realise that membership by innocent association could be just as damning. "I would guess she came over from Belfast to find Daley once she heard he had escaped from prison. It might take time for relatives and friends to become concerned."

"It's still a complication; having the body here. And if this place belonged to the man Con shot, the police will be here as soon as they find him. This wasn't a good move." Steinbach scratched his head. Young shoots were already coming through and they itched. He stared at a window whose curtains were still drawn across. He stood up. "It's falling apart. I can feel it. It's time we split." He turned suddenly, his cold eyes on Patterson. "Don't you think?"

Patterson shrugged. He could do without the Germans; his battle was with the Provos and although Steinbach and Ulla had proved their use, he would prefer to be without them. Yet, for a reason he could not define, he was reluctant to see them go. They helped to keep Daley reasonably stable. Perhaps he saw little difference between any of the terrorists and would like to see them all blown from the face of the earth. It was fanciful thinking. He said, "It might be some time before the police find Conner. We would be all right for tonight. Anyway, where would you go?"

Steinbach transferred his gaze to Carmel. "That is the problem. Maybe it would be better for us to leave Britain and

211

go to Holland. We have contacts there. But the whole of Western Europe is a high risk area. Things will quieten down after a while but who knows when?"

"Why don't you go to Eastern Europe?"

"Are you mad? It is worse there than here. They are all looking for us. They've nurtured, fed, financed and even trained us, but suddenly we are an embarrassment to them. They would now use us as specimens to show their good faith with the West." He reached across the bed to place two fingers at the side of Carmel's neck. Without any noticeable reaction, he said, "She's dead."

Patterson stood up. He had expected it but was no less dismayed. Women like Carmel did not stand a chance. "Don't tell Con. We don't know which way he'll jump."

Steinbach nodded slowly. "Perhaps if we clean her up he will be happier."

They found a flannel in the bathroom and wiped away the congealed blood and pulled the blankets up further to hide the stains on her dress. She appeared better and Patterson checked the pulse himself to find that Steinbach was right.

They switched off the light, went downstairs and Patterson said, "She's sleeping. Hans cleaned her up." When Daley moved towards the stairs, he added, "Let her rest, Con," and with a certain truth, "She looks a little better."

Daley seemed relieved. But a glance at Ulla convinced them that she had seen through the ploy. Somehow they had to get through the night and plan the next day. They started to explore the small house to discover for how long it might be useful in the event of a siege.

Flynn panted heavily. It was so dark in the alley, so quiet, that he was almost afraid to move, seeing a threat in every shadow. The escape from the immediate ring of police had been harrowing and he leaned against a wall wondering just how he had managed it. The euphoria of success had gone some time ago. He had no feeling of satisfaction, though relieved, but they had got Mike Mooney and he dare not go back to the digs where he kept his gear.

His clothes were torn and oil-stained from crawling under

212

cars, his hands grimed and greasy. It had not been easy and often, where the gap was too narrow, he had been forced to come out from under into the street itself. Yet he had not been seen and he believed it was because he had edged nearer to the starting point of the search.

Now he was some distance from the hub of the police search but was nervy and, as it was well past 1 a.m., he felt as if he was alone in the world, yet, perversely, one move would bring them all running and the alley would be blocked off both ends. Without the comfort of Mooney's presence, Flynn had nothing with which to bolster his flagging confidence.

He could not stay in the alley all night and he could not go back home. Nor could he look for fresh digs at this time of night and in this condition. He needed daylight but that would expose his terrible state and draw attention.

As he leaned against the wall he noticed that half-way down the short alley were two bollards; he could just see their faint reflection. He was not at all sure where he was and certainly not which direction to take. To increase his misery it started to drizzle. During a terrible moment of depression when he could see no future beyond the wet comfort of the wall which supported him, he felt like giving himself up. He staggered along the wall to the end of the alley to look out at the line of darkened terraced houses.

The mood passed and old hatreds returned and there was no way a lousy copper was going to arrest him. He patted the gun in his pocket and some of his confidence returned. Maybe the police had not sussed out his digs yet. But first he had to find a telephone.

When he did find a kiosk it was on a street corner and looked like an illuminated island waiting for the first passing copper to spot. Who used street pay phones at this time of night?

He went inside, checked that he had enough change, and dialled a number. Standing in the cubicle of light was like advertising his whereabouts and the light worked against him; he could not properly see outside, or if anyone was approaching. A sleep-laden voice answered and Flynn said quickly, "It's Danny. I'm sorry to wake you at this time but

213

I'm in trouble. Billy Conner has been shot dead through the head, probably by Con Daley, and the police have picked up Mike; they'll try to pin the killing on us because we were there. I'm on the run and in a callbox. I need help."

There was a long pause the other end of the phone then a deep voice, no longer sleepy, and with a faint Dublin accent said, "Where are you?"

"I haven't a bloody clue. I can give you this number if that will help."

"Give me the number and hang up. I'll ring you back so we won't be cut off. Meanwhile go to the nearest corner and look at the bloody street name and the district code. When you have it stay near the phone but out of sight."

The exasperation in the voice induced Flynn to say, "Look, I know you don't like being contacted. I didn't know what else to do. I'm sorry. I'll do as you say." He hung up.

As Flynn was already on the street corner it took him no time to obtain the name of the street he was in and that of the road that cut across. He went back and waited in the tiny front garden of the house opposite the kiosk.

The night closed in once more and he stood behind a low wall watching the oasis of light on the corner. Time passed, nothing happened and he began to wonder if he had given the wrong number or if it had been taken down incorrectly. A car passed at the junction, the driver so careful that he was probably drunk, and once he heard distant footsteps. An upstairs light came on in the house across the street and flicked off shortly after. Flynn was getting worried. It must have been twenty minutes before the phone rang and as Flynn hurried to the kiosk he almost panicked into believing that he had forgotten the street names. He was in a cold sweat by the time he lifted the receiver.

As Flynn put the phone to his ear he wanted to shout a protest at the delay but would not do it to this man. "Danny," he said weakly.

"I couldn't ring back sooner. Finding somewhere safe for you took a little arranging at this time of night. And I had to fix transport. The accommodation will be safe for a couple of nights, then we have to think again. Wait there for the car. I

214

don't know what make will be used. And I don't know how long it will take. Just be there. When the car arrives, climb in the back. On no account get in with the driver; I don't want him recognised, okay? Now give me the details and he'll be as quick as he can but you might have a bit of a wait. And Danny, don't ever ring me again. You know the procedure."

It was almost an hour before Flynn heard a car approach. Little had happened while he waited except that the weather had worsened and he was now soaked through. Visibility was bad but gave him an additional curtain of cover. Shortly after hearing the sweet hum of an on-coming car, he saw the distorted dimmed headlights through the streaks of rain. He did not leave the garden until the car slowed down and pulled over to glide past the corner and then pull in.

Flynn watched and thought it was easy for the driver to pick out the kiosk. As the car stopped, the rear door opened and Flynn hurried towards it. He was shot down by a hail of bullets from a silenced SMG and crumpled on to the wet pavement in a dead heap. He never knew what happened. The door closed and the car pulled away.

"I've arranged a stake-out for Conner's place."

"Can't we just go in, sir? We are losing time and Jamie is in danger."

Gaunt passed across the thermos. "It's a toss of the coin. There might be useful phone numbers and addresses in there. On the other hand, if there are, someone will come for them. I would like to see what happens. If we go in and leave our mark it will warn people off. Ideally, we want to get both callers and incriminating evidence. I shouldn't have to tell you that we are dealing with people who know how to use the law against us. They can do what they like, kill who they like, but we have to go by the book and be good boys and girls. And Jamie Patterson is involved by his own choice. Nobody is any longer sure of his motives."

"I am sure. I told you what they are." Donna found the chair hard, the room tiny, considering the amount of work they were trying to get through.

"I know. But you're prejudiced. Here, have a biscuit."

Gaunt rolled the packet across the small table and Donna turned up her nose.

"I can see the weevils from here. So Mooney hasn't come up with a thing?"

"I didn't expect him to. It was a wonder he didn't deny his name. I think it's time we went home. There's nothing more we can do tonight. I doubt we'll find Flynn now. That was a bad slip. We should have got him." It was three in the morning and they had drunk countless cups of coffee.

The hunt for Flynn had widened but nobody was optimistic. At 4 a.m., just when they were about to leave to salvage what was left of the night, the news came in that a police patrol had found Flynn's body riddled with bullets in the gutter. He had been dead for no more than half an hour. The shots had woken no one but now the whole district was crawling with patrol cars and the police popularity ratings had sunk to below zero as house-to-house questioning had started.

Identification had been quick; Flynn carried a UK/Ireland time table and his prints and description had been faxed immediately to Belfast who had responded at once. This news was passed to Murder Squad who immediately informed C13. It was slick work but did not make up for the fact that they would have preferred to have found Flynn alive.

Gaunt stared thoughtfully at Donna, all notion of sleep gone. This was a blow. "They're getting desperate; killing off their own to protect others."

"Does it change your mind about raiding Conner's place?"

Gaunt inclined his head, acknowledging that it was a good question. "We're pretty sure who killed Conner. A raid won't help in that direction. I'm after as many as I can get. A team is already in position. They were there within an hour of finding Conner." He could not know that Patterson, Daley and the two Germans had arrived well before Conner's body was found.

22

Patterson faced Steinbach across the small, plastic kitchen table. He was uncomfortable about the whole situation, and he was certain that so, too, was Steinbach. They had to move somewhere, and there had been little time to think about it. But doubts were now setting in.

Ulla and Daley were resting on top of separate beds in a room upstairs. Before Daley had turned in he had peeped into Carmel's room, held back by Steinbach who was insistent that she should not be disturbed. It was not the right time to tell Daley that Carmel was dead. There might never be a right time, he was too emotionally disturbed over everything, including the fact that Carmel had obviously slept with Conner. This enraged him more than anything, although he had clearly intended to desert her, and again that strange, self-justifying hypocrisy, convinced him he had been betrayed.

That Steinbach had restrained Daley, when at any other time death, no matter whose, left him unaffected, indicated that he too was well aware of the increasing dangers.

In a strange way Patterson and Steinbach got on together. They recognised the same dangers and had a percipience about events. As they sat, tired out, but still alert, the hackles on each were bristling with unease. They sat sipping Conner's coffee, occasionally speaking in a desultory way until Steinbach said once again, "It was a mistake coming here."

Patterson pushed away his mug, leaving a wet ring on the plastic, and repeated his own question, "Where else could we have gone?"

"I know. But the police will come here when the priest is found." He had developed a habit of calling Conner 'the priest'.

"That could take some time."

"And they might already know."

Patterson gazed at Steinbach and wondered how he had ever become so cold, so unfeeling of everything. He was far from being a coward. Steinbach was the type to go out with blazing gun. Although he had kept Daley away from Carmel's dead body in order to avoid a situation, Patterson felt that the reason had not entirely been that: he had wanted to spare Daley a degree of anguish. And he had shown odd touches of care when he had cleaned the blood off Carmel's face. It was contradictory, and therefore, in this context, dangerous.

"If they do, they'll be outside now." Patterson had been a long time in replying. His three companions were all deadly dangerous in their own respective ways. But a bullet is a bullet no matter who fires it or why. Although he was comfortable with Steinbach at this moment, he knew it to be a false solace. He had never felt so vulnerable. But there was another reason. He wanted to search the house on his own. Somewhere here Conner must have kept notes of some kind, names of those he dealt with even if they were in code. There had to be something in the house to supplement memory.

Steinbach took his pistol from his hip pocket and placed it on the table. "Everything must remain the same. The curtains must stay as they are, everything. Where the curtains are drawn back we must keep well away from the windows. There must be no indication that anyone is here. We must not go out until we are sure." He screwed on a silencer.

Patterson considered it prudent to do the same if only to convince Steinbach that he agreed with him. "Let's see if there's a back way out while it's still dark."

One of the advantages of sitting in the kitchen was that it faced the rear of the house and was not immediately overlooked. Conner, who seemed to have been security minded, had fixed both curtains and roller blinds to black out the light. Every room had heavy drapes, which when properly drawn across were as effective as 'black out' curtains.

They switched off the kitchen lights before unlocking the door with the keys Daley had taken from Conner. Patterson stood by the door with Steinbach just behind him and opened the door a fraction. The early morning chill made them shiver. They slipped outside and pushed the door to and stood to one side of it.

The drizzle had stopped some time ago but the air was damp and penetrating. As far as could be seen, the garden was nothing more than a small yard, full of litter and a stinking refuse bin. A cold wind stirred dead leaves, making them rustle like shifting gravel. As their sight adjusted to the darkness they could make out a wooden fence at the bottom which seemed to back on to the yard of the house behind; a typical back-to-back. Houses in either direction faded into the gloom.

They could not have explained their caution in what was a protected area, seemingly away from prying eyes, yet they showed that unspoken understanding that indicated something was wrong. Without comment, they eased to one side of the yard, careful to pick their footsteps among the rubble, and stood side by side with their backs against the wall.

A few minutes later there was a slight noise from the fence and someone climbed over from the yard of the rear house. Then another shadow slipped over. It was difficult to see them and once over they stayed against the fence where they could not be seen at all.

Patterson reached up to close his hand over Steinbach's gun, indicating that they should not fire until sure of the opposition. If it turned out to be the police he knew he would not be able to fire, but how was he to find out? He was highly anxious now and hoped Steinbach, who was alert but cool, would not notice his agitation.

A third and a fourth figure appeared but none of them as yet moved forward. Patterson and Steinbach stayed absolutely still; numbers were against them but they had the advantage of surprise. It was impossible to fire accurately; it was far too dark and the intruders obviously wore dark clothing to make it almost impossible to pick out against the fence.

Nothing happened for quite a while. In little more than an hour it would begin to lighten. Someone moved forward tentatively and in a strange quirk of light and movement it could now be seen that he wore a hood.

Again Patterson gave Steinbach a warning touch. Surely it could not be the SAS; the time factor seemed to be all wrong and they seldom did operations as speculative as this. And somehow he did not think it was the police. His main problem now was to stop Steinbach from firing; he might well have picked off the advancing man even in the bad light. Just who the bloody hell were they?

Suddenly Patterson thought he knew. If he was right then almost certainly Conner had been found to provoke this kind of action. He felt better too about firing. He put his lips to Steinbach's ear. "IRA. For Daley. We'll scare them off." Even so close he was not sure Steinbach heard him.

The one figure was fairly clear but what about the others? Once they started firing they would give their positions away, even allowing for the silencers absorbing most of the muzzle flash. It was a dangerous game to play and Steinbach was an old warrior. He wanted better odds and held his ground; some people did not scare off. He and Patterson had not been seen simply because they were standing well to one side and had not been anticipated.

A second man was now following up behind the first. Single file was a strange formation but the nature of the yard did not offer too many alternatives. Again Patterson whispered into Steinbach's ear and this time they both sank to their haunches.

The first man was now past them, on the way to the back door, and the second man was drawing level as a third man left the fence. They were now strung out making an impossible target to get in one attempt. The fourth man was still invisible against the fence.

Patterson and Steinbach lay prone. It was difficult with so much scattered about the yard. They now faced the house. A few feet away from the wall was what looked like an old pear tree which had shed its leaves. Patterson pulled himself towards it the next time the man advanced a stage. He crawled until he was behind the bole of the tree. Steinbach stayed where he was as cover for Patterson who was now almost out of his sight.

Patterson could not now see any of the men as his vision was cut off by the tree. But he could see all the windows at the rear of the house. He raised his pistol to aim at the window of the room Daley was in. He was firing at an angle and hoped it would make the difference between a neat hole and cracking the glass. He fired, the subdued flash hidden by the tree, and the plop of the shot confusingly from anywhere and almost instantaneously covered by the sound of breaking glass. Almost immediately he fired again, this time at the kitchen window.

The sound of breaking glass was so loud in the confined space of the yard that Patterson thought it was enough to wake the whole street. The approaching men threw themselves flat, and Daley could be heard swearing upstairs. No lights came on and none were expected.

Patterson fired again to smash another window and this time produced a reaction from the raiders. Crouched down they ran back to the fence to disappear against its shadows as Steinbach fired a shot after them. One of the men retaliated but the shot was wild and cracked into the wall well clear of Steinbach who fired again as the men spread out and jumped for the top of the fence to roll over one by one. There was no sound of their retreating the other side of the fence as though they were just waiting there. But it was extremely doubtful that they were.

Patterson dashed back to Steinbach, annoyed that the German had fired at all, and yet he knew he was right. The raiders would believe they had walked into a trap. On reaching Steinbach, Patterson crouched beside him. They were aware that Ulla and Daley would be at the upstairs windows waiting for a target to fire at.

Steinbach called out softly, "Hold your fire. We'll explain when we come in." He had used German to identify himself to Ulla who would pass it on to Daley.

Patterson and Steinbach approached the fence cautiously, well separated. They found one man at the foot of the fence, alive but unable to move. They picked up a machine pistol which he had dropped nearby. He was groaning with pain but it did not stop them from searching him; he had been hit in the stomach. They tore off his hood and carried him towards the house, this time Patterson calling up a warning to Daley.

Once inside the kitchen they closed the door and switched on the light. Ulla and Daley came racing down the stairs to join them.

"Do you know him?" Patterson snapped at Daley.

The man was in his early twenties, ginger-coloured hair, freckled face and pale skin. The sweat of pain was standing out on him.

Daley stared, shaken and confused. "No. Are you saying he's a Provo? Search him."

"We have. Nothing on him."

"So he could be anyone. Police, maybe."

"He would carry identity."

"SAS, then. They wouldn't."

"And they wouldn't have pissed off, or if they had they'd have been back. It's down to you, Con. They were after you. You've more than had your hand in the till for them to take this kind of risk. What aren't you telling us?"

Daley glared malevolently at Patterson. "You be careful what you say, wife-killer. Don't try that on me; it's you that's hiding something." He looked down at the young, twisted face, saw the widening stain creeping through the fingers of the hands clasped over the belly, raised his gun and fired. The body would have slumped to the floor had it not been for Steinbach holding him by the hair.

"What the hell did you do that for?" Patterson shouted.

"I did him a favour." Daley shrugged. "I didn't shoot him in the first place. If it's not good enough to get Carmel to hospital it's not good enough for him. He was dying anyway."

It was true, the man would not have lasted the rest of the night. But Patterson was convinced that that was not the reason Daley had shot him. "Bloody marvellous," he said. "Now we'll never know who sent him. Or was that your intention?"

Had it not been for the presence of the Germans, Patterson believed Daley would have tried to kill him. He was still hiding something; he must know who had sent the men after him. "Okay," Patterson said. "Now you're satisfied he can't talk what do you intend to do with him?"

"Put him in bed with the girl." Ulla spoke scathingly, showing her disapproval of what Daley had done. She was not disturbed by the killing but by the unprofessional nature of it; they should have tried to find out just who the enemy was, just what they were up against, before ending a young life.

Patterson thought Daley would go berserk. He turned on Ulla, his face red with rage. All that prevented him from trying to kill her there and then was her gun levelled at him, and her proud eyes, challenging him to try. And the fact that Steinbach, now standing behind him, would protect Ulla.

"That's a terrible, barbaric thing to say," Daley spluttered at last. "Fancy saying that. To put the dead in with the living."

"She's been dead since the boys took her upstairs." Ulla was intent on hurting him now, to push him to the limit. She had suddenly had enough of Daley and needed only an excuse to fire. "They tried to protect your feelings but they're not worth protecting. We're all on the line because you're hiding something. Jamie is right, nobody takes stupid risks unless it's for something really bad. Nobody would go this far just because you dipped into the till; they would take their time for that. So what have you done to upset them so much?"

"Take it easy, Ulla." Steinbach surprisingly tried to ease the situation. He did not want something developing inside the house to distract them from what might be happening outside.

Patterson backed Steinbach up although satisfied that Ulla was right. Four men had been sent out, presumably to get Daley, and maybe there had been more. There had to be a very good reason indeed.

Suddenly Daley flopped, whether genuine or opportunist was impossible to tell. But he flopped on to a chair, his head between his hands, and appeared to be crying, occasionally moaning "Carmel", to himself.

Patterson watched for a few seconds and then left the room. There would not be another opportunity like this. He went into the box of a room on the ground floor that Conner had used as a study, felt his way to the window and made sure the drapes were across. He went back to the door, closed it, and groped for the light switch. There was an ancient, small metal filing cabinet, and a roll-topped desk which was open, its top scattered with papers. Conner had clearly not been the tidiest of men. Patterson sat in an old creaking director's chair, its leather torn, and started to go through the desk contents as fast as he could.

He tidied as he went because it was easier to avoid repeating his search. Most of the correspondence related to the various bogus businesses Conner had run. Yet there was no sign of bank or cheque books. So items of importance were kept elsewhere. But he continued on section by section, drawer by drawer. He found it ominous that none of the drawers were locked. As he worked he was puzzled by the fact that Daley had made no effort to do what he was doing; it should have been in Daley's interest to find out if Conner kept any written information appertaining to the IRA, if only to hide or destroy it. Unless he already knew that Conner had none or, more likely, kept it elsewhere.

When he had finished with the desk he forced open the locked filing cabinet but again found only letters connected to various phoney business activities. Nowhere did he find a single reference to anything that could be construed as being tied to the IRA. No names, not even Irish dance evenings. In fact there was nothing to show that Conner had even been Irish.

Patterson went back to the director's chair and swivelled round in it to survey the small untidy room with its overriding smell of dust. But for the recent dates on some of the letters it could easily be assumed that this study had not been used in months.

There were other rooms to search but Patterson had come to the conclusion that there was nothing incriminating to tie Conner in with the IRA in this house. Yet still he was not satisfied.

He slid from the chair and on to his hands and knees and started to probe under the desk itself. There was a gap between the desk and the wall but not big enough for him to

angle his head to peer up it. Crouched in the knee hole he slid
his hand up the back of the desk to feel something stuck to the
wood. He tried to get in further in order to get a better grip
when he felt a slight draught of the door opening and a pistol
was pushed into his back and Daley's murderous voice was
asking, "Just what are you looking for, Jamie me boy?"

Gaunt slipped into the back seat of the car and said,
"Anything?"

The two men watching in the front could hardly keep
awake. Their relief was slow to come through. Nobody liked
these hastily arranged surveillance jobs. Good positions were
difficult to obtain in the middle of the night when cars were
parked the night through. Daylight would enable the police to
approach households in key positions but scratch jobs at this
time of night were seldom satisfactory.

Apart from two cars either side of the front of Conner's
house, but not close enough for detailed observation, there
were men stationed in doorways with a better view. The local
police had been requested to keep away in order to avoid
complications. A car was parked at each end of the street so
that the nearest turn-offs could be watched and should cover
the street running parallel behind.

"Nobody's gone in since we've been here. I would guess
there are heavy curtains. No sign of lights." The detective
yawned, "As dead as the proverbial . . ."

"Or as dead as you'll be if you don't keep awake and your
eyes skinned. We're dealing with professional killers."

"We've done well over our time, sir. The relief is late. It's
difficult to keep awake."

"And I've been up all bloody night. There will be no relief
for me. The slightest twitch in that house and I want to know.
Let me down and you're out of C13."

Gaunt limped slowly to the other positions. He wore rubber
soles and kept as close as he could to the house line, aware that
he was the most likely to be seen from across the street. He
checked on every man on duty in the street and picked up
nothing positive.

The shots had all been silenced and had been at the back of

the house. The nearest man to Conner's house thought he heard glass being broken in the distance; could have been milk bottles, almost anything, but nothing further had happened. No lights had showed at any time. There was a problem because a street light was right outside the house and lights behind it might be difficult to detect. But he was certain there had not been any.

Gaunt returned to his car stationed round the corner, and drove round the block. In the street running parallel to the one Conner's house was in, there was one house with lights on in an upstairs window. The odd landing or night light could be detected elsewhere. He was not sure what he was looking for, except that a man like Conner would have a back way out. But Conner was dead. And so was Flynn. And Mooney was not being at all helpful. And nobody knew what Patterson was really playing at. Perhaps Donna Smith was right, Patterson simply wanted to take out as many IRA as possible, no matter how. But that could lead to being exactly like them, and he believed that Smithy thought so too and was worried sick. He drove back to the Yard where he had rigged a camp bed in his office; with luck he would snatch an hour or two.

Donna Smith was too tired to sleep, and she had too much on her mind. Her main concern was to get Jamie Patterson away from the other terrorists . . . *the other terrorists?* Was this how her mind was working? Had she already accepted that he was as one with them? That was impossible. No man could change that much, it simply was not in his nature. Yet she found it difficult to believe that he had not had his chances to cut loose.

She twisted and turned in bed while she tried to make excuses for him. But others had lost loved ones to the senseless killings of the IRA and, to a lesser degree, the Loyalist paramilitaries who were less organised and not nearly so well armed. But the intent on both sides was the same. She knew he had been terribly upset when she had left Ireland but there had been no real option. She had done good Intelligence work among the females of the IRA species and it had become far

226

too dangerous for her to stay. And Patterson was needed in Belfast and, anyway, could not leave his mother in the state she was in at the time.

It had all been a hopeless mess and they had become the victims of a futile war about something she accepted as an insoluble issue. As she saw it, she was no longer fighting idealists whatever the strength of their original cause, but out-and-out terrorists who made a living from it and had come to like the taste of blood. She knew Patterson felt the same way, but his feelings had hardened considerably after his mother was fatally injured. And that worried her. She should never have left him. It was easy to think like that now.

Smithy sat up and put the bedside light on. Her employers had found a good apartment for her and paid her a London allowance. She was extremely useful to them. She swung her long legs out of bed and prayed that Patterson could cope. He was tough and resilient and determined, but even these qualities, given the nature of the opposition, was often not enough. And what galled her the most was that, so far as she knew, he was totally unaware of her presence here. Was there some way to warn him? To try to make contact?

She stood up and wandered to the kitchen to make herself a cup of cocoa. There might be a way. She would be roasted if Gaunt found out. But she had to try.

Patterson felt the gun, recognised the voice, and said, "Just what the bloody hell do you think I'm doing?" He continued to grope behind the desk.

"I've just about had enough of you." Daley's voice wavered. "I don't trust you. I never did but something has changed in you I don't like at all. It will relieve my mind if I put a bullet in your skull."

"Well, that's your usual way," Patterson said coolly. "How many more are you going to kill? And has it solved any of your problems?" But his confident tone did not reflect his deep fear. Daley was becoming more trigger-happy by the day.

"Answer the bloody question. What are you looking for?" Daley's despair was barely below the surface.

Patterson eased his way from under the desk knee-hole and pulled himself up. He turned to face Daley and said far more easily than he felt, "Put that damned thing away, Con. I'm doing what you should be doing. I'm searching for names."

"Provo names?" Daley could not believe his ears. "You've just sentenced yourself to death. What would you want with Provo names?"

Patterson appeared exasperated. "We were attacked out there, you silly bugger. Hans and I were almost killed and you were close to it. Someone knew you would come here. Now how would they know that? How did they know Conner wasn't here?"

"Perhaps they didn't." Daley shook his head as if in pain. "Perhaps they were after him."

"Don't talk wet. They could pick him off any time. They must have found him and assumed correctly that you would use his pad for a day or two. And they must be satisfied that you topped him. I'm trying to find any clue that might lead us to them."

"Why? Why would you want to know? To hand them over to the fuzz? To do a deal with them?" Daley was close to being hysterical. He had been upstairs to see Carmel and the remorse had set in again.

"I could have done a deal with them at almost any time. Your brain has become addled. I could have shopped you ages ago. When will you get it through your thick head that my problems are the same as yours." Patterson indicated the desk. "I've been right through every drawer. He obviously keeps his important stuff somewhere else. These guys are going to come back with greater numbers and will be better prepared. You should know they won't give up. So where are they coming from, Con? Who are they and where are they holed up? You don't seem to bloody well care. Well, if you have a death wish, we haven't. That's what I was doing."

Daley stared as if he had not understood a word. Patterson knew he was but a trigger pressure from being shot and that he would have no time to go for his own gun. He was awkwardly placed to dive and the room was tiny. Daley appeared mad just then.

"He's right," said Steinbach from the door. "We need to know where they are and who they are; we might be able to get to them first. Why did you not look into this yourself? You know what to look for."

The only thing that stopped Daley from firing was the fact that there was someone in front and behind him. When he turned back from acknowledging Steinbach, Patterson had his gun out. He shrugged and lowered his pistol, but his eyes still smouldered as if he was suffering a personal nightmare. Perhaps the attempts to kill him were finally getting to him.

Patterson suspected that Steinbach had been listening beyond the door for some time. Nobody seemed to be willing to sleep any more; too much was happening. They traipsed back to the kitchen, the wind cutting through the blinds from the holes in the windows. Ulla had made another pot of coffee in an attempt to keep them awake until daybreak. They sat round the plastic-topped table as they had before and Steinbach said to Daley, "There must be a back way out."

Daley looked blank. "I don't know. Conner knew most of the London crowd and he had his uses because he had so many contacts and 'ins' to so many places. But the real secret work hadn't touched him for some time; he had blotted his copybook. If he was anyone of real importance this place would be constantly staked out and there is no way I would have suggested coming here. If there's a back way out I don't know it."

There was a long silence as though nobody believed him and this rattled him into bawling, "I don't bloody well know."

"Another shout like that and everyone will know," Patterson snarled at Daley. "Why don't you go out the front and tell them?" But Patterson was deliberately getting back at Daley in order to re-establish himself. And when that brought no reaction added, "Hans and I know. We saw them come over the back fence. My guess is that one of the rear houses belongs to PIRA. Maybe even the one immediately behind. If this house is being watched by C13 they would cover the two ends to see what emerged from the street behind. There's been

229

no shooting, no rumpus. Those killers have not left the other street. They are still there."

"The police might not be watching us." Daley was deliberately unhelpful.

Ulla laughed scathingly; of all people, she was best able to ruffle Daley. "Are you saying that your ex-friends know Conner is dead but the police do not? Just how have you survived, little man?"

Patterson knew how Ulla could get under Daley's skin. But instead of turning on her Daley was apt to turn on Patterson, who said quickly, "Con assumes the worst like the rest of us. There's no point in going over it."

Steinbach was holding his mug of coffee, listening and making up his mind. He said quietly, "Ulla and I are leaving you at the first opportunity. We'd go now but I think the police are at the front and the flanks, and Con's nice friends are at the rear. We need to know what we're up against first." He gazed at the two Irishmen. "I wanted you to know what we intend to do. No hard feelings." He raised his steaming mug. "The best of luck all round."

Another silence during which Ulla winked at Patterson as if to say, 'We might still have time to make it'.

"Is there any particular reason?" Patterson asked after a while.

"As a group we are falling apart. We can cope with the police but Con's friends are an unknown issue. It would help if we knew why they want him so badly. We would then know the strength of their intent. But he seems reluctant to tell us so we must form our own ideas. It is therefore best that we split up."

"And what are your ideas?" Patterson asked bluntly, watching Daley as he spoke.

But Daley gained complete control of himself as he saw danger mounting against him. "You know nothing about me. And it's a private fight, not yours."

"It's no longer private if it brings us into the firing line. And I don't think your problem will go away." Steinbach was speaking softly, but there was a challenge, as if he had thrown down the gauntlet to Daley.

230

In the face of real danger Daley was at his best, overriding his neurosis. An issue was being forced and a dangerous tension was building up. "You had better be very careful what you say, Hans. Or better still, say nothing at all."

"Once we've gone it's your own problem. But while we are here it's all our problem because it affects our safety. It already has. And that problem really came to a head in Germany, did it not?"

Daley paled. There were no hands on the table now and Patterson guessed they were where his own were, below table level pointing their respective pistols at whoever they considered to be the danger. Patterson was not at all sure why Steinbach was forcing the matter until the German said, "Eugene Lynch was a friend of mine. It has taken me a few days to piece together what happened to him. Had he not offered me the key to the apartment I would be no wiser. But he did. And he went to Libya with you to raise funds and arms, and you both received a beautiful bonus. Both. A shame that the only man who can bear this out died in London in a road accident. Very convincing too, or the Libyans themselves would be after you."

Daley sat back, relaxed, with a smile playing around his lips. "The pressure's got to you, Hans. What a load of crap."

Steinbach did not move but his gaze was frightening yet seemed not to touch Daley. "But you were in Germany the same time as Eugene?"

"No."

Steinbach placed his pistol flat on the table and kept both hands in sight away from the weapon. He gazed easily at Daley, almost mockingly. Very quietly he said, "You are a liar."

23

There was the faintest sound from the blind as a breeze caught it through the broken glass. Then the refrigerator clicked on to startle them; at any other time it would not have been noticed. Nothing had changed. Steinbach's pistol still lay flat on the table as did his hands. All eyes were on Daley.

Daley himself was very still, his wiry frame tensed. And he was ghostly white, thin lips tightened into a line. Below the table his pistol was aimed at Steinbach's guts but Steinbach himself seemed to be relaxed, although his gaze was cold and challenging.

Daley was just a fraction of pressure away from firing but one thing stopped him. Ulla was aiming at him just as he was aiming at Steinbach. He could get Steinbach easily enough but he doubted he would live long enough to know. He briefly wondered where Patterson might stand in all this but he was across the table from him and he could not see his hands.

The silence lasted no more than a few seconds but seemed to be an eternity. The tension was difficult to bear and had to break.

Daley found that he could not back down completely. It was not a matter of losing face but of stubbornness coupled with self-righteous belief. "I'll kill you later for that, Hans. But why did you say it? You know it isn't true."

"You were there," said Steinbach evenly, "and you blew Eugie up. It only made sense when we came here."

"Mother of God, why would I do that to my best friend?"

"Because only the two of you knew about the apartment. It was a great place to hide and when that use was gone, worth a considerable amount in that part of London."

"But it belonged to the Libyan. We couldn't touch it."

Steinbach laughed. "Don't insult me. A bent lawyer could have fixed the ownership with no trouble at all. If ever it came to light it would be long after you had sold it with false documents. You probably have a copy of the original purchase. You would have made a fortune. The lawyer might have had his cut, but you would probably have taken him out as you did the others. From Day One you intended to have that apartment as a haven and as an investment. You killed your best friend to get it."

Surprisingly Daley appeared to be more relaxed. His hands slowly appeared without his pistol and he clasped them behind his head. "And you worked all this crap out by yourself?"

"It was easy. It added up as we went along. You could not know that Eugie would pass on his key to me, or anyone. That was where it started to go wrong for you. That and the fact that your old 'friends' seem to be after you for something else. Maybe they don't know about the apartment. Maybe they found out about Eugie, though. And maybe you got greedy and betrayed a few of them for extra money. I don't see us as associates any more. We take our affairs more seriously."

Steinbach seemed to lose interest in what he was saying. He pulled out his share of the money from the bank raid and started to count it. But suddenly he looked up and said to Daley, "The only reason I haven't blown your treacherous head off is that it would be counter-productive at this time. We have enough troubles."

Daley was smiling widely. "I've got to hand it to you; that was the best bit of bullshit I've heard in a long time. It would be nearer the truth if I told them it was you who killed Eugie, and you killed a morgue attendant for the key to the apartment. He told you all about it and *you* saw the opportunity. I should have realised earlier. You've spun that cock-and-bull to confuse the other two and because it might come out. There is no way I could have killed Eugie. We were mates. I'll get you for this, Hans. My God I will."

Steinbach continued to count his money as if he had not heard. Ulla sat blank-faced, switching her gaze between Steinbach and Daley. She did not like Daley, but was totally aware of the utter ruthlessness of Steinbach. So far as she knew, Steinbach had no real friends. She knew he had helped Eugene Lynch and that they had co-operated, but it was quite normal to liaise between the groups. She was puzzled; men like Steinbach did not need an excuse to break away from the others; he would just do it. She wondered what he was up to. It would not worry her if he had killed the Irishman in Germany. She did not like foreign battles being fought on German soil.

During all this Patterson had said nothing and his expression gave nothing away. The only effect it had on him was to make him feel better about what he was doing and what he intended to do; if he could.

Dawn was creeping in but the drapes and blind would remain in place no matter what the light outside. The biggest problem in moving around the house had been in going from one room with curtains drawn and lights on, to a room with them drawn back. They could not allow the light to filter from room to room, so lights had to be switched off when moving about and they could not afford to forget.

As daylight crept in they took turns in using the solitary bathroom and this took time. Conversation was now almost dead. Steinbach and Daley not only did not speak to one another but chose to avoid looking at each other. Steinbach's appraisal had created a very difficult situation and Patterson could not understand why he had done it at a time when co-operation was vital for their safety.

Ulla made breakfast and the result was her own indictment on the deterioration of comradeship which had set in. In the end Patterson settled for toast made from stale bread. Basic stocks of most foods were good, an indication that Conner was prepared for siege.

For safety's sake they had to organise watches and they took turns to go round the house to see what could be seen outside. It was a tedious job with caution the mainstay but the result was that they saw little and the tension between them mounted and at times was explosive.

At ten in the morning the telephone rang. It broke an uneasy silence with the impact of a fire alarm. It was the loudest intrusion yet.

They were again sitting in the kitchen because it was the most difficult room to observe from the outside. No one moved but the bell kept peeling out until Patterson rose and Daley yelled at him, "Don't touch it. The house is supposed to be empty."

"Carmel is here. Someone might know."

"Then they'll think she's out. Leave it. It is probably a trap."

Patterson sat down again. Daley might be right. It was a Catch 22 situation: if it was the police they might assume the place to be empty and raid it. After a while the phone stopped and the silence was almost painful.

Patterson rose again. "I don't like the atmosphere in here." He left the room with no one commenting, and wandered into the hall and then back to the study. He crawled under the desk and reached for the thin package he had located there. While he tried to pull it away there was movement in the hall. He wrenched as hard as he could and tore the package from the back of the desk and backed out fast. As he stood up he sensed someone outside the door which he had left open because that was how he found it.

He rammed the package inside his jacket and hoped it would not show. There were soft footsteps and he sensed that there were two people near the study door. He stepped behind the door and was glad that he did because someone looked in the study and then withdrew. Ulla and Steinbach started to talk in German. It was almost as if they were in the room but as Patterson understood no German it did not help him. The exchange was heated at times, particularly from Ulla who seemed very angry. But Steinbach remained unruffled and after a while they moved off.

Patterson slipped from the room and went upstairs to the bedroom he shared with Daley. Daley was already lying on his bed when he went in.

"Close the door." Daley mouthed the words rather than uttered them.

Patterson closed the door and sat in the only chair in the room, a sad relic from the wrong end of the Portobello Road. The small house was having a claustrophobic effect after the luxury apartment.

Daley sat up and moved to the end of the bed to be nearer Patterson. In a whisper he said, "I'm going to kill Steinbach. I need your back-up to take care of Ulla."

"Here? You're mad."

"Why? We've already got two stiffs in the next room. Another two will keep them company." He seemed to have recovered from the sad death of Carmel remarkably quickly.

This was a complication Patterson did not want. "You think he's going to hang around and let you do it? You've picked on the wrong man."

"He's after the apartment; rent or sell, it's worth a packet. He can only get it with me out of the way. Don't you see? That's why he spun all that bull about me and Eugie. I must get him first."

"I want no part in it. It's your fight."

"You're hooked in whether you like it or not. If he gets me, as sure as hell he won't leave you around to tell the tale. And it will be two to one against. You wouldn't come out alive, Jamie."

Events were going from bad to worse. What they really needed to do was to get away from this house and go their separate ways. It was not going to happen. Patterson said, "Just now you didn't trust me. Now you're in the firing line you want my help."

"So this is your chance to prove yourself." Daley smiled lopsidedly. "I couldn't argue after that, could I?"

As he sat reflecting, Patterson realised they were simply progressing from one killing to another. If it were the Provos he would do it from a deep sense of justice; he could not face the word revenge.

"He won't be expecting it," Daley continued to push.

Patterson stared in disbelief. "Why the hell not? He's a pro to his trigger finger."

"Because he's so goddam sure of himself, that's why. He doesn't rate me. He has Ulla and she's pretty deadly for sure. But he's got away with it so often he think he's unassailable."

For a moment Patterson thought he was going mad. He stared hard to make sure it was Daley speaking. But Daley could have been speaking about himself, yet it had not, and

236

would never, occur to him. He had killed and killed again, by no means always in his cause, yet it meant no more to him than it meant to Steinbach. Every killing was just one more corpse.

Patterson did not know what to say. He had created the position he was in and could have no complaints. It was Daley he needed, not Steinbach, and it was true the German would think nothing of killing him. He had to make up his mind.

To help him, Daley said, "I know a way out and four will be too many."

"What makes you think you can rely on me?"

"Because if I take Hans out Ulla will go for us both. Whatever happens we would have to get her." He watched Patterson closely and added, "I don't understand your problem. It's them or us."

"When would you plan on leaving here?"

"Well before midnight."

"And where would we go?"

"We'd either have to sleep rough or find a small hotel for the night."

"And then?"

"Go abroad. Anything. Rob another bank. We just need time to sort ourselves out. There's still the cache in Hertfordshire. They wouldn't expect us to go back. There's money in that stuff. It would fetch a bomb on the underground market." Daley smiled at his pun.

Patterson had made up his mind but it was important to take it a stage further. "How many more pistols are there in the cache?"

"Maybe half a dozen. And some machine-pistols. Why?"

"Because we need to change the ones we've got, particularly after taking care of Ulla and Steinbach. Too many used slugs can be traced back to those guns. Leave ours with the Germans to confuse the police. We can pick up new ones at the cache."

"So you'll help me? It will just be the two of us together again."

"I'll help provided we think things through properly. It does not stop at killing them." Patterson was thoughtful for a

237

while. "Once we're out of here we'll split and meet at the cache some time later in the day."

Daley was immediately suspicious. "Why? What's wrong with staying together." If he did not trust Patterson he needed him just the same. And if they killed the Germans Patterson would be as committed as he.

Patterson said scornfully, "Because they've been looking for two Irishmen together from Day One. We can't go looking for late digs together. We split; we meet up later. And if you're afraid of my not being there you'll have to put up with it. What would it matter one way or the other? Sooner or later we'll have to split. But as it happens I need stuff from that cache as much as you do."

"I don't like it."

"Then that's too bloody bad. I'm not going to wet-nurse you at every turn. That's the way it will be or we don't do it. Please yourself."

Smithy put the receiver down. She had been stupid to try. Her degree of desperation showed in the fact that she had left Scotland Yard to make the call from a public callbox. It had been easy enough to get the number, it was in the directory.

Even if someone was there, how could she know Patterson would answer? And if he had answered, what the blazes could he have said if the others were there? As Smithy went back to the Yard she felt ashamed. She had behaved like a rookie; not a rookie, a love-sick girl whose dormant feelings for a man had burst out with the remorse of someone who had made a bad mistake and did not know how to rectify it. She went back to check if there was any fresh news.

Gaunt had his men better placed and had received the co-operation of some of the neighbours, noticeably those opposite Conner's place, and one of the adjoining houses to fix special microphones to the walls to pick up any sounds there might be. He was not even sure whether anyone was in the house, although somebody along the street had reported seeing a man and a woman calling late the previous night.

That sort of evidence was always dubious. At night and

from a distance, it was not always possible to be precise about the place of call. None of the near neighbours had heard anything, the shootings had been in the dead of night with barely a noise. One or two people thought they had heard glass breaking but they were all used to milk bottles being smashed by vandals at night.

The other difficulty was that Patterson and the other party held most of their discussions in the kitchen, which did not adjoin either of the connecting houses. And when they talked in their bedrooms they did so extremely quietly so that the other couple did not hear.

Gaunt had trembler microphones in the house across the street, to pick up vibrations from the windows, but the front of the house still had its curtains drawn so he was up against it in observation terms. Yet he retained the gut feeling that someone was there. It was a question of making a decision of when to go in. If he knew for certain someone was there he could co-opt the SAS. And he did not want to have an evacuation of the nearest houses without good reason.

Gaunt was used to these frustrations. The whole business might turn out to be abortive and that would be far from being a first. But he might be up against highly dangerous and skilled terrorists; he had to be cautious. It was difficult to keep his men out of sight, and he had to arrange it in a variety of ways.

When Smithy arrived he was in the house across the street and she was dressed as a nurse.

The mounted binoculars were not manned because of the drawn curtains in Conner's house. The directional 'mike' moved from window to window without success. When Gaunt tried to get use of two houses in the street behind he had met with some hostility and no help and a check revealed that one was occupied by an ex-villain. But in any event he doubted their value because the height of the fence only allowed a view of the upper windows. He had both ends of the street covered as he had the previous night. His men were armed.

24

"I need to know the escape route should anything go wrong."

"If Steinbach gets me first, you mean?" Daley shrugged the possibility away. "Sure. Hans might have worked it out for himself. Straight over the rear fence, down the garden and out by a side alley. Simple."

"Are you saying that the Provos chasing you went out into the street behind?"

"No. The fuzz would have seen them. One of the houses is owned by an old lag. He met some of our boys in prison and has done odd jobs for us. We use him for transit. He gets paid well enough. They would have stayed the night then pushed off one by one as the opportunity occurred."

"If they were so near it was a wonder they didn't come back."

"No. They knew then that we were waiting for them. They wouldn't take those odds."

Patterson found it difficult talking in such subdued tones. He said, "You talk as if you're still in the Provos. How do you know about the place behind?"

Daley lay back on the bed again. "You forget I worked in London for a couple of years. I knew Billy Conner from way back. He's lived in this place for years. I went to Libya from here." His eyes glazed over as he reminisced.

Patterson sometimes thought that if Daley could put the clock back he would have done things differently. When he spoke of the Provos he seemed to do so wistfully. He was a man who would always need someone and he had left the comfort of their numbers. Patterson himself was a poor substitute and one of the enemy, which illustrated only too clearly Daley's need of anyone at all. He had made a terrible mistake and there was no way back.

As Patterson studied the prone figure of Daley it was difficult to imagine him as a multi-killer, but there was no mercy in the man; he still could not forget the callous killing of the innocent farmer in Ireland and the way he had killed Conner. He was tempted to raise the Libyan issue but a strong instinct held him back. He might never know the truth of it but there was little separating Steinbach and Daley; in different ways they were equally cold-blooded.

Patterson had learned what he wanted to know and he rose from the old chair and said, "Okay. I'll help. But for God's sake give me fair warning."

Daley turned his head, undisturbed by what he intended to do. "No problem. Just be ready as from now."

"Right. I'm off to make my will."

"What!" Daley shot upright.

Patterson signalled him to keep his voice down, then whispered, "Just in case I finish on the dust heap. There are a couple of items I want to leave to someone. I've got to find a paper and pen." He grimaced. "You can witness it when it's ready."

Daley was confused and suspicious again. He could not understand why anyone would want to make out a will. It was like a death wish. "Don't take too bloody long. We can't put this off."

Patterson closed the door behind him and noticed that Steinbach's and Ulla's door was closed and no sound escaped. Ulla's love life was on hold while they solved the current problem. He poked his head in the room where the dead couple lay together in the same bed like a sign of some sick sexual ritual. They looked as if they belonged to one another; they were young, pleasant looking and prematurely dead because of a way of life they had chosen; it had lasted no time at all.

He went downstairs to the study, sat at the desk, no longer caring who saw him, and searched for a blank sheet of paper and a pen. He printed just a few words and folded the paper in half, sealed it in an envelope and slipped it in his pocket. He wrote another note, this time addressing the envelope and also tucked it away. He then wrote a short will during which time

Daley came in and stood behind him, watching. He could feel Daley's suspicion oozing into the room, and was not surprised that he had come in. He folded the sheet over leaving enough space to add the name of the witness. "Sign here," he said.

"I'm not signing anything I haven't seen."

"Then I'll get one of the others to do it." Patterson pushed the chair back and stood up. "It doesn't matter to me who signs it."

Daley was put out; he had not expected that reaction and he did not want Patterson fraternising with the enemy at this crucial stage. "Okay, I'll do it."

Patterson held the paper flat for him. As he leaned forward he felt Conner's envelope slipping from his inside pocket; he would have to be more careful. "You'd better put an address. Not the Maze. Where you lived with Carmel will do." He was sure, that just for a second, Daley's thoughts were so obsessed that he had to think who Carmel was. When that was done Patterson slipped the will in the same pocket as the rest.

Daley said, "Let's get it done. When I rub my nose I'm going for Hans. You take out Ulla. They're coming down the stairs now. Make sure your bloody silencer is still on."

The small hall was not the best place for a shoot-out, Patterson thought, but there was nowhere in the house where it would be ideal. It was a bizarre, briefest of thoughts, for as he and Daley left the study Steinbach and Ulla were almost at the foot of the stairs.

The grim expression each exuded was almost a signal in itself as though they all had the same deadly intent. As the Germans stepped into the hall they separated to split the target. Patterson wondered if he was being fanciful because he was very much on edge. Daley had yet to give a signal that he felt sure they knew what was about to happen. Yet they, too, had done nothing.

Daley said quickly, "When do you reckon on leaving?"

Steinbach appeared slightly amused. "Some time when it's dark. And you?"

"We'll wait until you've gone. It's best we don't all leave

242

together." It was the first time since their row in the kitchen that they had exchanged words.

"Well, in spite of everything, the best of luck," Daley said. "I hope things work out for you."

"And you, too."

It was a crazy exchange. Patterson could now see why Daley had not given a signal; Ulla had positioned herself behind and to one side of Steinbach so that Daley himself was blocking Patterson's line of fire. If Daley moved away it would look too obvious. Patterson leaned casually against the wall; in the narrower part of the hall there was nowhere else for him to go.

The whole scene was unnatural and the dreadful sound of muted voices added to the unreal atmosphere. Something had to give and it did. Daley decided he was badly placed and moved down the hall towards Patterson who then moved back towards the kitchen making it even more difficult for him.

Patterson could see that Daley was trying to create a situation which suited him in the cosy belief that he could out-think Steinbach. Daley was so intent on what he was doing that he missed the obvious. He presented Steinbach with the target of his back and Steinbach shot him before Patterson, whose view was blocked by Daley himself, could warn him.

Patterson never forgot Daley's look of pain and surprise as he crumpled in front of Patterson who fired before Daley hit the floor. Steinbach spun round, shot in the shoulder and for once blocked Ulla. Patterson fired again and jumped for the stairs to race up them and wait for Ulla to appear. He heard Steinbach crash down and then there was the kind of silence he detested. Ulla was down there, armed and unhurt and he had no idea what she was doing.

Patterson knew that Daley was dead and for a moment he suffered a crazy sort of loss. But he was not sure about Steinbach. He waited on the landing, safe while he was there because Ulla could not reach him without showing herself. But she cut off his retreat.

Then she called up very softly to him, and even in such moment of tragedy managed to get a sensuous element into

243

her tone. Her whisper drifted up the stairwell. "They are both dead, Jamie. That leaves you and me and their money to split between us. We don't need them; they were both mad. We'd make a good team, Jamie. Wouldn't we?"

She spoke as though Steinbach had never existed. There was no regret, no sorrow, no threat of revenge. But maybe that was her way of expressing a threat. She wanted him to come down.

Patterson did not reply. She could not be sure where he was and any move she made towards the back of the house would bring her in view at some point. For the moment he held the advantage but could not stay there for ever.

Again Ulla's voice floated up. "I could have killed you . . . easily. I had a clear view. Think about it."

He did think about it. When he winged Steinbach the German had spun to block Ulla out; it had probably saved Patterson's life. But still he did not answer. Let her sweat. But it did not help his own escape.

Both floorboards and stairs creaked and could give his position away if he moved, but he could not stay there. There was a sudden flash of movement in the hall as Ulla dashed for the kitchen and he was far too late to fire. He was not sure that he could have done so, even given a slower target. It was a crazy time to be old-fashioned about women so he convinced himself she had been too fast for him.

He moved just as quickly before she settled. He kept to the edges of the landing and stepped across to the bedroom where the corpses of Carmel and the young IRA man lay. It was a room which overlooked the back and the curtains were drawn across.

He wedged a chair under the door handle, whipped off the sheet that covered the bodies, and started to tear it into strips. As he worked, the two bodies lay side by side and their hands touched as lovers' might.

He made his rope, tied it to the bed, drew back the curtains, opened the window a little at a time, and climbed through. He had no idea whether or not the house was directly watched from the back; the only certainty was that Ulla was somewhere beneath him with a gun and she was deadly.

He climbed down and stood with his back to the wall. The kitchen was to his left and he stepped forward a couple of paces to see that the windows were still covered. He picked his way through the rubbish towards the fence at the bottom of the yard, occasionally glancing back. When he reached the fence, he felt exposed but there was no movement from the kitchen. Ulla would have to go into the yard to see the knotted sheet, but it could easily be seen by anyone in the rear houses and Patterson knew he had little time.

He climbed the fence and went down the other yard, almost a garden with two small, very tidy flower beds. He skirted a small pond set in the concrete, and headed for the back door. Gun in hand he rapped on the door, banking on the visitors from last night having long since gone.

A short, fat, midde-aged man opened the door, and said, "I didn't expect you back so . . ." He tailed off as Patterson rammed the gun at his head. Patterson towered over him and looked down on a balding head and a putty-wet face. Scared eyes stared up.

"Anyone else in?" asked Patterson, and when the man shook his head added, "If you're lying I'll blow your head off."

"No. No. There's no one here."

"When are they due back?"

"I don't know. Look, that bloody gun is screwing a hole in my head."

"What about your wife? Where is she?"

"You're bloody joking. She walked out with the kids years ago. Look, what have I done? You don't need the gun."

"Inside."

They walked down a narrow passage, into a room, neater, but otherwise very similar to the one in Conner's house. Patterson took up position near the door so that he could see out into the passage and cover the room as well. "Have you a car?"

"An old banger. It goes, though."

"I want to borrow it just for today. I'll pay for the hire."

"Sure. No problem. But who the hell are you?"

"I'm one of the bunch the Provos tried to knock off last night, operating from this house."

"Never! I'd never let those bastards use this place. Why do you say that?"

"Have you got a name?"

"Ernie. Ernie Dipper."

Patterson smiled. "Ernie the Dip, more like. Have you access to these people you wouldn't allow in here? And don't bugger about, Ernie, I haven't the time, and one more corpse won't matter. How quickly can you get hold of them?"

Ernie's gaze strayed to a Mickey Mouse telephone. "Just a phone call."

"Good." Patterson took out one of the sealed notes he had written and passed it over. "It's important that one of the boyos receive this at once. Life or death. Probably yours. It's in the note and to save you steaming it open, states that Con Daley will be at the Hertfordshire cache at three this afternoon; he intends to plunder it. I am not the police and this is not a police trap. Now let me have the keys of your car." Patterson peeled off some notes. "I want a receipt."

Ernie Dipper handed over the car keys, his gaze darting everywhere, searching for a trap and an escape at the same time. He did not understand any of this but he knew he had better pass on the message as soon as he could. "It's an old Austin. Blue and rust coloured." He turned to a modern bureau while Patterson watched him closely. He scribbled on some paper and eventually handed it to Patterson. "So you can prove you didn't nick it. There's the receipt and the registration number is down there." He looked up at Patterson, not at all sure of what was happening. "When will it be back?"

"By six this evening. I won't be using it until this afternoon but don't want to come back for it. Is it topped up?"

"It's always topped up." Ernie managed a nervous grin. "Never know in my line; I believe in being ready."

"Okay. You can walk to the car with me as if we are friends."

They went out through the front door and stood chatting by the car. They were both satisfied that there were police cars stationed near each corner. In this role Ernie Dipper was at his best, having had ample practice. His association with

Patterson appeared friendly and, from any distance, close. They even shook hands and Ernie waved as Patterson drove off, lingering a while until the car had turned the corner, before going in.

Patterson stopped at the nearest post box and dropped the second note in. He had been unable to find postage stamps at Conner's place but knew that the address was sufficient for it to be accepted. It was still early morning as he drove out of London and into the country, under a pale sun just emerging from rain clouds. The air was damp and cold, but the heater worked and the old car was well tuned up and the tank full as Ernie Dipper had claimed.

Over the last few days Patterson had got so used to being with Daley that he now felt the loss. Daley had died still full of himself, so cocksure that he had everything under control. To have taken that view with someone like Steinbach was crazy and he had paid for it, not fully understanding what had gone wrong right at the end. Daley had died not really knowing himself and he had taken his deadly complexities with him.

Patterson had often had to restrain his hatred for all that Daley stood for. So far as he was concerned circumstances had forced them together and Daley had become an instrument to achieve an aim and, though dead, was still fulfilling that part. But it was impossible to be forced into a predicament with a man without learning a little about him and without changing some part of an opinion even if it meant strengthening the hate. As he saw it, Daley had stood no chance from the beginning and would have finished up the way he had whatever he did. Daley was a born loser who had tried to bring off the big one and had been quite amenable to murder and betrayal to succeed. Some of the prisoners would have got him if Steinbach had not.

And yet Daley had paradoxically needed the help, and often just the reassuring company, of a recognised enemy in Patterson, to an extent that had allowed ridiculous risks like the early telephone calls, as though he trusted Patterson even while doubting him; he had been right in that Patterson had tried to protect him. But only for his own reasons. As he drove into the Hertfordshire countryside Patterson took a long look at himself. This would be the last attempt at his battles against what he saw as evil before he became part of it. Perhaps he already had.

He thought of his sister dying so young, and his mother in so much agony, and he considered the more recent proxy bombs in Northern Ireland when the Provos had roped fellow Catholics in their own cars which were packed with explosive. He felt sick to the core, and had no regrets at what he was about to try. In a way he was glad that Daley had died the way he had; he had at least gone cleanly.

He reached the turn-off well past Tring where he bought another spade, and took the meandering path through the woods to the area of the cache. It was half-past ten when he started to dig. The car was tucked some distance away and he was a lone figure on the site.

He knew roughly where to dig but had to change direction now and again. Everything he wanted was there. Guns, ammunition, enough Semtex to use on several big jobs, detonators, fuse wire and command control apparatus. There was nothing on site he did not know how to handle. Once he had exposed what he needed the rest was fairly simple; a matter of patience and extreme care. There was no need to fix detonators to the separate packs of explosive; one massive eruption was sufficient to blow the lot.

It took Patterson two and a half hours of uninterrupted work before he was ready. He left one command controlled detonator partly exposed in order not to provide any kind of shield for the signal, and loosely covered it with leaves. The button box he placed in his pocket.

By the time he was satisfied the site looked natural there was only an hour and a half left to the rendezvous. He had cut it very fine, for they were certain to be early. On the other hand they may well have been watching. In which case they would not come at all.

He retired to the wood where he and Daley had first gone, hid himself while retaining a view of the site, and waited.

At two forty-five he found it impossible to take his eyes from the site although he did not expect anyone to be there. But it should be under observation by now. At three he was sweating in spite of the cold. At three-fifteen he believed he had failed. They had seen through the ploy and were not coming.

At three-thirty he was ready to leave. There was no sign of life, not even wild life, and he knew that soon he would have to give up. Two minutes later a gun pressed against the back of his neck and a grating voice with a London accent said, "Bird-watching?"

Patterson had concentrated so much on the site that he had done what Daley had done – overlooked what might be happening behind him.

"Stand up," said the voice. "Move over to the site. Hands on head."

Patterson knew it to be futile to pretend he did not know what was meant. He had been there too long. He rose and stepped ahead of his unseen captor, and moved towards the site as others emerged from the trees and the dead ground around it. There must have been half a dozen men plus the one behind him; all were armed. They were a peculiar mixture from the fairly well dressed to the near dowdy. The oldest was about forty. They were hard men and as they spoke among themselves while watching his arrival, Patterson recognised a variety of accents: London, Birmingham, Liverpool and certainly at least two from Ulster.

"Where's Daley?" called out one of them as Patterson arrived.

"Search me. I was banking on him coming. It was his idea. We were to meet here."

A tall Ulster man eyed Patterson with scorn. Patterson thought he recognised him from a mug-shot of a Provo from Armagh called Mick O'Leary; a hard man and they did not come any harder.

"You mean you were setting him up?"

"I've been on the run with him for days. I've had enough. He's a nutter."

"Oh, he's that all right. He must have known what you were doing." There was menace in every word.

"It looks like it."

249

"So you must be Jamie Patterson. Did he ever buy that story about you killing his wife?" O'Leary was grinning widely.

"It worried him for a bit. I don't know whether he bought it though."

"You can't win them all. So what are you doing here, Jamie?"

"I wanted to make sure he arrived." Patterson knew he was finished. These men would never let him go.

"You wanted to see what we would do with him?"

"If you like. I had to be sure he was off my back."

O'Leary gazed round at the others as if to seek an unspoken agreement. "Well, you are not going to find out one way or the other, are you?"

"May I put my arms down now, they're aching?"

"Poor bugger. His arms are aching. Where is Con now?"

"As far as I know he's at Conner's house, though I expected him here. It was his idea for us to meet here."

"The house has the police all round it. How did you get out?"

Patterson was slowly lowering his arms, keeping them well away from his body. "You know how I got out. I don't know what the fuss is about; you want Daley, I tried to deliver him to you. It didn't work."

"Then why didn't you take him out yourself?"

"Because he's not my fight. He's your problem and I reckoned you would prefer to deal with him."

All seven men were standing around in a group, smiling away, feeling that they were not entirely empty-handed although the big one had got away. Patterson's hands were almost by his side now and in that second O'Leary saw the obvious and his expression changed drastically.

The instantaneous belief that Patterson would not blow himself up held his gunshot up by just a fraction. Patterson threw himself backwards and sideways and thrust his hand in his pocket just as O'Leary fired and caught Patterson in the chest as he hit the ground. Barely knowing what he was doing Patterson found the button and detonated the Semtex. The roar and the massive flash was something he took into

250

oblivion. He had a faint impression of floating at great speed and a huge pressure all round him. He did not see the mass of dismembered bodies hurtling through the air. Nobody had a chance to scream. Life was over very quickly, scattered far and wide among the grassland and the trees, some later to be recognised as human remains. And with the human flotsam went the arms by which they lived, shreds of metal and wood searing through the air accompanied by the fire-cracker sound of exploding ammunition. Patterson had taken his final toll.

EPILOGUE

An ashen Donna Smith said, "How is he?" For five days, many times a day, she had been asking the same question. She could see him wired up and full of tubes and a frame over what had once been healthy legs. There was little she could see to recognise yet she had stayed hours, and even slept in an ante-room until Waring considered she was ruining her own health.

The shot had almost killed him and the complications of removing a bullet while in the state he was in after the enormous blast had raised little hope. Yet against the odds he had survived the operation but was still unconscious.

"Go home, Donna." Peter Gaunt had said the same thing so often he was tired of his own voice. There was nothing they could do, not even the doctors and the surgeons who had already done everything they could. It was down to Patterson himself and he had no idea of what was happening.

Gaunt and Donna sat miserably in the ante-room as they had been doing on and off since Patterson had been transferred to a London hospital. The conversation always came round to the same thing – Smithy had been right: Patterson had executed a wild justice in taking out as many PIRA as he could. They had found the shreds of the package in the tatters of his jacket and the tiny pieces of paper were still being painstakingly put together and already had provided important names.

What had largely saved Patterson from the worst of the blast was his act of diving before he detonated the Semtex, and the almost fatal bullet which had knocked him flat at the crucial moment. Most of his clothes had been blown off, as were his shoes, and his shattered legs and feet had provided a nightmare for the orthopaedic surgeon. The explosion had been largely upwards and out and Patterson's prone figure had avoided the worst at ground level. Nevertheless it was a miracle that he was still hanging on.

Commander Waring, once in control of the situation, had issued a press release stating that eight men had been killed in the explosion, all thought to be members of the IRA. There had been no survivors. Attempts were being made to identify the remains.

The sheet from the upstairs window of Conner's house had been seen by a patrolling police car and Peter Gaunt had decided to raid the house. Ulla had stood her ground in the kitchen, killed one policeman and wounded another, before being shot dead. The discovery of the other bodies had given the newspapers their biggest story in years. It had been a bloody affair from the moment of the breakout in Ulster.

Ten days after the bullet was removed from his chest, Jamie Patterson was still unconscious and the doctors expected the worst. Smithy was left alone with him and only she retained hope. While he breathed there was always hope. She sat holding his hand and willing him to recover, believing that he would. The hospital staff could only marvel at the way he held on. Donna was showing a remarkable faith and some of it transmitted to others. Some began to believe with her and a new hope began to grow and an ancient faith to strengthen.